THE TAPESTRY

THE
TAPESTRY

MARGARET ALLEN

Matador
Unit E2 Airfield Business Park,
Harrison Road, Market Harborough,
Leicestershire. LE16 7UL
Tel: 0116 2792299
Email: books@troubador.co.uk
Web: www.troubador.co.uk/matador
Twitter: @matadorbooks

ISBN 978 1803132 648

British Library Cataloguing in Publication Data.
A catalogue record for this book is available from the British Library.

Printed and bound in Great Britain by 4edge Limited
Typeset in 11pt Minion Pro by Troubador Publishing Ltd, Leicester, UK

Matador is an imprint of Troubador Publishing Ltd

To Maura, Kwame, Taali, Namali and John

CHAPTER ONE

Washing her grandmother's lifeless body, Selina had experienced the truth of so-called dead weight. Frail as she had become in these last months, it had still proved surprisingly difficult after the ablutions to manoeuvre her unbending and uncooperative arms through the long sleeves of shift and overdress. The very fact that those unwieldy limbs were also withered and desiccated made the determined effort she was obliged to employ all the more difficult and distressing. Awkwardly pulling and tugging at clothing as stiff and unyielding as she herself would soon become she reflected on the pity of it all. These garments had been put away long ago, reserved for the special occasion that might come, but of course never had. Instead they would now adorn her body for the occasion of death, rather than in preparation for the life-changing invitation or encounter for which they were initially made. Sewn then in the never-failing hope and anticipation that the best might yet come, they had languished a lifetime as unseen and quietly unfulfilled as the woman who had made them.

There had been no need to close her eyes. She had done that for herself as she had surrendered unresisting to those other forces that would now take charge of steering her dismasted vessel. Maybe too she was weary with the world and its ways, and glad enough to be done with having to look at it. Whatever her fading motivation had been, in the end she had slipped away so quietly and in a manner so devoid of fuss or drama that Selina had not been aware of exactly when she had finally crossed the dividing line between here and gone. Stepping outside the door for the briefest of moments to stretch arms and back, and to take in a good deep breath of air free from the smell of death, she found that in that short space while her back was turned, her grandmother had departed this life without ceremony, leave taking or bestowed blessing.

She had died much as she had lived. Not so much living really as simply existing, and she would leave as little impression on the world she had just departed as her wasted body would leave on the straw mattress on which she was stretched. Selina sighed and shook her head as she finished dressing her, and then laid her out with hands folded across her breast before the stiffening set in. Her final act of respect was to comb and braid her hair and tie up her jaw with a binder. Then she gathered some sweet herbs from their small but well-stocked garden and laid them round about her. When all was done, she cleared away the water and washcloths, knowing she must sit with her a while before she went to fetch the priest.

She had not been close to her grandmother; their relationship defined by the fact that she had never called her anything other than 'Grandmother', and she in her turn had remained 'Selina'. No sweet, affectionate pet names had evolved naturally in the course of their one-to-one shared life. It was a life in which nothing had ever been done or said that was unkind, but also one where if there was no evidence of disaffection neither was there any of affection, of displeasure or pleasure. Such spark of emotional life as might yet have survived unquenched in her grandmother's shrunken heart was channelled entirely into her needlework for the church and it absorbed her totally. It was her livelihood but also her reason to be. As she sewed, she became lost in executing her exquisitely perfect stitches, consumed by her own ability and the results of it. Maybe through gloriously enrobing God's ordained intermediaries she found a reciprocal sense of also being of use to the Divine, her work in its own way no less a vocational gift and calling.

But as they had never talked about such things, Selina could only guess at the reasoning of her head and heart. The bare facts of her life were known to her only from her own mother's telling; a tale in which it seemed that everything that was going to happen happened early on and then was over. Barely started before it was finished.

In her long-forgotten girlhood, her grandmother had been seduced by an itinerant mummer. He had come into and gone out of her life with careless but potent brevity, like an incubus whose dreamlike visitation had an adversely tangible outcome – her own mother's birth.

Selina's grandmother had raised her child on her own with scant sympathy and even less assistance, but her salvation was in her exceptional ability as a fine needlewoman. For in recognition of this, the church had given her free tenure of a humble dwelling and a meagre stipend in return for fashioning vestments, altar cloths and whatever else the house of God had need of. With her eligibility for procuring a legitimate husband and helpmate irredeemably compromised this then had been both work and penance ever since. And she had accepted it without complaint or rancour as her just deserts, the wages of sin inarguably allocating her place in the scheme of things. The mummer never came back nor did she seek him out. Instead she supplemented the church's barely adequate provision by taking on commissions from the better heeled, and thus kept body, soul and child safely steered away from total privation.

Over the years, despite living a more or less hand-to-mouth existence, her grandmother, like many others, had still managed to put aside a few coins every week to ensure a coffin of some ilk, a simple service and a marker for her grave – stone if funds ran to it, wood if not – when the time came. A pauper's burial was the dread of the impoverished and to be avoided at all costs, the resulting shame and stigma untenable. No matter that they would be dead and gone, they still would not escape such considerations, for it was common knowledge that you would languish in Purgatory or worse for all eternity should your mortal remains be left to rot in unhallowed ground. Selina hoped her grandmother's work over the years for the church would have earned her a decent resting place whether or not the adding up of her contributions fell short of the mark.

Fortunately, when her own misbegotten mother grew to maturity, she met with better fortune than a vagrant opportunist. Her head was turned by a handsome, able and entirely suitable young man encountered at the annual May Day fair – the accepted trysting place for seeking and finding a partner. She left with him, glad to go, shed her bastard status and start a life of her own in another settlement. The distance between them meant Selina saw her grandmother rarely at first and finally not at all and news came but sparsely.

There was traffic enough from place to place with pedlars, story-tellers, tooth-pullers, actors and acrobats coming and going, all of whom you would be a fool to trust if you seriously wanted to send word.

Few could read or write, so for the written word you needed to employ two scriveners, one to pen the news and another to read it at the other end. Added to this burden of expenditure was the cost of the purveyor of the missive. In a climate where dubious dealings were normal commerce, it was all too likely that while on the road the bearer would spend his fee at a wayfarer's inn and thereafter lose the incentive to fulfil his side of the bargain. Were he to be caught and challenged, he could always plead that he had been ill-used on the road by brigands, which being indeed so prevalent would be hard to disprove. Another possible choice was the wandering friars who were undoubtedly honest and who would also refuse payment other than a morsel to sustain them along the way. But they could lose themselves and all sense of worldly matters at any time if they were caught up and whirled away in a divine rapture. In transcendent holy madness, all else was as nothing to them, a fact that, when all was said and done, meant they were no more reliable than the rest.

Her parents had thrived in their committed endeavours

with a sound beginning and the promise of a prosperous future ahead of them. Her industrious father apprenticed as a youth to the guild of weavers, had achieved the position of journeyman and aspired in a matter of a few years to become a master in charge of his own business. Being thus secure, they had been able to send word to her grandmother through guild and church channels to come and join them, but she had refused their generosity. Her restricted life had come to entirely suit her and she sought none other. So, for all her early years, Selina and her two older brothers, Daniel and Edward, knew nothing at all of their mother's mother, other than that she was alive and apparently well, or well enough.

Then that assured confidence that came with the belief that all was well and good with themselves too, had in a matter of a few short weeks been turned on its head.

Every once in a while, which none could either predict or prepare for, a number of unfortunate villages would be visited by the Pestilence. Some but not all, and where it came from God only knew, and whom it would take likewise as unknowable. But like an ill wind it blew where it would, and with relentless malevolence into the mouths of its chosen victims, like the foul breath of a grave-risen vampire. There were few who could survive that kiss of death. A whole generation might be spared the coming of this baleful miasma, and when it did come sometimes it would seek out only the aged as its chosen victims. Then, in that pitiless culling, there would come a strange silence from those corners in homesteads where the old beldames sat. Often lame or otherwise impaired in their dotage, they were still able to sit long hours spinning to the accompaniment of the sweet hum of the wheel. As they span the wool with practised hands into fine thread, they supplied the weavers like Selina's father, who then wove it into good cloth before they in turn passed it on to the dyers and fullers.

This time however it wasn't just the crones and gnarled old men who were silenced, nor those at the opposite end of life's journey, the babes-in-arms and little children. More inexplicably it was visited on those in their prime, young still and full of vigour. Selina's father qualified as a perfect candidate, and then her mother also. She would not leave his side for a moment in her devoted efforts to save him, so in health and in sickness they were not parted but went out through death's door together, though Selina and her brothers found scant comfort in that.

Nor were they the only ones going through that ominous portal, far from it. By the time the accursed scourge had run its course through the borough, in and out of the houses, seeking and scything, the populace had been decimated.

Stunned with grief and shock, Selina, Edward and Daniel were denied the consoling comfort of ritual. With so many to bury there was no time for the normal niceties, and indecent haste was the order of the day. The stern but soothing poetry of the burial mass was reduced to a hasty ceremony, lacking all dignity, said as it was at mass interments for no one in particular. And there were no eulogies and no gatherings afterwards. No time to talk, to praise and lament. No time to come to terms with or make sense of it. No time at all for any of the things that they were in sore need of.

Her brothers at least were provided for. Willingly following in their father's footsteps, they were already serving their apprenticeships and living in their master's house as was the custom. But Selina had no such option, and at the awkward age of eleven it wasn't easy to know what to do with her. With orphans abounding, there were none willing or able to take her in, so she was made to pack her box and was packed off to live with her grandmother, though neither had been consulted on the matter.

Selina had travelled with her few personal possessions on a wagon loaded with cloth bound for the coast, from whence it would be transferred aboard a ship setting sail for France. There, fine English woollen material, unlike herself, was much sought after. She wondered what it might be like to stow away on such a vessel, and what adventures, good or bad, could be had starting afresh in a new country. She could not imagine she would feel any more lost, alienated or abandoned in France than she did at the moment where she was.

Edward and Daniel had each other, the familiarity and security of the master's house and their friends, the other apprentices learning their craft alongside. It was the nearest thing you could get to your own family. Saving pestilence or accident, their road ahead was mapped out precisely. All they had to do was follow the path. If only she had been a boy, she too might have bided there with them, instead of being disposed of with neither consultation nor consent.

When she had stumbled down from her unconventional transport, weary and disorientated, her grandmother had received her with an uncomplaining resignation. It was an attitude that mirrored exactly her acceptance of the sinner's stance, for a fall from grace so she believed, must ever have continuous retribution heaped upon an unworthy head. So, having declined joining her family, preferring her simple and solitary existence, she nevertheless took Selina in without any evidence of resentment.

Selina, though arriving forlorn and desolate, soon found that the very lack of any emotional charge in her new homestead had an unexpectedly beneficial effect – it was calming. It soothed her tumbled and undisciplined desperation. The placid daily round was reliably consistent and after so much tumult and turmoil, it provided an unforeseen but welcome sense of security and sanctuary. She was not unhappy.

She found her feet in routines that gave her purpose but were not overly demanding. She gradually took over all the household tasks – cooking, cleaning, laundry and the care of the little garden plot – leaving her grandmother free to concentrate on her needlework. This arrangement suited them both, and had the additional benefit that with more time for sewing a little extra money was coming in. This gave life a welcome degree of breadth and leeway now there were two of them rather than one to sustain.

Selina grew to love her small garden almost as much as her grandmother loved her needlework, and for want of a little animal to lavish affection on, all her caring went into the plants she nurtured. This manifested in an abundance of produce. From such a modest space came prodigious yields. They ate well, and her grandmother saw to it as her side of the bargain that Selina was decently clothed for all seasons.

From her non-church commissions, she often had left over remnants of velvet, silk, satin or cloth of gold, but none were allowed to dress above their station and, like her own unworn finery, they could only be put away unused and wasted. When she was alone though, if her grandmother had gone to the church or for a fitting, Selina would open the chest where they were stored and feast her eyes on the sumptuous colours and stroke the opulent textures. They awakened in her a need for beauty, a yearning for something more than basic necessities and serviceable homespun.

With the Pestilence she had lost not only her parents, but the particular lifestyle and status that would have been her entitlement. Cloth of gold may have been the preserve of those of noble birth, but silk and velvet were allowable and available for those of her rank with wealth enough to pay for them.

The four years Selina lived with her grandmother had gradually seen her sense of grief and displacement lose their all-consuming power; though they were still an essential part of her, they no longer defined her. And the quiet that had suited her at first was now fast becoming more burden than blessing, for the chest of exquisite offcuts stirred that something in her that had nothing to do with the self-effacement and timid humility that her grandmother so willingly embraced. Her mother and father may be dead and gone, but the strong and vital blood that pumped through her veins was their legacy, and it was stirring in her the qualities of courage and assertion.

As she sat on a stool beside her dead grandmother, her primary feelings were of sorrow and regret on her behalf for a thwarted life only half lived, but there was none of the searing inconsolable grief that was so much a part of losing her parents.

Also, her grandmother's death had happened at a time when Selina was already aware that, no longer being the broken little creature that she had been on arrival, change must come. Whoever she was now, or was becoming, she knew for a surety that continuously living in obscure isolation was no part of it. Like her brothers, she had served her apprenticeship in that accomplishment and was fully certified. It was time to move on, but to what she did not know, for her life and her choices were still not her own to make; they were not in her remit. The priest would come when she summoned him, to attend to her grandmother and pray for her immortal soul, and as the church owned the dwelling, what happened to her next and where she went from here was very much church business. Once again, death had forced irrevocable finality not just for the dead but for a whole way of life, and, as with the Pestilence, there could be no arguing nor bartering that would buy you grace or remission from your fate. But this time she was ready for change, and old enough now to refuse to be forced into what did not suit her, or so she fervently hoped. Her grandmother's devoted service would surely also buy her that consideration.

She stood up then, ready and willing to take the first step into whatever was to come next. But before she set out, she first gently pulled the coarse cotton sheet up over her grandmother's chilled body, already so clearly devoid of anima. However, she found she must stop short of covering her head, for she could see that in the little while since death had occurred, her grandmother's face had changed, but not in the same way as her body. Rather than stiffening, it had gently softened. The deeply etched lines around eyes and mouth smoothed out as the accretions of a hard life had been stripped away to reveal a wholly unsuspected sweetness of mien. One that must have been there in the very beginning, before destiny riding roughshod over her hopes and dreams had obscured her original nature. Marching time had over-printed her face with very different but indelible markings, finally changing her features irrevocably into those of a completely different woman. The revelation of this unknown aspect of her grandmother stirred a novel tenderness in Selina and a resultant sense of loss. She was in bereavement now, forever bereft of any chance to get to know her grandmother better, to discover the person she had been and truly was. It had not been possible in life and now in death it was too late.

Selina gently folded the sheet back then, leaving it tucked neatly just beneath her chin, more as if she was preparing her for bed and sleep than laying her out. Then resolutely she crossed to the door and took down a light woollen shawl hanging from the peg on the back. She wrapped it tight around herself and well up over her own head so that from the side her profile could not be seen. It was April and the warmth of spring could already be felt as the land woke to the vigour of new life, but Selina covered her head not against a possible chill in the unsettled and unpredictable early season but to show she was in mourning. She closed the door quietly behind her also out of respect, for though her grandmother could not be roused by the harsh noise of clumsy movement, and there were none other present to take offence, it offended against her own sensibilities. Turning then to step onto the narrow, well-worn track to the church, trodden smooth as stone over time by her grandmother's constant comings and goings, she was aware of the auguries of this particular journey with regard to herself.

Spring was the wrong time to die, but it was the right time for new beginnings. She had received no last blessing from her grandmother to ensure good fortune, but as she made her way she beseeched instead her sorely missed dead mother to grant her this. If it was possible to influence worldly matters from her heavenly abode, she implored her to demonstrate she was still her mother wherever she was, and to do her utmost to guard and guide her in the life ahead. She didn't want to mimic her grandmother's lifestyle in any way if she could possibly help it.

CHAPTER TWO

The priest had returned with her, bearing the tools of his trade: vestments, oil, holy water, candles, bell and sacred writ. As he set them out, Selina withdrew respectfully to stand beside the door, giving him enough space to perform the sacraments and an essential distance from other close human contact while so doing. Watching from her discrete position as he celebrated the offices, she readjusted the shawl around her more loosely. She still kept head and shoulders covered though, no longer as a sign of bereavement, but as she would have done were she in church.

For in donning the vestments, the clergyman became at once an ordained man of God and the simple room a sacred space. It seemed as if the robes in themselves had the power to imbue divine authority. He kissed the holy symbols, lit candles, and then applied oil and water to her grandmother's body, all the while intoning the hypnotic murmur of ancient chant and prayers for the dead. Revered over centuries, the rhythm coupled with the smell of incense and the chime of the bell was the long-established accompaniment to the soul's journey home, and it provided great solace. Selina added her own amens where they were required with a very real sense of the need to participate. Her grandmother, thank God, was finally being given what she had yearned a lifetime for, the full benefit of the church's rites, and Selina was glad. They had been denied her parents and that lack of absolution pained her still on their behalf. She added her own silent prayer, asking that through their family connection blessing would come at last to them all.

Afterwards, when the priest had put away all that he had brought with as much care and attention as he had in setting them out, she sat with him at the rough-hewn but well-scrubbed table. She offered bread, fruit and curd cheese, along with spring water and some ale, simple but acceptable fare. Although for a man of the cloth wine would have been more appropriate, there was none to give him. She abstained herself as was proper, and the priest took a little of the bread and cheese as was also fitting, and they talked of her grandmother and her devotion to her church and church work. In his summation, he assured Selina that in the execution of those duties over the years, she had more than earned forgiveness for her sin and he promised a good plot and a decent headstone.

He shifted on his bench then to face her more directly and she knew the talk was now to be focused on herself and what was to become of her. She waited to hear what had been decided. The priest was recognised as a good man, one you could put your trust in. Of middle years he had the look of a born contemplative, and, although rather austere, he strove always to practise what he preached in sincere imitation of his Lord. But there were others who were not so exemplary and who might dismiss her situation as a trivial inconvenience of little, if any, concern. Her fate depended on whose opinion held final sway.

Leaning forward on his elbows, although his long, narrow face expressed genuine concern, he maintained appropriate formality as he addressed her.

"Selina, it is known that you do not have your grandmother's skill with a needle, but even if that had been the case you could not take on the tenure here, being a young woman on your own without a chaperone. In due course you might well return to your brothers when they are established and able to receive and support you, but in the meantime we have to find other provision for you.

"You will of course remain here until your grandmother's funeral, which as custom decrees will take place after the third day. Also, there will be those who knew her who will wish to call in and pay their respects during that time, and it is your duty to receive them and accept their condolences. Then, after the interment, you will gather up all of yours and your grandmother's accoutrements and clean and prepare the dwelling for its next incumbents."

If he was stating the obvious and taking his time to get to the point, she was aware that his deliberations were not an evasion, but a need to demonstrate to her that whatever the outcome proved to be, it had been arrived at with due consideration after exploring all possible options. Nothing had been lightly done. He emphasised in his preamble that Mother Church was deeply concerned for each separate member of the fold, and sought to guide all souls onto the straight and narrow path; male or female, none were excluded and all were precious before the Lord. She refrained from any impatient interrupting of this tedious paean of religiosity, for in the face of such earnest piety it would have been regarded as impudent, and the more so given her age and sex. But indeed, she was now in no great hurry to learn what awaited her, for she could already tell from the carefully composed look on his face that what the priest was about to tell her might not be to her liking. He inevitably got around to it nevertheless.

"There seem to be no known relatives on your father's side, so for want of family we have found a placement for you that should suit all concerned admirably." His words belied a look of uncertainty, one that for an 'honest-to-God', straightforward man was singularly out of place.

"We have been in negotiation with a woman of good character and elevated status in need of a companion and an assistant. She is long widowed and now, unable to manage on her own, has sought the church's help and guidance in selecting a suitable candidate."

He paused then for a moment, but Selina remained silent, for already her heart was plunging, rather than sinking, in response to the little she had heard. Ominously, it sounded as if instead of change, her life was going to repeat itself, and living alone with only an old woman for company was again to be her lot.

No doubt the church's thinking was that given her situation, she must be quickly fettered to protect her virtue, lest in close dwelling and association with her grandmother she had become contaminated by her sin. For Satan, having once got his wily foot in the door, would lose no opportunity to beguile her into following in the same unfortunate footsteps.

The priest then confessed the apparent cause for his disquiet as he continued to make his case.

"She is not of our diocese, thus I have not been able to meet or talk with her personally, but there can be no arguing with the fact that her station and domicile are quite beyond those which someone like yourself could normally hope to attain. This therefore can only be viewed as an exceptional opportunity.

"She is, I understand, without issue, thus it is not unreasonable to suppose that in time, if you prove yourself worthy, you could become more akin to a daughter or granddaughter than a serving lady's maid. This is an extraordinary chance for you, Selina, to advance yourself by pure merit. You served your grandmother well, and in the time you were together you have mastered all the domestic arts, save expertise in needlework, thus you are well qualified and deserving of this boon."

He sat back then, looking at her expectantly, but also as if in seeking to persuade her of the situation's merits he had finally managed to thoroughly convince himself. Selina however was not persuaded, and now that he had concluded his presentation she felt able to question him without the risk of seeming impertinent, but she demurred cautiously.

"Father, would it not be necessary for a meeting to take place first before commitment? As you yourself say, you have not had the chance to meet her and so become acquainted with her preferences. It is possible, is it not, that she may not take to me and will therefore feel obliged to withdraw the offer?"

She judiciously avoided pointing out that the same could apply regarding her own reaction.

The priest frowned, looking more than a little affronted by such ungrateful quibbling, for had he not just presented her with a gift that most would regard as an answer to her prayer? There could be no question that she would not suit, he insisted. She was diligent, of good temperament, and adept in all the skills required. In accepting this placement, her immediate future would be secure, and, maybe in the course of time, even her fortune too.

Seeing no easy way out of this non-negotiable entrapment, Selina in desperation threw caution and etiquette to the winds.

"Father, forgive me, but I must speak my true mind in this matter.

"I have lived with my grandmother these last four years, and though she was good to take me in and I am most grateful for that, she made no alteration in the life she led that took my different and individual needs into account. Over the years she had become incapable of change, even had she wished it, thus by her choice we lived apart from the rest of society. A separation that means there will be few, if any, coming to pay their respects. She was close to nobody and this must be known to you. She had no friends, and because of that nor did I. Her life was joyless and empty, but she was elderly and totally resigned to her lot, believing it was the price she must pay for her redemption. She denied herself everything that would have been enriching. Her only satisfaction was in her sewing, for she saw each stitch as a small payment to reduce her debt of sin, but it was at a never-ending cost and consumed her entire life. There was neither space nor entitlement for anything else. What she might have been in other circumstances remained forever untried, and her restricted life shrank more and more over the years. Father, I have committed no sin, but in living that parched existence I too have been punished, even though blameless. To tell me that now I must go and do likewise, living again in isolation with another old woman whose limited life will dictate the manner of my own, is no blessing that I can see.

"There must surely be some other choice. A placement with a family or within a community perhaps, where there is normal human contact and companionship. Father, I beseech you – do not insist that I do this, for rather than the gift that you describe, to me it seems more akin to a curse."

The priest, who had previously responded to her doubts with a mild but slightly irritable reprimand, now looked at her with a mixture of shock, confusion and doubt. Her reasoning and the attendant emotion had hit home with its justifiable sincerity. She had made her point convincingly, and there was no way he could evade addressing the legitimacy of her claim.

He shifted uneasily on the bench, sitting in a more upright position as if to regain his shaken authority, but he couldn't quite suppress a sigh of acknowledgement.

"Selina, you have made me aware that, as a young person, your place in life and your requirements do not necessarily always align comfortably with the requirements of an older person at a very different stage."

He paused, and then firmly composed himself back into the role of church functionary and ordained instrument of religious infallibility. There could be no arguing with God's will as administered by the clergy. The laity was ignorant in such matters and therefore needed to be told what was good for them.

"The fact does remain however that this is truly a great opportunity for you. This woman's circumstances in no way resemble your grandmother's, and there is no reason to suppose she lives in isolation, quite the opposite. The high-born are used to a lifestyle that embraces all the rich benefits that come with wealth and status. The impairment of advancing age may have limited her activities to some degree, and this is no doubt why she now has need of a close and able assistant."

He then inadvertently admitted the more significant cause for the church's decision.

"But that apart, the truth of the matter is, I'm afraid, that there is no other suitable placement at the moment, or at least none that we could commit to without reservation. None can judge without experiencing the actual truth and reality of the thing in question. This applies to yourself and I admit in this case to me also, therefore I will make sure that the priest of that diocese keeps an eye on you and informs me of how you have settled in. I cannot interfere directly in things that are not of my own parish, but I can and I will keep informed."

He stood up then, making it clear beyond all doubt that the exchange was at an end, the matter settled, and that there was nothing more to be said. For Selina, there was still a great deal more she needed to say but she knew she must bite her tongue; arguing her case further now could only do more harm than good. She would lose his support if he judged her difficult or wilful, and she might have need of that in the future.

But his presentation had not made sense, and she wanted clarification on the obvious discrepancies. If this woman lived in society with those of her kind, why would she need to go to the church to find a suitable candidate for a companion? Surely there were those about her who would best fill the role – why go outside her own parish in the search? The oddest thing of all, though, was that a woman in her position would be bound to already have a close lady's maid in attendance. It had nothing to do with age, but station.

As he donned his cape, she gave no outward sign of her concerns, but submissively opened the door for him with a little curtsey to demonstrate respect for his office and meekly accepted his blessing in return. Then he was gone, leaving her alone with her dead grandmother.

*

The priest's departure left Selina painfully aware that the door had also closed on hope. Her fate seemed uncompromisingly sealed. As she considered the dismal prospect of a repetition of the life that had gone before, she had instinctively gone into her garden and worked for a spell, glad there was still light enough to see what she was doing. She had the need to be there. The little plot had always been her sanctuary and private place. Here she could retreat, free while she tended the plants to think the thoughts that she could share with no one. As she eased out a few stubborn tares, she pondered on who would care for it when she was gone. What manner of person might they be, and would they appreciate and tend it as devotedly as had she? It would hurt her to be parted from it, but, truth to tell it was the only thing that she would miss.

She determined then and there, that if she must leave behind her beloved garden, she would at least take the chest of remnants with her. They did not strictly belong to her, but nor did they belong to anyone else. And those beautiful fabrics that had cheered and delighted her in a life short of such pleasure, she would not have them lost to her. If she folded and placed her own garments over them, should any man attached to the church pry into her possessions, he would not dare show indelicate interest in the items with which women clothed their bodies, especially if the undergarments were displayed conspicuously on top.

She would take too her grandmother's work box, the scissors and shears, the spools of thread and skeins of silk, the needles, pins and stays, and the measuring tapes, for no one could argue that these were not rightfully hers. She may not have the same rare ability as her grandmother, but she could sew to a good standard and she had a mind, now she thought about it, to fashion herself a wonderful patchwork tunic from the contents of her acquired treasure chest. It would be like Jacob's amazing coat of many colours, a dazzling rainbow of kingfisher iridescence, a feast for the eye and all the senses, and it would be fit for a princess, even if she herself didn't actually have occasion or opportunity to wear it. But that reminded her of her grandmother's wasted and unworn finery, and she promised herself at that moment that whatever she created from such a glorious palette of radiant possibilities, it would not be hidden away, doomed to be no feast for the eye but rather food only for the moths.

If, on the face of it, once more she had no choice in what befell her, being entirely at the mercy of the church authorities, at least now, she reminded herself, she was old enough and robust enough to resist their imperious dictate if she had to. The priest had admitted that what had been decreed was not the best, but the only option. She would go, as go she must, but if it proved to be a dreadful incarceration with a crabbed old woman, then she simply would not stay. She would run away. Somehow or other she would make her way back to her true home, where she would find her brothers and they would take her into their care. In the joy of reunion, they would never allow her to be wrenched away from them again, nor forced against her will into any form of conscription imposed by officious outside forces.

With the possibility of escape firmly planned, visualised, and ready to be put into action if and when needed, she felt less helpless and more in control, strong and sure in her own ability to act out her resolve. She stood up then, and with the light fading fast, brushed the dirt from her fingers before rinsing them in the rain-water barrel. There was a new moon just appearing in the darkening heavens, and she made a wish on it for good fortune in all her endeavours. Her mother had named her for the moon, the planetary body that governed all women's lives, in a rejoicing to have given birth to a daughter after her two sturdy sons. Thus, Selina felt an affinity to both as she silently voiced her invocation. Then she went back in to her grandmother.

She lit candles, putting two of the sconces at her grandmother's head and two at her feet, and, unhooking the simple little wooden crucifix from the wall above her mattress, she placed it under her folded hands. Then she settled herself on the stool close by to keep watch with her through the first night.

CHAPTER THREE

Over the three days, one or two called in while Selina still sat with her grandmother throughout most of the daylight hours. But they came more out of curiosity than respect, and, when they saw there were neither viands nor good ale on offer, they did not linger. Selina, aware of their paltry motivations, made no attempt to detain them, neither did she desist from displaying her contempt with a look of chilly disapproval. If they had refrained previously from calling in to check that all was well with them they need expect no welcome now, nor were their hypocritical condolences countenanced and were hardly acknowledged.

After the third day, when the watch was finally over, the fourth, the day of the funeral, dawned clear and bright, the sun ascending in full spring glory and the birds too in full-throated, exuberant song. Again, Selina thought ruefully that this was a time when to be alive was joy enough, and no time for anyone to be done with living.

The two gravediggers, men of few words, had come at first light and lifted her grandmother into an unadorned and unlined coffin, then waited outside whilst Selina placed cushioning under her head and cloths around her to keep her body firmly fixed. She had picked some cherry blossom and put this in alongside and at her feet. When it was done to her satisfaction, she called the men back in, and without further ado they nailed the lid firmly down. It seemed such a noisy and brutal act that she could not refrain from wincing as the last glimpse of her grandmother disappeared for ever from view. Then the coffin was carried out to the handcart and loaded on. There was neither horse nor hearse nor cortege for her grandmother, just one man pushing and one man steadying and Selina following on behind.

But Selina had dressed in her best, and wore a fine, soft, dark blue shawl, draped carefully over head and shoulders. She carried a bouquet of blossom tied with a purple satin ribbon from the chest. If such colours denoted higher ranking, she did not think anyone would challenge it on such an occasion, that is if it was noticed at all which was hardly likely. She would honour her grandmother in whatever way she was able. This was the completion of her circumscribed life, a life in which all she earned beyond subsistence went to pay for her death, a situation that had Selina wondering if it might even have been better never to have been born at all.

When the little procession arrived at the church door, the men lifted the coffin from the cart, careful to keep it level, then heaved it onto their shoulders and carried it inside, where they deposited it on waiting trestles near the altar. Her grandmother, spare to start with, had finished a mere wisp of a creature and she was no taxing weight for them to bear. Just as she had neither plumed horses nor stately hearse, she had no pall bearers to solemnly process her to lie awaiting her final mass, only these two rough fellows in peasant dress as escort.

Selina's grandmother had given birth to a child but with no husband had been deprived of the sacrament of a nuptial mass, and Selina was not even sure if her mother had been baptised, but assumed, given her status, most likely not. This then was her grandmother's one and only legitimate entitlement to any sacred rite as seen in the eyes of the church she had served all her life, but now being gone from the world could not relish.

A lifetime's privation had provided only the most scrimped and meagre ceremony, but at least Selina was heartened to see that there were many containers of spring flowers, blossom and catkins still there fresh from Sunday. The sweet smell of them mingling with the incense was like a promise of eternity. And their almost gaudy vividness was such a defiant statement of vigour that it seemed to even dare challenge the sovereignty of death itself. She placed her own bouquet on the coffin, where as if catching the triumphant stance of those of its kind, it glowed in the scintillating shafts of sunlight streaming in through the stained-glass windows; the fiery light making it seem almost luminous against the pale, unpolished wood. No amount of money could have purchased anything more beautiful, Selina thought, and she gave thanks for the gifts of springtime free for all.

As the priest prepared himself, a few others from the church came to join her. They served in one way or another, each according to their abilities just as her grandmother had, and thus had known her, inasmuch as she could be known. They came now to her departing with respect and kind regard; Selina, expecting none but herself to be present, was immeasurably moved and grateful, and gestured her acknowledgement involuntarily with a hand touching to her heart. They nodded in sympathetic response.

And so, her grandmother had a gathering about her in her final hour before burial that she could not have foreseen, but would surely have given thanks for. How could she not? Why was it that she had chosen to exclude herself so completely from the warmth of human contact and comfort? Was it shame, or had she simply forgotten how to reach out and receive such life-enhancing gifts? Her disposition had suited her far better for the convent than the hurly burly of the marketplace, and she could not, or would not, respond to offers of friendship and inclusion. But alas so be it, it was the spilt milk that was now beyond regret.

At the interment, her fellow mourners stood a measured way back as befitted those who were not close family, and so Selina concluded her relationship with her grandmother with a solitary sprinkling of dirt that clattered on the coffin lid with noisy disrespect for the dead. All then withdrew and dispersed, leaving the gravediggers to pile the earth back into the space, 'Earth to earth'. And so it was done, the brief ceremony and the little life, both over.

*

She returned to the dwelling, which, while it never felt like home, now without the presence of her grandmother seemed even less than it was before. She had occupied it for so many long, uneventful years, that it did not seem possible that either could be separated from the other. They had fused into a co-existence that was as indivisible and enduring as any relationship you could think of. Subdued she may have been, but nonetheless the emptiness that resulted from her absence was stark, and the place, small to begin with, strangely seemed now even more shrunken as a result.

Selina remembered well the warmth and vitality of her own family home. The four years of living with her grandmother had not erased it from her mind, thank God, for that memory had sustained her through bleak times, when the lack of demonstrable affection seemed more than she could bear. She had not lost recall of gaiety and laughter, of a sense of belonging, of loving and being loved in return. And this she knew was what gave life its savour, and she would find it again, even if in the quest she had to run the risk of striking out on her own in a dangerous world.

She had a day to clean and pack up; not long but long enough, seeing that between them they had so little. The table and benches belonged to the church and the straw mattresses would be burnt along with her grandmother's clothes. The few crocks would be left behind, as Selina could not foresee having any need of them in her new placement, and should she abscond she would hardly burden herself with anything that might hinder speed. Whoever came next, and she had not heard tell who they might be, they were welcome to them.

Her mother of course had also spent her childhood and growing years in this place, and from what she had told of them they were little, if any, different from Selina's own experience. She had been the physical manifestation of a fall from grace. Her very presence, being as it was a constant reminder of iniquity, had resulted in the stifling of any natural maternal instincts. So, her grandmother had raised her with only a conscientious sense of duty and obligation, but fortunately too with a clear understanding that the child herself was innocent of any sin. Thus, like Selina, she had been well cared for, but with no evidence of a loving impulse behind that caring.

Maybe her own mother had been more like her absent father, the mummer, for there had been a life force in her that was irrepressible and not to be denied. She would not settle for an allocation at the bottom of the heap, no matter what her mother or anyone else might decree was her rightful place in a God-given order. Her errant father had ever remained nameless and unknown, except for the fact that he had made his living in dumb show and displayed no sense of moral rectitude. But perhaps his adventuring way of life, though reprehensible, was passed on to her mother as inherited forcefulness, and to Selina also as a saving strength and grace.

The mummer and the details of his life were lost for good and all in the mists of times past – her mother had been lost to the Pestilence, and her grandmother to old age and natural causes. Now she too would soon be gone. Whoever came to occupy the dwelling next would have no connection or concern for those lives lived out here beforehand. They would disappear irretrievably and be as forgotten as if they had never been. Surely though, it had to be that something of them must survive and persist, some echo of their lives absorbed and retained in the fabric of the structure, an imbuing not so easily completely wiped away. Who could tell? And she herself would return, if she returned at all, only to visit her grandmother's grave and would have no reason to revisit the house.

At the end of the day, though, with mattresses and clothing incinerated and the ashes raked away, the dirt floor swept clean and table and benches scrubbed, there was no visible trace left of their habitation at all – the garden the only clue as to what manner of folk had previous tenure.

The chest and her grandmother's sewing box ready at the door, Selina, now with no mattress, settled down on her shawl on the floor to await collection on the morrow. She had been instructed to be ready early, when some form of transport would be sent to fetch and convey her to her new placement. Neither the priest nor any other person had volunteered to send her on her way, nor accompany her on the journey. She felt very much abandoned, with only her own resources to call on. She would depart from this place and this parish with no calls of "Good luck!", no cheery waves nor "Godspeed"s. None would miss her or suffer from the lack of her presence, as unacknowledged she was borne away to heaven only knew where. It was not a comfortable feeling. She knew she would get little sleep that night, but it would not be because of the hard floor she was forced to lie on – her mind not her body would keep her awake.

She had wanted change and it had come to her bidding. Eager for new experiences and a fuller life, she had invited it in, but she had little hope that she would discover what she sought ahead of her. However, she concluded, she would find out soon enough what manner of place and employer awaited her, so there was no point in the meantime filling her head with fruitless speculation. It might all turn out well and good, with her fears and doubts proving wholly unfounded.

Her fitful dozing was evidence that she had not reassured herself with hopeful optimism. Her uppermost feeling remained one of extreme foreboding, illustrated when she did sleep by dreams of dungeons and barred windows. Waking in the early hours from such torment, she roused herself, and fearing more of such things, sat up on the stool for the remainder of the night. When the deep dark started to give way, she went out and said farewell to the dwelling and to the garden that she could no longer call her own, and as first light came bright enough, she gathered more of the pink frothing blossoms that had decked her grandmother's coffin. She filled one of the remaining crocks with them as a token of goodwill and welcome for the newcomers. She hoped they would be young and lively, not old and weary, and that they would fill the place with happy noise. It was what it needed as much as she did herself.

Then she sat on the chest by the open door and waited for the conveyance that would transport her to whatever it was that lay ahead.

Chapter Four

She heard the transport coming before she saw it, the plod of hooves and the accompanying occasional snort of a horse picking its way along the track still heavily rutted from winter. The oxen that regularly passed on their way to the fields had given it rough usage, and, as they drew nearer, Selina could hear the grumbling curses of the driver who was no doubt having a hard time of it with the steering. Then they rounded the curve and came into view, a small one-horse carriage, covered but far from fancy. This could not be the main mode of transport for a woman of high ranking, but presumably a more modest affair for regular conveyance. As Selina stood up and hailed him, the driver called out a "Whoa!" to the horse, and, pulling back on the reins, brought the carriage to a halt beside her. Climbing down stiffly from the position up front, he arched his back, clearly aching from the journey, as he indicated the chest and box.

"Is this coming along with thee-self?"

At Selina's confirmation, he loaded it on the shelf at the back fashioned for that purpose, and, covering it over with a stout cloth, roped it firmly in place. While he was thus busily occupied, Selina asked, "Is it a long journey, how far distant from here?"

"Best part of the day to get there, but we will stop for a while when the sun is directly overhead for sustenance and to stretch our legs. And the nag will need a rest and a bag of hay, and then when he has filled his belly and got his breath we will be back on our way. He is an old fellow but good and willing. I will not have him ill-used, and we have already made the journey the other way around."

Selina asked if this meant they had travelled overnight.

"No one of sound mind would be on the road in the hours of darkness. That is when every cut-throat and raving madman is abroad, preying on hapless folk caught by chance between safe havens. Not just them neither, bad as they are. There are the phantoms that roam freely in the black of night and all manner of devilish things released from hell, that will steal not just your purse and your life but your soul too, God help you. No, we stopped at a hostelry from sundown to sunrise, with four strong walls and the company of others doing the same."

With that he opened the carriage door for her, putting a hand under her elbow to help her in for courtesy's sake only, for it was plain she was well able to climb in unaided. Then they were under way.

It was a slow and bumpy start, with Selina hanging on to the strap provided to stop being pitched about, but when they gained the main route it proved easier and more comfortable going and they trotted along at a steady pace.

The landscape rolling past quickly became new and unknown to her. Although she had lived in the region for four years, she had seen but little of the terrain any distance from the dwelling, and she felt as if the blindfold of restricted vision was at last being pulled from her eyes. So much to see, so much to experience, so many possibilities in a world that had suddenly expanded in every direction. Her spirits rose just looking at it all, and as they came into more populous places, with noise and bustle and many people going about their business, she was completely enthralled. Folk were inspecting the wares on sale at the stalls and through open windows, and the vendors were loudly extolling their virtues. The centres of the streets were occupied by carts and strings of packhorses. At the sides crowded citizens in every kind of dress, friars in black, white, and grey, men-at-arms, roistering groups of lads who had entered schools or religious houses, those returning to their lodgings with their 'bastards' or daggers in their belts alongside their leather purses, coxcombs parading with long hair, furred cloaks and shoes chequered in red and green. She had not seen the like since she was eleven years of age. It released in her a flood of memories that were almost overwhelming in their intensity. That remembrance was like a homecoming and reclamation, for here was the rhythm and energy of daily life as she had known it and had been part of it without ever realising what a simple blessing it was. She yearned then with a desperate homesickness for her parents, her brothers, friends and neighbours, and the life that had been hers. This awakening of her childhood past seemed to completely fill her, wiping away entirely more recent times as if they had hardly happened, as insubstantial as dreams. And in that restoration, she became again fully herself, just as her grandmother had in the transformation of death.

She had existed in suspended animation for four years, waiting for the key that would release her from confined inertia back again into the world she had lost. No wonder, she thought, that the dreams of her new placement were of barred windows and dungeons, for she had a great fear of being cast back again into the same or similar prison having only just gained her release. God forbid!

When the sun reached its zenith, they pulled off the thoroughfare alongside a small inn as promised, and after the driver had uncoupled the horse from the shafts and given him over to the care of a stable boy who would attend his needs, only then did he see to their own. They settled at a table and waited for the food to come. All were served the same dish: a substantial stew of meat of some kind and root vegetables, no doubt from a diminishing winter store. There were only a few others so they could sit apart and the meal came quickly. Selina was not used to so much meat. She and her grandmother had plenty enough, but generally the poor could not afford to eat meat, save for feast days. Though she had never felt in any way deprived by its lack, rather the opposite, she was hungry and applied herself willingly to her trencher and all that was on it. The driver encouraged her to eat her fill as funds had been provided for all the needs of the journey.

She was warmed by his being mindful of her and looking to see she was well served. Just as he couldn't settle to his own food till he knew the horse had his portion, she had the impression he would be as caring with anyone or anything in his charge. She had never known a grandfather, but had she then this man would fit the image in her mind's eye. He was stocky rather than stout in his ageing, and weather-beaten as were most that were not of the merchant class or in other employment that kept them out of wind and weather. His hair and beard were trimmed, his tunic and hose clean, but more than all this, good indication as it was of character, it was his expression that marked him clearly as a decent and kindly man. He said his name was Jacob and it fitted him exactly, almost as if he'd grown into it and what it represented. Selina felt able to speak to him freely of her concerns and had the need to do so.

"The woman I am going to serve, who must also be your own employer, I have no knowledge of her, not even so much as her name. Could you tell me what manner of person she is and what I might expect in taking up residence and close association with her? Then I can prepare myself for our first encounter."

Jacob, raising his eyes from his food, gave her a somewhat doubtful look that reminded her too much of the priest's countenance for her comfort or peace of mind.

"'Tis true enough that I am in her employ, but my work is all about what has to be done outside the residence, and the fact is I never go inside the house, and she never comes out. My orders come from her but not direct, so I have no actual dealings with her personally. Truth is, young mistress, I have neither met her, nor even so much as set eyes on her in the several years since my engagement."

"But you must meet and talk surely to others whose work is within the house and know well her temperament and her ways?" Selina insisted.

He sighed. "There is only the one who has direct dealings with Madame, the chatelaine, and it is she who conveys to the rest what is required of us. The day before yesterday, she bade me prepare both horse and carriage for this journey. I was to fetch you and bring you back, but why, or for what reason or purpose, was knowledge to which I was not privy. That is always the way of it. We simply do as we are bid and ask no questions, for in all other respects she is a fair and generous employer. That is more than good enough for most of us."

It was not good enough for Selina.

"But why does she keep herself so apart, and what need has she for the likes of me if she already has someone close to her to do all her bidding?"

The sense of alarm that had suffused her dreams, now burst through into full consciousness. It looked ominously as if once again she was doomed to be confined with an old woman, who, in seeking isolation for herself, imposed it on others regardless of their wishes. This time, however, it seemed certain it would be even more restrictive. Her grandmother had been benign and unassuming in what she inadvertently demanded. This woman sounded more absolute in her rulings and maybe even ruthless in applying them. And if she kept herself away from all society, for whatever reason, would that not also be her own fate, literally to be locked in with only the chatelaine having the keys to her freedom to come or go? She looked earnestly to Jacob for reassurance.

Jacob looked troubled, and he took his time to answer, searching for the right words but also for the truth, for, as Selina had seen, he was an honest man and he would not play her false with blandishments or deception.

"There are things I cannot tell, not from withholding but because I am ignorant of such matters. As I said, most of us there are uninformed about most things. What I can tell you though, is that there is no evidence at all that Madame would in any way be other than good and fair in her dealings with those in her employ. I have not heard of anybody that has had cause for complaint. But when it comes to asking why she sees no one nor allows them to see her, now as to that, I have to say, there is much gossip as to the reason, but 'tis no more than tittle-tattle and most likely all nonsense. Nevertheless, I shall inform you what is supposed and then you will know as much as I.

"They do say that at some time, a goodly while past, some terrible accident, mishap, or malady befell her that caused the ruination of her features, and, having before been feted for her beauty, 'twas a dastardly thing for her to bear.

"They do also say that she was not widowed, but that her husband deserted her afterwards in her hour of need. Because he could no longer countenance to look 'pon her he took himself off, disappearing like a thief in the night, and wherever he went he has not been heard of, nor from, since. Now that would be a mightily cruel thing to do if it were true, but as for that I can only say, if it was indeed the way of things, 'twould make sense of it all. And it be only natural that ever afterwards she be unable to bear for others to see and judge her as her husband had, better surely to let none have the chance and thus save herself from more such distress and misery.

"As for the chatelaine, she is now long in the tooth, and, judging by the way she grumbles and groans, likely finding the aches and pains of age are overtaking her willingness and ability to fulfil what is required of her.

Mayhap that is why you have been fetched, to learn the ways of that station and take on the role when she be no longer able?

"As I have said, there is no certainty in any of this, but it is all I can offer, for in any case you will know the true facts of the matter soon enough. We will be on our way when you have cleared your platter and the nag is ready for the shafts. Now I shall go and settle the debt and see if they have some apples for the road for all three of us."

*

They reached their destination with the light fading fast, and Jacob, who had refused to urge the horse to a speedier pace, was clearly relieved to have made it home before they were overtaken by the perils of darkness. The journey back had taken longer, as the fatigued horse had needed to mind and husband his diminishing strength, but whatever frightful possibilities the night might have held, Jacob had refused to take the whip to him.

They had travelled the final stretch through dense woodland, which had also given some cause for alarm, despite it adjoining home territory. For dim as it was now, and at any time or season, it could be the hiding place for who knew what manner of mischief or mayhem. But the track was firm from constant use, the going good, and they came to no harm. Yet Selina was only too aware as they passed through the thick of it, that the obvious isolation of this place seemed accompanied by inaccessibility, a considerable hindrance to any plan of escape. She might flee from one danger, only to be faced by another even greater.

As they emerged from the thinning trees into a more open landscape, Jacob called back to her from the driving seat, "Put thy head out and take it all in, for we are come to thy new home."

The horse, also recognising his surroundings and all that it entailed, found his second wind and eagerly picked up pace. Selina, leaning out of the carriage, peered ahead over his bobbing ears.

The residence, built on a promontory, raised it above all else to dominate its environs, but its appearance as they approached was mainly obscured by the high wall that surrounded it. Only the roof and chimneys could be seen, but without doubt it was a goodly sized manor house. Round and about it were dwellings and other buildings, barns and stores all set in clearings with orchards, crops and grazing for animals. There was a sense of orderliness and of all being neat and well-tended, but the fact that it also looked like a settlement entire unto itself in the middle of nowhere did nothing at all to reassure her. Her fears were mounting, but she tried to hold on to the fact that Jacob, clearly a good man, was resident here in one of the dwellings, and he had never heard tell of any bad thing with regard to the woman who presided over it.

He stopped the carriage in front of a large arch carved into the house's encircling stone wall. It was fitted with double-fronted doors of such formidable size and strength they would have not been amiss barring admission to a fortress. Alighting and taking hold of the knotted bell rope to the side, he set up a strident clanging that roused the rooks just settling for the night in adjacent trees. In indignant response, they answered back with their own raucous clamour. Yet, despite this strident shattering of the peace, it took some while before there came the rasping of a key in the lock from within, followed by the opening of a small door set in one half of the larger pair.

The woman revealed, standing there with her grasp still on the big metal key in the lock, had a heavy chain around her waist to which it was attached along with many others. She was stooped, but whether from the burden of their weight or from other causes Selina could not tell. Dressed in black, with hooded eyes that appeared the same colour in the gloom and a sharp nose, she had the look of one of the crows that had complained noisily at their arrival.

"What took thee so long, Jacob? I've been ready for my bed this long while."

"We did not dawdle, and stopped but the once at noon, long enough only to get a quick bite. There and back was a task for the nag with the carriage and two of us to haul along. We have had only apples since, and those well past their best. We are all in need of better fare. I'll untie the boxes and bring them inside, then I will get this good old fellow to his stall for a rub down and his supper. He has earned his fodder this day."

As he went to the rear of the carriage to attend to the two boxes, the chatelaine came closer to Selina and scrutinised first her face, and then, standing back a little, examined her from head to toe. Finally, she spoke.

"My eyesight is not what it was, but you have the look of a young woman who might manage well here. There are certain qualities that are necessary – strong body, strong mind, and an ability to see beyond appearances. But we will not talk of such things at this late hour. Come inside and I will show you to your quarters where you will find all you need, then you will be fetched in the morning for your breakfast and to learn the details of what is required of you."

Jacob came then, carrying both chest and box with surprising ease. He obviously was used to such demands on his strength and was in no way extended. He placed them on the floor inside the door, and then, touching his forelock, he took his leave of Selina.

"I do bid thee goodnight. I trust you will sleep well and I shall look to see you again as soon as maybe."

She thanked him for all he had done and echoed his hope that they would see each other again soon. Meaning every word, she was loath to see him go. There was no doubt that, brief as their acquaintance was, she valued it, and of his being close at hand.

Then, with a further touch to his forehead as he nodded to the chatelaine, he turned about and went back to see to the horse.

The chatelaine watched him go for a moment before ushering Selina inside, and, after laboriously shutting and relocking the door behind them, paused briefly in her tracks to add, "My name is Abigail, and you may call me by it, though none other has that privilege."

Selina following behind sought to make out all that was about her, hard as it was becoming in the gathering gloom. They crossed an inner courtyard along a stone-flagged path that led to the main entrance of the house which had sturdy double doors set in a pointed arch, though not on the same formidable scale or structure as the outer pair. The arch itself was part of a square two-storey tower that fronted the building and marked the way in.

The doors opened directly into the heart of the house, the spacious hall where there were torches burning in twisted metal wall brackets that threw enough good light to see to the farthest corners. A fire roaring on the big open hearth was well set in a deep fireplace served by a cavernous chimney. Atop was a stone mantelpiece elaborately carved, with the intricate patterning all picked out in colours of red and blue.

The room's main item of furniture was a long trestle table that occupied the centre and substantially filled it. Along with the sturdy benches on either side were two handsome carved chairs at the head, presumably for the lord and lady's use. An ornate and similarly carved chest fashioned from dark, oiled wood stood against one end wall, with a tall matching cupboard holding rows of pewter plates and goblets at the other. The walls themselves were all hung with rich red and brown tapestries showing lively hunting and hawking scenes.

Selina had needed to halt on the threshold, brought to an involuntary standstill by what she beheld. Never before had she seen anything quite so fine, nor so grand and impressive. It demanded a demonstration of reverence and respect akin to that required before entering a church. But despite the grandeur, there was also a pervasive air of warmth and welcome palpably present that she had not expected. Yet for all that, and the fire throwing out full heat and light, there was none there to benefit from its splendour. The place seemed entirely deserted, with not even a hound or two keeping vigil. Well, the hour was late and maybe all had taken to their beds, and the dogs banished outside for the night.

Having come at last to her new abode, whatever she might have envisaged beforehand fell well short of the actuality, and was so far removed from her grandmother's humble dwelling that, other than the possibility of similar confinement, there could be no comparison. When the priest had said that very thing, she had not appreciated how vast the difference and distance between the two domiciles could actually be.

Abigail moved slowly across the hall to a large screen at the far end, painted vividly in blue, red and gold, and she beckoned for her to follow. Her speed, Selina guessed, was not so much to politely give her the time to take in her new surroundings, but because this was her normal gait. As she thus proceeded, Abigail informed her that behind the screen, hidden from the view of those in the hall, lay kitchen, larder, bake-house, buttery and brew house, but they were not heading for these. Rather, their goal was a little winding staircase tucked between hall and domestic premises.

They took the stairs which led up to the next floor at Abigail's measured pace. It opened out at the top to form a broad landing that divided the chambers leading off to left from those to the right. Pausing for a moment to get her breath, Abigail put one forefinger to her lips, and with the other pointed to the left hand where the door of the immediate room was a little ajar. Inside could just be glimpsed a comfortable parlour lit by the light of several candles. It was the room that Madame occupied all the hours of daylight, Selina was told in hushed tones, and none entered there unless specifically bidden. Beyond that was her bedchamber, likewise out of bounds lest invited.

Observing the signal for silence, Selina merely nodded in acknowledgement of the information. But instinct also warned her that it would be wiser not to ask any questions at this stage, however much she longed to. Abigail was still assessing her and would almost certainly be on the lookout for any display of inappropriate behaviour or indelicate curiosity. That Abigail would be fiercely loyal to the woman she served she did not doubt, so she must be wary and not give her any cause for disquiet. As with the priest, there was a time when holding your tongue was the best policy.

Turning to the right, away from Madame's quarters, Abigail shuffled along a passage with doors at intervals to one side only. The opposing wall was interspersed with tall, narrow windows, though what they overlooked she could not tell, the hour being too late for seeing. When they reached the third chamber, Abigail halted by a door of a size that hinted the room beyond was likewise of no paltry dimensions, indicating to Selina that this was to be her accommodation. Grasping the ringed handle, she turned it, letting the door swing wide, then stood aside for Selina to enter before her. Selina had enough time and alertness about her to notice that there was a key in the lock. It was on the outside, but at least it was not on the chain at the chatelaine's waist. She went in cautiously, and, uncertain as to what she would find within, craned her neck, trying to see as much as was possible before fully entering.

The first surprise was indeed how spacious the chamber was, more than four times the size of the whole of her grandmother's dwelling. The second, and greater, was the fact that it was furnished with a four-poster bed hung with curtains. Beds were a sign of station and status, and certainly not normally provided for people such as herself. Her parents had plans for one as soon as funds could comfortably allow, but in the meantime, like their children, they had slept on straw mattresses on the floor. They could not have envisioned Selina having a resting place such as this, nor of it being fully endowed with pillows, sheets, blankets, and, beyond belief, a patterned velvet counterpane – a fact that had her jaw dropping. Eyes and mouth both wide open, she spun round to face Abigail in search of explanation. How could she be entitled to occupy a chamber clearly fit for the most noble in the land? It made no sense and was beyond all reason.

Abigail proved she was not devoid of humour by failing to fully hide a smile at Selina's reaction. It was clear she was enjoying her astonishment.

"Madame Isabella wants all in her employ to be well-housed, well-nourished and well-content. She does not care for change, and thus does her utmost to ensure that, by providing no possible cause for complaint, none would wish to leave her service.

"You will have her particular concern as you will be privileged to be closer to her in your duties than all, save myself. To that end all here has been provided for your utmost comfort and should prove, I think, to your complete satisfaction.

"There is a choice of dishes on the chest under the window for your supper, and I am sure you must be ready for them after your long journey. There is also an ewer of water and a bowl that you may refresh yourself. On the morrow, your things will be brought up to you, though Madame will provide new attire for you as is suitable for your position in her service. There is just a nightgown left for this night at present. Tomorrow I will come for you when she is ready to receive you. Meanwhile, I wish you a good night and trust you will sleep well. Do not leave your chamber. It is not permitted to wander about during the late hours, nor is there any need, as tomorrow you will become fully acquainted with the premises and the way things are conducted in the household. Now I will take my leave of you. It is past my normal hour for retiring and I weary easily these days and find any extra demands on me overtaxing. My own bedchamber is the first we came to and closest to my Lady's. Till tomorrow."

Abigail retraced her steps then with a weary tread that reminded Selina of the horse, and it was reassuring to register the fact that neither had been dispensed with, despite both being clearly no longer quite fit for service. It was reassuring too to see that Abigail, even as she was prohibiting night wanderings, had made no move to lock the door, sealing her within.

Selina closed it herself, but did not remove the key to set it in the door on the inside. Whatever challenges the situation might present, there seemed no danger lurking here within the house that required bolting her bedchamber door. Turning then to give her full attention to the place she had been allocated, she sat gingerly on the bed to test it, fearful of any damage to the exquisite coverlet. It gave beneath her weight and felt wondrously soft. She found, on drawing back the covers, that the mattress was overlaid by a deep feather topping. No straw here.

The supper dishes on a salver beneath a muslin cloth were such as she had never encountered – breast of some kind of uncommon fowl, fine white bread made no doubt in the bake-house, butter and a variety of cheeses. Preserved fruits reposed in a dish with nuts and other sweetmeats, but as to these she could only guess what they might be. Putting one in her mouth and testing it with her tongue brought her no nearer to an answer, other than it was delicious.

Beneath the window that must overlook the inner courtyard, the large, elaborate chest on which the supper dishes reposed was of the kind used to store clothes. She opened it but found it empty, no doubt in waiting for her own apparel, both those garments she had brought with her, and presumably those too that would be given her as Abigail had suggested. The final item of furniture in the room was an ornately worked wooden chair that stood alongside the bed and was dressed with a chair-back that matched the bedcover.

Of all these furnishings, splendid as they were, none were the dominant feature of the room, not even the bed. The thing that unerringly drew and held your eye was the wall-hanging opposite the bed, and this not just because of its size, though it was very large, almost covering the entire wall it embellished.

After folding the coverlet back, Selina settled herself cross-legged on the end of the bed opposite it, compelled to give it her full attention. The distance between them and the perspective gave the sense of it almost being an extension of the room; the two were on the same plane making them seem connected. It was more colourful and intricate than those in the hall, and it did not repeat the hunting themes they favoured. Indeed, it appeared to have been wrought by entirely different hands. Depicted here in vivid detail and clarity was no bloodlust pursuit of hapless animals, but a scene of pastoral perfection.

A broad, shallow brook ran from left to right, dividing the setting in two. In the lower half, youths and maids were sitting in a flower-studded meadow, communing together or fashioning daisy chains or their like. Some were wading in the crystal waters and bending to examine water lilies or golden fish. Others, with musical instruments of diverse kinds, were making music to which those gathered danced in circles or in pairs.

In the top half, above the brook, the landscape stretched away to the tree-lined slopes of rolling hills which in turn gave way to distant blue mountains with snowy peaks. These towering monuments of nature were of compelling but mysterious beauty. They magnetically attracted but also disturbed, with a sense of being possibly perilous should you dare try to scale them. Reaching as they did up to the heavens, they were holy places and inhospitable to souls who might prove unworthy.

In the foreground, on the nearside bank of the brook, animals had come to quench their thirst but also to allow themselves to be greeted by some of those gathered there who were stretching out inviting hands towards them. Hinds with their fawns were accepting their caresses. Hares and leverets, red foxes and otters with their cubs and all manner of other beasts were assembled in biblical accord, while behind and above them a majestic stag, crowned with many branched antlers, and a pure white stallion kept watch.

She would have continued gazing mesmerised for much longer, but like Abigail she needed desperately to sleep and it could no longer be denied. With little the previous night, and the day-long hard shuddering of the carriage, her mind and body craved their rest. Rinsing just face, hands, arms and feet grimed from the journey, she put her creased and dusty garments in a tidy pile on the chair, then gratefully pulled the fresh cotton nightgown, left beside her pillow, over her weary head. Crawling into the feathered bed was like falling backwards into clouds, and she slept almost before her head had reached the satin-covered pillow.

CHAPTER FIVE

Selina awoke to see a pitcher of fresh water and a towel left in readiness for her on the chest. Laid out neatly over the back of the chair were a girdled robe and a silk shift, replacing the pile of her own soiled garments of which there was now no sign. Alongside the towel, a large, silver hand mirror with matching comb and hairbrush had been placed, and on the floor beside the bed a pair of soft leather slippers were ready and waiting for her feet.

Who it was that had affected entry so silently that she had not been roused or at what hour they had come she could not tell. But surely such stealth could not have been achieved by Abigail with her unsteady gait. That she had not locked the door would have been evident to anyone who cared to look, the key clearly visible on the outside bearing testimony. But whoever it was that had slipped in and out like a wraith, leaving no clue as to their identity or time of coming, had quietly delivered these things to her, then kindly chosen to leave her sleeping rather than waken her.

And such a slumber it had been. She had never before to her memory slept so long or so deep, almost as if bewitched. Fatigue and the soft enveloping of satin bed sheets atop the feather bed had totally claimed her, drawing her down into fathomless oblivion. Maybe no surprise then that she had not heard her nocturnal visitor. But, be that as it may, the arrival of washing water and apparel, whoever had brought them, must mean it was time to rise.

She threw back the bedcovers, thinking to dress quickly and seek out Abigail, until she became mindful of the instruction that she would only be fetched for breakfast and a meeting with Lady Isabella when the time was right. Nevertheless, she would prepare herself now in anticipation of that time, for it could be imminent. Standing on the towel she rubbed and rinsed quickly but thoroughly with the wash cloth, for the garment laid waiting for her she could see was very fine indeed. Fashioned from a rich, brocaded cloth, it was of gentle fit but with a girdle of plaited gold silk that would serve to draw it in and keep it neatly in place. There was a heavy brooch of jewelled bronze at the breast for the same purpose, though the silk shift beneath was designed to serve if necessary as a modesty vestment.

The shift itself, simple as it was, felt extravagantly luxurious against skin accustomed to rougher covering. But it was the brocade robe with its weight and splendour that stayed her in wonder when she had donned and draped it about herself. How could it be that she was adorned in such a garment? Knotting the girdle around her waist, she carefully fixed the bodice with the exquisite jewelled pin then smoothed all down with hands that felt too work-coarsened for contact with such finery. With the enrobing done, she next took up the silver brush, and, first removing any tangles, restored the gloss and smoothness to her hair with vigorous brushing. When that too was completed to her satisfaction, she plaited it into a single long braid which she wound around the top of her head like a coronet. This was achieved by patting and fixing all neatly into place purely by touch as was her usual way, till she minded that she had been gifted a mirror. Raising the heavy silver looking-glass up in front of her to check that all was in order, what she beheld again stopped her breath. For beyond all doubt, she could see from the evidence of her reflection that with a change of garb it was not just apparel that had changed, but everything. Like unto the strutting coxcombs who, parading in their fine feathers, demanded respect in the vainglorious assumption that their splendour warranted it.

But the image she herself now presented had no base in false vanity. It was rather an acknowledgement that she did indeed have the look of a person of noble birth, her appearance no longer at variance with that of her bedchamber. Upon such evidence it had to be owned that, more than anything else, it was the clothes you wore that defined you, and anyone knowing nothing of her true origins, upon encounter would defer automatically to her perceived rank.

She had brought with her the chest of remnants from the old dwelling in brave hope that in fashioning some form of rich and colourful attire she might combat the expected drabness of her new placement. Though, even should that be achieved, she had feared she might never have opportunity or occasion to wear that which she had created. Now here was that notion turned upon its head, for beyond all reckoning she was presently as splendidly adorned as any princess.

As she tentatively moved about the chamber, unused to the weight and length of the robe, and trying to accommodate and become accustomed to both, she considered the possible reasons for such fine raiment. This was certainly not suitable wear for the domestic duties she believed she had been engaged to perform, but nor were last night's supper dishes the expected and appropriate humble fare for a serving girl. By way of explanation, Abigail had said Lady Isabella did not like change and strove therefore to make sure all in her employ were well content. Jacob had also said as much. But this went way beyond what could be construed as a good employer caring for those who served her.

For Jacob had owned, too, that when he had been sent to fetch her and bring her back, he had been given no knowledge as to why or for what reason. Merely accepting that this was the way of things for all in her service, he seemed content to ask no questions, feeling more than compensated with secure employment, so if she was secretive as well as reclusive that was her business and no doubt she had her reasons.

While she must wait as calmly as she could for Abigail to come and take her to her first encounter with this uncommon woman, Selina sat back down on the end of the bed to resume her examination of the Tapestry till such time as she was summoned. Being mindful now as she settled of her new clothing as well as the counterpane, she was unable to be at ease with either. Feeling as she did like an impostor masquerading in someone else's finery, for she could construe no possible reason for such entitlement.

But putting that conundrum aside and engaging again with the vivid imagery, the first thing that drew her attention now was a figure in the immediate foreground that she could not recall from the previous viewing. A young man, solitary and gazing out from the idyllic tableau as if he was searching for something, or someone. He seemed at odds with, or detached from, his surroundings and those about him, as if he were lost. She wondered what such a figure signified in an otherwise apparent paradise. Maybe it had a biblical interpretation as the animals did, but whereas they were in union and accord, he perhaps represented the lost soul or the prodigal son. Looking at him with his back turned to his companions and their happy pursuits, she wondered how she had failed to note him on her first viewing, for he was a compelling character and difficult to overlook. No doubt she had been too weary to take it in. All else though appeared to be as she recalled, with no other note of discord; well not quite the same, because now of course she was seeing it in the light of day rather than by the light of candles. They had cast a different, more diffuse illumination, and the attendant shadows could easily cause misinterpretation. Head on one side, she pondered that possibility, for in all truth it did not appear quite as she recalled. There was a sense of subtle difference, though she could not name what it was, other than in attributing it to the change of light.

Further thought was brought to an abrupt conclusion by a gentle tapping on the door, and she leapt to her feet as if stung. It opened then to reveal Abigail on the threshold, peering enquiringly in at her.

"Ah! You are dressed and ready, good. Let me take a look at you and see if you are fit to meet my Lady."

She came a little into the room and stood, holding on to the bed post while she inspected Selina's transformation.

"Yes, you look well. I think she will not be disappointed, but first we will take you for your breakfast, and the hour is presently too early in any case for us to disturb Madame. She takes time over her own toilette and breakfast, and sees no one till both are completed."

She turned about then and gestured for Selina to follow. They returned to the landing, where, with Abigail's slow and careful negotiation of the stairs, they descended back into the main hall. Though the fire was still ablaze, as before the place was echoingly empty, the only difference being that now two places had been laid at the long trestle table, and the fare for breakfast was ready and waiting. Abigail led her to a setting half way down and indicated that this was to be her place. She herself would not be joining her, she said, for she ate sparingly these days and had already had all she wanted. Meanwhile, there was business in the kitchen that required her attention, so she would see to that and leave her to enjoy her meal.

Selina asked for whom the other setting at the head of the table was laid, and should she not refrain from beginning her own meal till they had come. Abigail paused for a moment then spoke quietly, "That is for my Lordship. His place is always laid though he might be detained, so feel no need to wait on him."

"But is Lady Isabella not widowed, or do you refer to some other kin?"

Abigail made her way determinedly towards the screen and the kitchen beyond, saying only, "There are no other kinfolk. I will be back to take you to Madame in a while."

Selina again held her tongue. It was clear that the topic was not to be pursued at present, if ever, and she would not risk doing anything to antagonise the chatelaine. Also, she did not want to cast Jacob in a bad light by repeating his suspicion that the lord in question had not died but taken off like a runaway. But why set a place for someone who would not come? And, if it was given to people to believe that she was widowed, no doubt to avoid the shame of abandonment, did not such a gesture confound that deceit?

Turning her attention then to the table and the breakfast dishes, she listened too for any signs of life in this vast space that seemed so devoid of it. You would expect some noise of busy activity coming from behind the screen where Abigail had gone to conduct her business in the kitchen, yet she could hear nothing. The only persistent sound was from the cracking of the great logs on the fire and the birdsong that penetrated in from the environs. Sitting there alone in such barren emptiness, she felt not unlike the figure in the Tapestry, adrift in a place where she was clearly out of her depth and did not belong.

She took some of the still-warm and fragrant bread. There was cheese alongside, and spiced cakes with their own rich aroma competing with that issuing from the fresh loaves. To drink, there was a choice between three flagons: ale, mead and water.

'Fine clothes and fine food, Glory be!' she thought.

In the usual way of things, most folk had only bread and beer for the break-fast, taking their appetites with them for the hearty midday main meal. Then they toiled through the second half of the day till the church bell tolled five, which was the hour for supper, the second and final meal of the day. So, like most, Selina was not used to having anything other than a piece of yesterday's loaf for breakfast, washed down with water from their little spring. Though in having that they had been exceptionally fortunate, for much of the water available was not pure and best avoided, ale being the safer and preferred choice. The contrast from the end of a stale loaf to the rich pastries and fine bread laid before her now, delicious as they were, rather than tempt her instead dulled any hunger she might normally have had. With none to share them, and so many uncertainties making everything unknowable, she had lost her appetite, and, like the chatelaine, ate little. She did not leave her place at the table, though, lest wandering in the daylight hours was also forbidden and she incurred the wrath of Abigail or someone else, even if none other was apparent who might be enraged.

There was certainly more provided here for breakfast than she could have done justice to, even had she been of good appetite. Was it really the case that the catering was to include his Lordship should he decide to return and take his place at table? How long had he been gone, and was there any sound reason to suppose that he would come back? Why welcome or wait on such a knave in any case? But she was making the assumption that what Jacob had offered as rumour only was the fact of the matter, when it could, as he admitted, be nothing more than gossip dreamed up by idle minds.

As she waited on Abigail, Selina perused again the tapestries on the walls here. Splendid as they were in their own way, they could not compare with the one in her chamber. Why then was it not displayed where it clearly belonged, in the Great Hall rather than hidden away largely unseen in an upper room? Questions, questions, would she be any the wiser at the day's end?

As if summoned by her disquiet, Abigail reappeared from behind the screen and informed her that the hour had come for her to meet Lady Isabella. She stayed Selina's first though with a gesture, saying she must make it clear that certainly at this initial encounter she should speak only when invited to do so. She must also refrain from prolonged gazing at her Ladyship. It was not permitted, and she should keep her eyes modestly downcast. She should be quiet and she should be decorous. It would be up to Madame how long the interview lasted, and there was no telling in advance how long that might be or the matters to be discussed.

"Surely it will be entirely to do with my duties and what will be required of me, though I must own that I am uncertain now as to exactly what these might be, given that the robe I am wearing for this interview is not the serviceable garment I would have expected. But then nothing is as I expected.

"The priest who made this arrangement said I was to be engaged as maid and assistant to an ageing and infirm woman because of my domestic skills, yet I have been received and treated more as if I was of noble birth than a humble servant. And you have told me but little, Abigail. Will you not help me to make sense of such a paradox, for surely I must have some understanding of what appears incomprehensible, lest I come before Lady Isabella misguided and ill prepared in my ignorance?"

Like Jacob, Abigail took her time and answered carefully.

"When you arrived, I told you that you needed to see beyond appearances and let that still be your watch word. Allow things to unfold at their own pace and do not try to force them into a pattern and limitation where they neither fit nor belong. If you can do that, then you will learn the ways of Lady Isabella and find profit in what you learn. Follow her lead. That is all you need to do, no more than that, and there will be no error. Now mind what I have said, and let us go to my Lady."

Once more they ascended the narrow staircase, and Abigail paused to regain her breath on the landing before she crossed to the parlour door. Knocking gently, she called in, "My Lady, we are come."

"Enter."

The single word sent a shock through Selina's tautly stretched nerves as, heart quaking, she followed Abigail into the chamber.

The room was darkened by heavy curtaining at the windows more than half drawn against the day. All was obscured in this curtailing of the light, but there were no candles burning in compensation. The resulting half-light created an uneasy and disorienting sense of not knowing what time of the clock it might be.

A large, throne-like chair, high-backed and draped with deep gold velvet, was situated with its back to the central window and against what light there was. The occupant therefore could be but dimly made out.

Lady Isabella sat motionless and regally upright in her majestic chair. She was wearing a dress of burgundy silk, elaborately embellished at hem and sleeve with gold embroidery, a patterning that caught such light as there was and glistened with its own luminescence. Her hands, resting on the carved scrolling of the chair arms, stood out starkly in the gloom, for they were very pale with long white fingers on which Selina noted was a prominent wedding band. Those hands did not strike her as those of an old woman, clawed and knotted with veins, rather they appeared as smooth and slender as would suitably grace someone of far fewer years.

She wore a headdress as was fashionable, but whereas many were large and elaborate, hers consisted of no more than a shaped and padded velvet band of a colour that matched her dress. Her hair was wound into a simple coil at the back of her head, but it was neither white nor grey, but still of its own rich, dark colour.

From the front of the headband, a heavy black veil fell to her shoulders, masking her features which could be but dimly made out. Her face, like her hands, was very pale, which seemed to give it an ethereal radiance that was not totally extinguished by the netting. But beyond the fact that it looked heart-shaped, further details were effectively hidden, so if it was indeed marred by accident or disease as rumour had it, such could not be ascertained, most especially at their respectful distance and in such poor light. It could of course be the case that the veil was not worn to hide and shield her from intrusive and unwanted inspection, but purely as part of the widow's mourning dress donned in bereavement.

After being ushered in and presented, there was but scant time to take in any more than a hasty impression before Selina had done as instructed and dropped her gaze to her feet. Standing still, and as motionless as Lady

Isabella, she waited for her to speak, but for a short spell she said nothing, and it was clear in that time she was being visually fully assessed.

When Lady Isabella did break the silence and speak, her voice was firm and clear without any hint of querulous old age.

"I trust that you are settling in well, Selina, in your new, and no doubt strange, surroundings. But these of course are very early days and I understand that this will take time and you will be given that.

"You have my sympathy on the death of your grandmother recently and also the loss of both your parents previously. To be twice orphaned is a hard and grievous thing to bear, and such loss is something I understand and am familiar with.

"I am reliably informed that you are adept in all the domestic arts, and have an exceptional way with growing things; that you are resourceful, diligent and of good temperament. Such information was conveyed from your priest to my own, though neither thought to mention that you are also comely. Maybe, however, they do not list that as a virtue.

"Laudable as your practical accomplishments may be, I do not need nor did I engage you for such talents. It is your qualities of character that are of far greater interest and value to me.

"You are now also without the ties and binding of familial obligations and commitments. That too is most fortunate, for it would be difficult if you had calls of duty beyond the settlement that claimed your allegiance. This domain of ours has necessary connection and exchange with the world outside, but as much as is possible it is kept to a minimum. We are self-governing and largely self-sufficient.

"Our excellent bake house provides bread, pies and pastries for all, likewise the brew house produces a sufficiency of ale and mead. We also have a trading agreement with the nearby monastery and exchange produce for their fine wines. We are equipped with our own smithy, oast house, physician, animal physician, chapel and folk of every trade and craft to fulfil all our requirements. From time to time nevertheless, even though few depart except through death or necessity, there arises a need to recruit new members into the settlement, and these are carefully selected by advisors. You have encountered Jacob and will appreciate his merits I am sure. He is in all respects a good man. And from what I have learnt your temperament is comparable, despite, or maybe because of, your restricted and difficult circumstances. In the right person with the right endowments, such tribulation, rather than undermining, can forge strength and fortitude. Your priest thinks highly of you and has asked to be kept informed of your progress. It would appear he needs reassurance that you have been well placed – that we will hope to relay to him in due course.

"There can be no doubt that you will have many questions, not least why you have been engaged if not for your domestic abilities, and why, apart from Abigail, you have encountered no one else in a house that should, in the normal way of things, be alive with bustling activity. I find such explanation tedious and tiresome, and I will leave Abigail to tell you much of what you need to know, as and when you need to know it, for in her I know I can have the uttermost trust. She has served me over many years and her devotion and fidelity are absolute. And yes, you are to study under her tutelage to take her place, though not only as chatelaine, there is more planned for you than that, but one step at a time, these things cannot be rushed. All will unfold in its due season, so do be patient. I will also continue to meet with you each day at this time, that we may become familiar with each other, for it is of the utmost importance that we are in accord.

"The robe suits you well, and Abigail will take your measurements that a complete wardrobe for all needs and occasions may be fashioned for you. The garments that you came with will be stored. They are not fitting for your new role and the life you will lead here, and so are best dispensed with, but they will be preserved, for perhaps you have attachment to them.

"There is a garden where you may take time for leisure, recreation and pleasure. It will be solely for your own use, and you may tend it and grow those plants that please you if you have a mind to. After the business of the life you shared with your grandmother, it might not suit you to be idle, but this choice I place in your own hands.

"On the Sabbath, the priest comes to me first in my private chapel that I may make my confession and take communion and where you will join with myself and Abigail for our private devotions. Your grandmother spent her life in service to her church and it will, I am sure, be essential for you to reflect her reverence. Our pastor then ministers to all that gather in the communal chapel."

"Finally, anything that you have need of, convey your want to Abigail and it will be attended to, save for those things which for whatever reason cannot be met, and I trust they will be few indeed. Tell me now before you take leave of me, are you pleased with your chamber and all in it?"

Selina, up till now completely silent in her audience with Lady Isabella, eyes downcast, listening strictly as a subject might attend to her sovereign, was startled to be suddenly called upon to comment. But it did now at last give her permission to look directly at the woman in whose employ she was contracted.

"My Lady, my chamber is far beyond anything I could have expected or indeed deserve. As yet I have no understanding of the reason for such exceptional favour, and cannot believe I possess any talent that could justify it."

As she spoke, she took the opportunity to try and see what she could of the face behind the veil. Lady Isabella was not the only one trying to get the measure of the person in front of her, but the net was too impenetrable in the limited light available to glean further information.

"Your response pleases me. It is well said and is a most promising start. Remember I am of considerable means, and it is my pleasure to amply reward those who merit it. Now I must rest, so I leave you in Abigail's care, and she has my permission to inform you of the running of the household and at least some of the history that brought it all into being. She is adept at knowing what can be divulged and what cannot, and how much you can digest at each sitting."

With that, she gave a small dismissive gesture with one pallid hand, and immediately Abigail moved towards the door with surprising alacrity. Hastily shooing Selina ahead of her, it allowed her time to perform only the briefest of curtsies. As soon as the last vestige of garment hem was free of the threshold, she shut the door quietly but firmly behind them, and then let out a sigh that suggested that the audience had been as testing for her as it had been for Selina, but, turning towards her, she gave an approving nod.

"You did well, child, and a good beginning presages favourable continuance. But come now with me and I will take you out to the garden Madame has set aside for you. You will be relieved to be outside in the light again, I am sure, after its exclusion in my Lady's chamber. She must have it so, but to someone in their years of youth and vitality it cannot be but oppressive. You will no doubt also be eager to become acquainted with as much of your new homestead as is possible or allowable, and I will conduct you in this."

Once again, they descended the winding stairs, but, at the foot, this time they did not enter into the Great Hall, but turned instead towards the utility premises.

Behind the colourful screen, Selina was surprised to find just a single large door, set in a deep recess with otherwise solid stone walls on either side. She had anticipated open access to larder and stores, and waited, uncertain now as to what might be encountered beyond.

Abigail selected a weighty key from amongst those on her belt, and inserted it into the scrolled iron lock. The door, though heavy, opened noiselessly, but not into rooms allocated for culinary purposes. Instead it revealed a long, narrow passage sided with blank walls, leading to yet another identical large door at the far end. The wall to the left would be, Selina ascertained, the outer wall of the building, yet it was devoid of windows and would thus have been rendered as black as pitch, had it not been for the two bracketed torches that showed the way. On reaching the second door, an alcove offset in the outer wall came into view, and set therein a separate door, small and studded and clearly giving access to the outside. Just as all others, this too was locked, and Abigail was obliged to search on her belt for the appropriate key. While she fumbled a little in the seeking, Selina, as she waited, became aware of sounds coming faintly through the larger door, muffled by its great thickness, but nevertheless the unmistakable noise of activity and conversation. Beyond doubt, here at last were the first real signs of others in occupancy, engaged in normal everyday pursuits. Much heartened by such evidence, she looked enquiringly at Abigail, hoping that she might also find the key to this entrance and take her through to encounter those she could hear.

"The sounds that I can hear beyond this door, are they from the kitchen? Is it here you came when you left me at breakfast?"

"It is, but we shall not be entering there, for see I have found the key for the garden and that is our goal."

Turning decisively away from the kitchen entrance, the chatelaine opened the little side door to a sudden rush of sound, particularly birdsong. Loud, clear and melodious, even the persistent cawing of the rooks that had scolded them on yesterday's eve was welcome. And carried on the gentle breeze were other calls, those of farm animals, oxen, sheep and hogs, with the occasional whinny of a horse. But above all, the voices of men and women too could be made out as they went about their appointed daily tasks. It was as music to Selina's ears. These were the sounds of community and fellowship that were so precious from childhood memory, and which she had sorely missed these last four years. Now here they were restored to her again in reassuringly close proximity. Her heart lifted with her fear of isolation thus diminished.

They stepped out through the doorway onto a gritted path screened by a high hedging of holly. With Abigail leading, they followed the way for but a short space, before finding themselves presently in a pretty square walled garden. It was laid out in patterned strips, with each strip allocated to a separate planting: herbs with sage, thyme, rosemary, saffron and nettles, and with flowers, lilies of the valley, geraniums, violets and roses just coming into bud. There were vegetables of diverse kinds too, and in each corner different fruiting trees – apple, pear, fig and quince. And, at the very centre, a stone bench set upon flagged paving beneath a medlar tree provided as perfect a place as you could wish to take your ease and survey it all.

Abigail sat down upon it with the sigh of one whose old bones demanded constant awareness and attention lest they suffer some hurt, then patted the bench beside her. Accepting the invitation, Selina settled with her, looking round and about at what had most extraordinarily been given her to do with as she pleased. It was so much larger than her own previous plot, one that she had cultivated entirely for sustenance, pleasure being born from necessity. That there were vegetables in this plot too seemed without any true purpose or reason. Why tend and harvest them when there were none here dependent on them for nourishment? Yet, for her it would seem an incredible indulgence to turn the land over entirely to growing flowers, for previously she had been intent on claiming every last inch of earth to grow only things that you could eat. But whatever you grew in them, all gardens were tranquil and delightful spaces, and this one was no exception and as lovely as you could wish. Was it not after all her own little garden that was the one thing that she had been sorely grieved to leave? To be given this, as the priest would say, surely seemed like an answer to unspoken prayer.

Its outer wall was clearly a part of the great wall that surrounded the house, both boundary and protection, but just beyond its great depth, close on the other side, was the settlement with all its attendant and compelling daily rounds as evidenced by the sounds she could hear. They vividly illustrated the activities so well, that to hear them was almost akin to seeing them. The lumbering rumble of heavy-laden wagon carts, the clatter of hooves over cobblestones, the bleating of sheep or honking of geese as they were herded from one place to another, and the faint but evocative snatches of conversation between the inhabitants.

When would she actually set eyes on them and be there amongst them that she might make good her avowed hope of meeting again with Jacob?

Abigail spoke then, as she smoothed her dress over her knees and gathered the keys into a heap in her lap.

"We must begin on your learning, Selina, for there is much to tell and much to know, and we cannot waste time for it is precious. The garden is a pleasant place to conduct your lessons if the weather be clement, and so I shall begin at once with the story of Lady Isabella herself, as all else hinges on that. But it is not a simple tale and cannot be made so for ease of telling.

"Again, some things cannot be divulged at the outset before there has been time for you to prove your fidelity, for it will be knowledge privy to very few and confidence in your trustworthiness can only be acquired with the passage of time. Nevertheless, I shall do my best and begin, as is always a good thing, at the beginning, but it will be but the bare bones in the first telling. We will flesh those out as time properly decrees. Now listen well."

*

My Lady was born here, her father a man of wealth, power and noble lineage, and as the only child she inherited all that was his. Her mother died of childbed fever after her birth, but her father did not choose to marry again; instead he invested all his energy and devotion in raising the daughter who was his heart's delight. He treated her in the same way as he would have done had she been a son, and so she grew with no sense of being any the less for being female.

All was well for most of her growing years, and she lived a charmed life with but few testing times, until one day a messenger came on a hard-pressed mount to find her father and beg his assistance for his own lord. He was a nobleman with whom there was a bond of allegiance, and both were pledged to come to the aid of the other should need ever arise. He called upon him now to honour that oath, and bade him come at once with as large a retinue as he could speedily muster. They were besieged and under attack from a fearsome band of outlaws, who owing allegiance to none were raiding and plundering mercilessly where they would. Hopelessly outnumbered, without help they could not hold out much longer, and would most assuredly all be slaughtered, then everything they had would be plundered and their home and lands laid waste.

Lady Isabella's father at once called on all in his service to don armour and vestment that they may rout the heathen marauders. They would see them off, or see them dead and gone back to the hell they came from. And let all rest assured that God would be with them as they rode out to save the innocent – they must prevail.

Many answered his call, and a strong and determined band of well-armed men rode out at the gallop to save their oppressed neighbours. Lady Isabella barely grown to womanhood must be left behind, but she was ablaze with admiration and awe at the sight of such as these. They were splendid to behold, and there was her father as she had never seen him before, the most magnificent of them all. With sword raised, he rode at the front on his powerful warhorse, and, as he put spurs to his stead, he gave voice to a battle cry that could have raised the long-dead warriors in their churchyard tombs, so compelling it was.

With those who remained, namely the women, children, the old and infirm, she waited the day out, desperate to know what the outcome might be. There was no way of knowing the strength of numbers, and, even with God's help, it would be hard to overcome the outlaws if they be very many.

Then, as the sun was setting, with the birds become silent in their roosts, at last she heard the sound of harness heralding the horses' return. Not galloping now, but at plodding pace they came into view, bloodied and wearied from battle. Of her father there was no sign. Racing to the first of them who carried a broken sword as evidence of the heat of battle, she seized the bridle and beseeched the knight to tell her why her father was not amongst them. He reassured her that he still lived and had not fallen, but in the furious melee, in which they had driven off the enemy with many slain, he had been seized by those who were the chieftains of the godless horde. They had preserved their own lives at the cost of their warriors and, as they retreated, leaving their men still in mortal combat, they were able to use the confusion of conflict to overwhelm her father and take him with them as their prisoner and hostage.

Although those who had ridden out to honour their pledge had prevailed, and it was a victory inasmuch as they had rescued the besieged, alas, it was also certain that the outlaws too had won a valuable prize. For most assuredly they would now demand a ransom that might take much of all they had in return for her father's safe delivery. They dare not risk tracking them down and attacking, lest they slay him in revenge. They must wait for their demands. They had no other choice.

They waited out four days before a messenger came astride one of the small but sturdy mounts they favoured. Unlike the great warhorses that had need to be able to bear the weight of a man in full armour, these, though of modest stature, were strong in neck and body, and their short but powerful legs rendered them well skilled in turning about at speed. It was believed that they were an ancient Norse or Celtic breed that, like their riders, in no way resembled their local counterparts. Neither man nor beast wore armour. Depending entirely on swiftness and dexterity, they regarded with contempt the cumbersome restrictions of breastplate, helmet, shield and unwieldy lance. The battle axe was their weapon of choice and they used it to deadly effect.

The messenger, bold in the certainty that his news and treaty ensured safe passage, approached the sentries with no sign of fear. He was escorted to a group of elders who had been waiting on his coming, impatient to hear the demands of this uncivilised band of wild men with regard to their liege lord.

Isabella, hearing the frenzied barking of the dogs at the coming of one they did not own as inmate, had rushed to an upper window to see who it was that approached. After four days she was distraught for lack of news of how her father fared, and if he had been tormented or ill used by those who held him.

Elders and emissary withdrew to the Great Hall to conduct their business, and Isabella crept silently down the winding stair till she reached the final curve. Here she could listen to all that passed without revealing her presence.

The messenger stated his clan's terms in measured tones, and, although his use of the language was heavily overlaid by an unknown accent, its solemn dignity was at odds with the reputation of his ilk for cruder exchange. He also took care to speak slowly and with great clarity, so all was readily understood.

He had no business with intermediaries. He said he would address himself only to the closest kin of his prisoner, for the decisions to be made were solely for the heir and next in line. None other had the right to barter for the lord's life.

The elders protested that the heir was in fact an heiress and little more than a child at that. She was incapable in her untried innocence of such negotiation and he must deal with them as spokespersons on her behalf.

But he stood his ground and repeated that his instructions were to deal only with the closest blood tie, and if that was a daughter then so be it. In concession, he agreed that they might stay and witness the exchange, but they must let her speak for herself.

Again they argued that such a burden of responsibility was too great for such as she, and Isabella, at her listening post, realised they saw her only as a pampered pet, overindulged by a doting father. They spoke from the prejudice of ingrained assumption, without real knowledge of her true merit, something her father never did. He had raised her certainly with love, but with no concessions to gender, and whether it was on horseback or in learned debate, he challenged her to extend herself to the utmost. These who stood in judgement of her were, she saw, not so much elders as elderly men of inherited rank, claiming authority purely on the grounds of birth and the presumption that with age came wisdom.

Taking hold of her gown then, and lifting it clear of her feet, she ran down the remaining stairs and into the hall. There, ignoring the assembly of elders, she strode past them to stand before the emissary, and in so doing contemptuously turned her back on them. Her stance was closer to the go-between than was fitting, but it gave forth a clear signal that here was no swooning girl. She was her father's daughter, and, because of it, all that he was so was she, and let none doubt it. She addressed herself solely to the messenger.

"I am Isabella, daughter of the lord you have abducted

and hold. State your terms and let us waste no time in posturing or bluster that the matter be speedily settled and he be returned to us with all haste."

The elders behind her immediately raised an outcry. This was not the way it should be done. Wily negotiation and gradual concession were the order of the day, not showing your hand too early. Hard bargaining proved you were strong men to be feared and not trifled with. Isabella, having gone straight to the end game without any understanding of due process, proved exactly their point – that a foolish girl could not do a man's job. The authority was vested in them, as evidenced by the ermine-trimmed robes they wore, and it was them, and only them, who could do business with the dangerous and uncivilised creatures represented by the primitive presently before them.

Isabella cut short their protestations with a single forceful, "Be still!" She added to make sure there could be no mistake as to her meaning, "You may stay only if you can hold your tongues. If you cannot do that then I bid you repair to some other place. Should I have need of you here, I will refer to you, but until such time you will record and bear witness only."

The elders knew that, whatever rank they held, in the absence of the lord of the manor, Isabella, girl as she was, outranked them as heir apparent. And should he fail to return, they had best remember that it would be her they must serve and answer to. They bowed in deference with an eye to that possible future.

She turned again to the messenger and now gave him her full attention. He was garbed in strange clouts, some kind of soft suede or leather breeches and tunic. His boots too were light and he wore nothing on his head. Beside herself in her courtly dress and the elaborate robes of the elders, fashioned as declaration of status, he looked decidedly under-dressed and yet somehow, too, unencumbered. And with a sudden flash of insight she also understood that maybe, from his point of view, such trussing might actually seem rather ridiculous.

Yet the garments which gave him this ease of movement, she could see were not rough cladding, being both well-made and well-shaped to his stature. They were a deliberate choice of apparel for good reason. Around his neck was a thick cord that supported a pendant wrought from some kind of gemstone that had been elaborately carved in intricate patterning. It was his only adornment. His hair, worn longer than was usual, was very fair, and he had the top section dressed into a twisted knot at the back of his head. His eyes were startlingly blue. When he spoke, she noted again his accent, which pronounced him as not of this place, or indeed of this land, so strange and foreign it sounded. His speech, his dress, and his manner all confounded what she had expected, the reputation of this outlaw breed being one of barely human savagery, yet he bowed courteously towards her as he made his address.

"My Lady, I would first assure you that your father is well. No harm has come to his person and he is in safe and comfortable lodging. To give proof of his wellbeing he asked that I relay to you the fact that it is fortunate that caterpillars do not wear shoes, for they would surely trip over their feet were they so to do."

The elders had trouble restraining their outrage at such jesting. The man must be a fool as well as a villain, and had clearly taken leave of his senses.

Not so Isabella; she knew exactly what it was to which he referred, for it was a merry thing her father would say to her when she was but an infant and still unsteady on her legs. It had continued for some long while because it never failed to make her laugh, and he delighted to hear her. But it had been a private jest between them and none else could have quoted it. It was the sure and certain proof she needed that her father lived. An involuntary exhaling of breath escaped her then, and with it she let go of the fear for her father's life. She restrained herself from grasping the messenger's arm in relief and thanksgiving, and begging him for further reassurance. Instead she answered him.

"I know well what it is you quote, and that only my father could have relayed it to you. You have my trust now in all else, so tell me straightway, what are your terms? You have me at a disadvantage, of course, for though I must bear in mind all that is at stake, and that the people must not be stripped of their homes or livelihoods in barter, in truth there is nothing I would not willingly forfeit for his sake."

The groans and snorts from the elders gave eloquent evidence of their despair at her disastrous inability to conduct herself and proceedings in anything like a proper manner. Their unwanted and unasked for contributions earned them no regard; instead Isabella, in anger that they could not see that she meant what she said, and would not unsay it, bade them leave the hall. Affronted but with no choice, they withdrew to wait without.

When the doors were closed firmly upon them and their outraged self-regard, Isabella addressed the messenger further, "Pray tell me now all that you have come to demand, for I would settle terms as swiftly as may be possible. Who is it that you represent and speak for, and do you swear that whatever is agreed upon will be honoured to the letter?"

"My Lady, you do indeed have my word on that, for I speak for myself as well as my kinsmen. My role is more than that of messenger here to relay terms back and forth between camps, for though you may not readily honour my station, I am the prince of my people and the terms are drawn up by myself and my family."

He paused then to witness Isabella's response to this declaration, and, duly noting her look of incredulity, he continued, not to justify, but to clarify.

"No doubt you supposed that the likes of us have no such conceits, living as you believe we do like animals, lawless and godless. I assure you that is not the case. Though our laws and gods are other than your own, we honour and live by their decrees as much as do you.

"You have requested that I go straight to terms and towards a speedy resolution. This I am most ready and willing to do, for it would serve us both well."

He smiled a little at first as he stated those terms.

"It is as well that you have banished your forum of old men; they have their own agenda and first and foremost would protect those interests.

"There is but one thing that is asked before the release of your father, and none under your patronage will be harmed or in any way the worse for its fulfilment."

Isabella, who had indeed been taken aback by his declaration of rank, was otherwise not uncomprehending of those things that he had stated. For it had been very plain to see from the start that this was no mere messenger. His bearing and manner clearly marked him out as of stature, and, wherever it was he came from, such things were self-evident and beyond dispute. Had she not known his origins, his conduct would have convinced her that they were of equal standing. Because of it, she hoped that the price demanded for her father's release and homecoming would reflect that affinity; that it would prove to be something that could be met without the threat of ruination for those whose livelihoods depended on them. But she braced herself, for despite such appearances this had been a hostile engagement with many forfeiting their lives, and, as the elders had said, hard bargaining must surely follow. She could not have anticipated just how hard the bargain nor how high the cost.

*

Abigail shook her head in remembrance, but then would say no more, declaring that they would leave things there till the morrow. It was enough for the moment. With that she rose a little unsteadily to her feet, whether from infirmity or from unsettling recall Selina could not tell.

CHAPTER SIX

Selina had been full of questions and of the want to hear more. Such a moment, she insisted, was not the place to curtail the history of Lady Isabella, but Abigail had been unyielding in her refusal to continue. She would answer questions on the morrow when they recommenced with the telling of what happened next, but this was sufficient for the day. Let her rather consider and reflect on what she had learnt thus far.

Instead, Abigail had given her a tour of the house so that she might get her bearings, and become familiar with what was, after all, now her own new abode. Yet still she refused to open the door into the kitchen as they passed it on their return from the garden. Though the muted noise of busy activity was still intriguingly apparent, her response to Selina's request to see beyond was met with a curt, "Not yet."

All the chambers, however many there might be, to the left at the top of the stairs were allocated entirely for the use of Lady Isabella, and therefore forbidden. Those on the right were all bedchambers, and besides Abigail's and her own were six others, all well-furnished and ready for occupancy, though upon inspection none were as large or splendid as her own. A small door at the end of the passage, she was told, opened onto a flight of stairs leading down to the far end of the hall, but inevitably it too was locked. The windows that had been blind on yesterday's eve, with naught to see but the night's dark, now showed a view of bare flagged paving, with gritted margins that spanned the space between the house and its formidable encircling wall. Starkly functional, the unadorned stone echoed the great double doors that gave entrance; the purpose seemingly more akin to fortifying than enclosing. The only relief from this grim outer austerity were the two enclosed gardens set within, for apart from her own there was apparently another much larger at the farther end. This was Lady Isabella's private sanctuary and retreat.

On the ground floor to the other side of the Great Hall were six empty rooms of varying size, each being furnished with a door that would have given direct access to the outside had they not been tightly fastened. Abigail said that nowadays they were not in use, but in times previous, amongst their various purposes, they had been places for minstrels, play actors and such-like to keep their instruments, props and paraphernalia, and where they might prepare themselves for performance.

The tower that housed the doors to the way in was shallow and but two storeys high, furnished with a single narrow, arched window above the entrance. The space in which the window was set, being too small to function as a chamber, was built no doubt for precautionary purpose only, to function as a look-out to see who sought entrance below.

It was clear that the house, for all its size, was laid out to a simple plan – bedchambers upstairs, Great Hall downstairs, and spare rooms with outside access for any purpose that might arise.

The heart and soul of the house, the very life force, lay within the kitchen premises, comprising the larder, buttery, brew house and bakery. For these quarters occupied a substantial portion of the building, and from here, at its very centre, just as with the hub of a wheel, came the power that gave point and purpose to the whole dwelling. Without its driving force, all would be as arid and wasted as the many unused chambers.

For as far as Selina could tell, there were but the three souls occupying the residential premises – three now but previously only two, and there was no bond of kinship nor other binding tie to forge them into unity. It could not then compare with the many who must be employed providing food and drink for the entire settlement, united together in fellowship and communal endeavour. Yet it was completely sealed off. Why?

At the end of the tour, which had taken longer than it might due to Abigail's laborious pace, they had returned to the Great Hall, where the midday meal had been served and was waiting in readiness. There were two places set, alongside the third for the absent lord in presumed continual expectancy of his attendance. But Selina did not remark upon it; instead, as they took their places and inspected the dishes before them, she ventured to ask, "With all the doors sealed, who is it that comes and brings the fare to table, and who brought the gown and washing water to my room whilst I slept, and who keeps the fire going? These things are attended to, yet none are in evidence."

Abigail took her time in replying. It seemed she must be ever careful in considering first how a question should best be answered, lest she say more than she intended or in some other way offend against an unwritten rule. Taking a little meat and vegetables from the generously filled platters, she spoke guardedly.

"In the morning I give keys to a select few who have need of them for these reasons. They are returned at the end of the day. The domestic departments have their own entrances and their own keys. There is a separate stairway at the end of the passage to my lady's quarters, identical to the one on our side. She herself is in charge of the door there and unlocks it briefly at certain times so that all she needs can be left on a chest within. And those given right of entry may not linger, but swiftly fulfil their purpose and leave. The fire will be left to go out at the end of May."

"But why keep the hall heated when there are none here to warm themselves, and may I not meet and speak with these that come to perform such services?"

Abigail, showing signs of irritation at so many questions which she clearly found taxing, answered briefly, "Not yet. I will tell you when the time is right. Now attend to your meal."

The chatelaine herself ate but little and was soon done, whereupon she raised herself up stiffly from the bench, saying it was time for her rest, after which she would wait on Lady Isabella. But before she withdrew she laid the garden door key on the table beside Selina, telling her she may come and go at her own pleasure. The door to the passage that served it would be left open till supper time, when all doors were locked fast for the night. She may also spend any time of her choosing in her own chamber, but for the moment she should refrain from frequenting other parts of the house.

Confirming her acquiescence, Selina enquired if her chest of offcuts, along with her grandmother's workbox had been delivered to her room. She was assured that such would have been the case. Abigail also informed her, before she left, that she would be served the final meal of the day in the hall, when the chapel bell tolled five. She herself did not partake of this repast, and Selina should not linger over-long with the meal, after which she must retire to her chamber till she was fetched for breakfast in the morning and her next audience with Madame. But the first task on the morrow would be the taking of her measurements that garments might be fashioned for her.

Selina thought it wisest to say nothing regarding the fact that if she saw no one there seemed scant reason for such an endeavour.

When Abigail had gone, presumably to her own chamber, Selina again ate less than she would normally have consumed. The food was delicious and plentiful, and she was loath to see it so little savoured for the sake of whoever had prepared it, but her appetite was dulled by her solitary state. Like the garments to be fashioned with none to admire them, a feast was to no purpose without good company to share it. At least she and her grandmother had sat together for the meals she set before them, in quietness maybe but in simple appreciation and gratitude too for full plates. And she had cleared her trencher of the rustic stew at the inn with Jacob alongside her doing likewise. If the way of things so far was how it would continue, then it would seem that most of her meals would be a lonely business. Abigail ate so little and with such distaste it was as if she was performing an unpleasant but necessary task. She was done with it as speedily as possible. Nor indeed was she the good company required to turn sitting at table into a festive thing.

But such considerations were of scant merit when she was mindful of her previous greater dreads. When she had been set upon the stool after a sleepless night waiting to be fetched here, she had feared much.

She had feared being locked away in perpetual exclusion with a miserable old woman, yet it had turned out Lady Isabella could in no wise be described as such, and she would see her for but a brief spell each morning.

She had feared isolation, but she was surrounded by many, even though they were tantalisingly out of reach.

She had feared a drab existence, with her chest of remnants being the only thing that might afford her any joy, yet, beyond belief, here she was clothed like a fine lady.

And finally, she had mourned leaving her little garden only to find she had been given ownership of one of much greater size and charm.

Those fears she had harboured beforehand were simple and straightforward. None had been made manifest, but what had replaced them was far from plain, and brought neither relief nor rejoicing, but rather confusion and unease.

When Abigail had stated at the beginning of her time here that she should see beyond appearances, for things were not always what they seemed, she had accurately described how difficult it was to understand the workings of this place. It appeared extreme in all its functions, yet, as with Jacob, none seemed inclined to question its peculiar oddities more than content to just bask in the benefits, particularly freedom from want. Mayhap over a period of time, that which was unusual eventually became the usual, and thus those involved saw naught amiss.

She finished the meal almost as hastily as Abigail, uncomfortable and self-conscious at being the only soul in the Great Hall at meat, even if there were none present to bear witness to her discomfiture. Every sound she made seemed to be echoed back to her at twice the volume, as if taunting her for being without the good company about her that would help absorb the unsettling din. Laying down her knife then with a deliberately defiant clatter, in its stead she took into her hand the key to the garden.

Crossing the hall to the door behind the screen, she found it unfastened as Abigail had promised, and she pushed its ponderous weight to one side, finding that a small but nevertheless pleasing sense of power accompanied the action. Apart from her own chamber, this was the first door that had yielded to her.

When she attained the one that gave entrance to the kitchen, unrestrained by watchful eyes, she pressed her ear against it. The cheerful noise of those behind, along with the clanging of pots, was thus made all the clearer and it raised in her an urgent need to alert them to her presence, to hammer on the door that divided them, call out and beg them to let her in if they only could.

Yet she did not.

Why, she was not entirely sure, save for the fact there was an instinct warning her not to break the rules, that it might well be dangerous to flout instructions and incur displeasure. But even more than this, she felt sure that those employed in the kitchen would not respond even should they hear her, for as Jacob said, they would do only what they were bid to do. Why do aught that might put their livelihoods at risk? If she begged their attention and acknowledgment unsanctioned by Madame, they may not thank her for it.

And after all, Abigail had said, "Not yet," which meant if not immediately, it would happen in due course. She must bide her time with patience.

She turned her attention instead to fitting the key in the lock of the garden door, and its ease of opening to the outside world brought her a compensatory sense of freedom. Stepping out this time however, she did not retrace her steps, but turned resolutely in the opposite direction from that taken in the fore noon with Abigail. In this direction, the gritted path should lead alongside the kitchen and she was hopeful of finding a window that served it. If meeting with those within was not possible, at least she might thus catch at least a glimpse of those she had heard.

But she had gone but a short distance before the way was blocked by more of the prickly and impenetrable holly hedging planted tight up against the house wall, and behind that was the inner wall that also abutted the building, continuing till it connected up with and became part of the garden surrounds – a wall behind a wall behind a thorny hedge. Was this constructed for defence against attack by such outlaws as she had just heard tell of, or was it perhaps as much to do with keeping folk in, as keeping them out?

Disappointed, but not overly surprised, she turned about then and followed the path to the garden, for clearly she had no other choice. In a large domain there was a strictly limited degree of unrestricted movement. The garden was like an island that could only be reached by a causeway, and was otherwise cut off and isolated from its surroundings. Completely containing all within its walls, lovely as it seemed, was it not in truth a veritable prison and herself the prisoner?

She sat down on the central stone bench, disturbed and ill at ease. She pondered on the story of Lady Isabella relayed to her here but a short while ago. She could not by any stretch of imaginings equate the bold and courageous young woman Abigail had described with the veiled, withdrawn and mysterious Madame who had chosen to lock herself away in permanent exclusion. And what had become of the others that had played their part in the tale: the elders, those who had ridden out in response to the call to arms, and the minstrels, troubadours and players who had frequented the empty rooms, giving them life and purpose? They had disappeared like the truant lord, but to where and what, and how long ago? For Lady Isabella did not have the look of a woman of a great many years, despite what the priest had assured her was the fact of the matter.

But what filled her mind the most after the morning's meeting was what her own role was to be. She had been told that it was important that they be in accord and familiar with one another, that it was fortunate that she was twice orphaned and without other kin close by, but not why such things were deemed necessary.

True, she and Lady Isabella were united in their experience of isolation, but hers was a deliberate act of self-incarceration for whatever reason, and not something suffered without either wish or want. What could be the point of the fine raiment and the best bedchamber for which privilege she provided no service? Doubtless there must be a reason for all these things, but what it might be was beyond conjecture. As she had wrestled with what might lie ahead of her before her coming, she could only accept the fact that nothing but the passage of time would give her the answers she sought. She must submit to that truth and wait on providence and God's good grace.

*

She had stayed on in the garden and become familiar with each and every planted thing that grew within it. It had been thoughtfully and knowledgeably designed, and all was flourishing, with never a tare in sight. Although it was designated as her own, she was all too well aware that someone else had created it and constantly maintained it most diligently. And presumably they would continue to do so, unless she insisted that her ownership be exclusive and none other be given permission to tend it. But she knew there could be no rightness in that, for it was not hers in the way her old garden had been; where all she had grown and cared for was cultivated entirely for the purpose of putting food on the table. And, should she lay claim to this place, then she would also be obliged to ask for all she had need of: tools, plants, and, if she was of serious intent, garb suitable for doing the work, for such as she was wearing would clearly not do. Madame had said anything she wanted would be supplied for the asking, but it required but little reflection to know she would not ask for this with neither right nor good reason, or indeed any promise of the fulfilment she had enjoyed in her grandmother's old dwelling – it could not be justified. Nor did she wish to deprive whoever had minded it thus far the right to continue. She could not do it nearly so well, her own experience being solely with things that were for eating, not ornaments for looking at.

But as with all such open spaces, little birds came to visit and search for food for themselves and their nestlings, and these she would nurture in the garden's stead, bringing them such fare as they would enjoy from the table. In her previous working with the soil, raising vegetables, they had come to garner those things they relished from the turned earth, and she had prospered from their company. Her parents' death having left her with a dearth of demonstrable affection, this legacy of emptiness was something they helped fill, particularly the robins and the blackbirds with their friendly way of being and their joyful singing. Now with spring come and with young ones to rear, they could be easily tamed. This would be a gladdening thing for her to do, and if she could have aught she asked for, then she would ask for a little table for their dining and a broad dish to hold water that they might drink and bathe.

When the tolling of the chapel bell gave signal to all who toiled to cease their labours, Selina went back to the hall for supper, feeling wholly undeserving compared to those she now heard returning from the fields, or those others she had harkened to in the kitchen. She had contributed nothing that earned her entitlement to the good viands that she knew would await her. For as Lady Isabella had noted, she was sorely ill at ease in idleness, feeling as useless and pointless as a peacock in a hen coop.

But when she did take her place at table, finding 'my Lord' still as stubbornly elusive as Madame herself, she found instead something else wholly unexpected by her setting: a little crock holding a posy of violets.

She picked it up and held the delicate flowers to her nose, inhaling their sweet scent, then, putting it back in its place, she looked upon it and considered who might have given her such a pleasing gift. Whoever it was, they must be acquainted with the fact that she would be alone at table, so there could be no supposing that they were intended for the chatelaine. This being the way of it, surely then they were given in kind regard, encouragement, acknowledgement, and, most of all perhaps, to reassure her that her situation was known to them and understood. If so, then she was immeasurably moved and cheered, but she reined in her gratitude lest she be foolish, misinterpreting what had been meant as no more than a pretty table decoration into a cause none had intended. Nevertheless, whatever the true intent, it lifted her spirits, and thus cheered she found her hitherto errant appetite and ate heartily and with appreciation of what had been set before her. She would have been glad to linger a while when she laid down her knife and spoon, in the hope that someone might come to attend to the platters or the fire, but, mindful of Abigail's instruction not to linger over-long, she waited but a short space before going up to her chamber.

As Abigail had foretold, the chest and the workbox were waiting beneath the window, and she was as glad to see them as if they were old friends encountered in a strange place. She opened both and found all in order, save for the fact that the garments she had brought and laid on top of the offcuts had been removed. Lady Isabella had indeed said it would be done, as they were no longer suitable in her new situation, but she felt bereft of her endowment, the little she had that was undoubtedly her own. And, simple as they were, her grandmother had fashioned them for her with as much attention as she used in her church sewing, proof of her own restricted but conscientious form of caring. Such sentiments apart, there was the consideration also that should she ever desire to leave this place for whatever reason she would have need of them. The rich clothing bequeathed her would render her conspicuous, and considerably hamper speed of movement.

In truth, she had found the wearing of the heavy robe the day long cumbersome and wearying. She must be ever lifting it to free the movement of her feet, and it dragged a little on the ground behind. Used to lighter garb that finished above her ankles, it was clear it had not been fashioned for quickness of pace, for the noble class had no such need, slow and stately grace being their chosen style.

Returned to her chamber, she was glad to divest herself at last of its restrictive limitations and the welcome freedom of naught but the shift. Upon reflection, she had understanding and sympathy for this outlaw prince with his unconventional style of dress for like reckoning.

Confined till morning within the bedchamber, she pondered on how she might profitably pass the day's end. She had endured no strenuous burden of toil that had wearied the body into early readiness for slumber, yet she could do naught beyond the room's confines. She determined then to make good her earlier pledge, and to work on fashioning a garment from the remnants. Her own garb confiscated, this would be a recompense. In the creating of new and singular raiment, she could claim whatever she made belonged entirely unto herself, and from the substance bequeathed to her from her grandmother. None other had a hand in it.

It came to her then that because of the diverse nature of all the fragments of material, it could best be sewn into a costume that a play actor might wear, a colourful jester with a cap and mask perhaps. And should she run away and be sought after, none would think to find her in such unlikely guise. Dressed as a wandering player, she could also present herself as a fellow and thus be twice as safe from detection.

She spread all the remnants about her on the floor and began to arrange them into a pattern. There were plenty enough for tunic, leggings and a cap with face mask. In scant time she was absorbed in planning how it should all be; sleeves and leggings would match with cuffs, elbows and knee pads picked out in vivid otherness, the tunic like unto a tabard with elaborate patterning emblazoning the centre. Cutting and pinning, she filled the hours till she must light the candles, and come that time she carefully gathered all together and stowed it away in the chest till the morrow's eve. Then she would press on with the work and gladly, for it gave her purpose and pursuit and she had need of such.

She saw a dish of sweetmeats had been left on the chest, along with a pitcher of water for drinking and another for washing. Beside them, carefully folded, was a fresh towel and a clean nightgown and shift for the morrow. When she had availed herself of all she needed in preparation for taking to her bed, she settled once more on its end in her nightgown and gave her complete attention to the Tapestry.

Her regard went at once to the lost soul, who in turning away from his happy companions seemed so conspicuously out of place and perversely forlorn in the midst of revelry. But there was something else too that she had not previously perceived. It was a sense of suspension, as if the diverse activities played out by those displayed had been caught and frozen at a particular moment in time. It brought to mind a game she, her brothers and others had often played in happy earlier times, which they had called 'Statues'. Those participating would dance to the lively beat of pipe or drum till, at a moment which none could foretell, the music of a sudden would cease, and all must on the instant stand as still and motionless as statues; those losing their balance or stumbling being declared out from the game. Then, after a short space when each must hold steady in their pose, the music began once more its lively caprice, releasing the frozen statues back to life and vigour till the next cessation.

There was that same sense here of waiting for the music to reanimate each soul out of imposed but temporary immobility.

As she thought on that old pastime, the freshly lighted candles started to gutter as if a strong draught had disturbed them, or perhaps an impurity in the wax or wick. The effect was to throw flickering patterns of both brightness and shadow across the Tapestry, and such light play did indeed seem to mimic a reawakening to life and movement. But as she contemplated the chasing, changing colours, she found she could not turn her head and look away. The shifting illumination was not just creating an illusion of all in the Tapestry as becoming animated, but of it being an actual fact, and, in a trice, they would come to vivid life, with herself having no choice but to bear witness to it. Hapless she found herself completely mesmerised, or maybe spellbound, and being pulled into an experience that she could not tell as to whether it be good or bad, but to which she had not given her consent and was not willing, for fear and doubt as to what it signified. Unable to unlock her ensnared gaze by turning away, she managed instead, with great effort, to close her eyes, and in so doing the spell was broken, but to be replaced in its stead by an unutterable weariness so that she must lie back upon the bed. It was as unto the night before, and she slept almost before her head touched upon the pillow.

CHAPTER SEVEN

Selina came into wakefulness instantly alert, and with a sudden and sure apprehension that something was amiss. The candles had burnt out, yet the chamber was bright with vivid light.

She saw the full, round moon filling the window was its source, and the shining beams streaming in were concentrated upon the Tapestry. As the candlelight had seemed like unto a touchstone that had stirred the woven effigy into simulated animation, the moonlight now effected the same.

But it was a fulfilled happening, for what was presently before her was no inert hand-worked wall-hanging with the appearance of motion, but rather it was as if the margins of the Tapestry had become the frame of a magic window. And looking through she beheld a scene of vibrant activity.

Here before her, living and having its being, was another and entirely separate world, but one in which she could actually experience the sights, sounds and smells of all depicted as they assailed her bemused senses. And in their so doing, they presented clear evidence of a true and actual existence playing out in front of her enthralled and startled gaze.

With no thought now to avert her eyes from what she could neither understand nor fathom, she crawled instead to the bed's end – the better to witness what was unfolding, like living theatre, the whole breadth and depth of the end wall of her bedchamber.

The musicians played their instruments, and the bare feet of the dancers circling through the green sward strewn with flowers caused the blossoms to release their scent, a fragrance that was carried up by the breath of gentle breezes to stir the leaves of fruit-laden trees, where birds sang and butterflies and dragonflies were borne up on the ambient current. The brook lapped the feet of the waders as they trod carefully round lily pads that gave shelter to the golden fish beneath. The animals moving gracefully around both dancers and those in the water mingled with and greeted them and were themselves likewise welcomed with soft touches and kind words.

And there, in the forefront of this blissful living tableau, was the misfit, with his back turned resolutely on an earthly paradise.

But because he was thus turned away from all going on behind him, he faced directly forwards, and this position placed him on precisely the same eye level as Selina as she sat bemused on her velvet counterpane.

On the instant that their eyes met, it was clear that he saw her, even though she was in no way a part of the picture world he inhabited. He started with shock and doubt, then involuntarily held his hand out towards her. She stayed stock still, uncertain in a confusion of conflicting responses.

Whilst never taking his eyes from her face, he moved forward till it was clear he had reached the very edge and limit of his own dimension and could come no further. But if he was restricted from physical progress, he could still give voice and he bade her earnestly, "Come, stand before me and tell me who you are."

Selina slid slowly down off the bedcover. Only the measure of a few steps separated them, and she took them, crossing the floor till she was close enough to reach out and touch him, if it was possible, or if she dared.

"Who are you?" he said. "Why are you here? Have you come to help me?"

She gave answer, hoping that if she could hear him and all the sounds of his domain, he too must be able to hear her.

"My name is Selina. I am but newly arrived in this place. I have not come to help you, for I know naught of your situation or what help it is you are in need of. How would it be possible to assist you in any case, seeing that we have neither knowledge of each other nor possibility of contact? I am here in the real and present world, and you inhabit I know not what kind of domain. Yet it is a truth that it seems we can converse across the divide between us."

He nodded assent eagerly. "Yes, it is so, and more than that, you can join with me here. You have only to stretch forth your hand with your eyes closed and I shall grasp it and pull you through."

Selina was at once aghast at such an offer and stepped back rather than forward, lest he grip her hand without her consent and drag her into some place and existence from which she could not return.

But at once he hastened to reassure her.

"Be at ease, you will be able to enter into this place and leave again as simply as stepping up into a carriage, from which after your excursion you step back down, safely returned from whence you came.

"During the hours of darkness you are at liberty to join me and will suffer no harm nor penalty that would entrap or imprison you. As long as you depart before the first rays of sunlight strike upon the Tapestry, no ill can befall you. I have knowledge of these matters for I am an unfortunate who did lose track of time here, and in so doing became forever a part of it. I am now in endless search to discover how I might remedy that error, yet have found no solution thus far. But you are surely sent to give me some answer, for I have never till now encountered such as yourself, that has a foot in both worlds."

Selina, who was still intent on keeping both feet firmly in her own world, enquired why, if he could pull her into his territory, he could not grasp some object other than her hand to pull himself back out into the bedchamber and reality.

"That I may not do, for there is an invisible barrier that I cannot penetrate from this side. You may pierce it with ease, but I can only grasp your hand when it has crossed that unseen but impenetrable screen that separates us. But please have faith and trust that all I have told you is nothing less than the truth and that you may join with me here without any risk of mishap, after which, upon my oath, I swear I will return you safely back well before sunrise. For if you are to help me do likewise, what would it profit me to play you false?"

Selina, allowing herself no time to prevaricate, without further ado stepped forward till she was close enough to reach out and touch the wall, whereupon she closed her eyes and thrust her arm towards him. There was a sense of coldness along its length as she was propelled forward, followed by a little shock akin to a sudden unexpected loss of balance, but then she felt the unmistakably strong warmth that came from the clasp of his hand. She opened her eyes to find she stood before him and that he was as humanly substantial as she was herself.

She was indeed also standing on the green grass of the picture world, and that too felt and appeared as real and actual as any, though the one great difference at once apparent was that all that grew and bloomed in this place presented itself only in its perfect form; each leaf and blossom showing a total lack of corruption. There was no hint of damage, disease, misshape nor malady of any kind.

Releasing her hand, he looked at her searchingly and she returned his scrutiny. Like the world he inhabited, he too appeared immaculate, despite his long sojourn, coupled with the despair and desperation of his predicament. For obviously, like all else here, he had been blessed by the charmed atmosphere he now inhabited and thus become immune to life's usual ravages. His spotless but colourful clothing would suggest that he was certainly not a field worker, and neither was the hand she had held coarsened from such hard usage. The tunic and hose he wore had good fit and style, but mayhap he had been gifted all this in losing himself here, where nothing that was either imperfect or uncouth could exist. His hair, worn without a cap, curled to his shoulders, and this she decided maybe marked him out as a performer of some kind. But her speculation as to his profession must wait then, for he spoke with much urgency attending his words.

"You are clearly the answer to the prayers that I have prayed most earnestly. For to meet again with someone from the other side is something I was beginning to fear might never come to pass, and my fate would be to remain here forever, trapped and isolated."

Selina, who understood something of isolation, could only doubt his experience as she looked with pleasure at the many who disported themselves round and about. Rather than exclusion, it represented the very answer to her own prayers for companions and community, and she confessed that she had no understanding of what he meant.

"Come, in a moment I will take you to meet with some of my companions that frequent this exquisite place, and you will find them very jolly and in perfect harmony with the paradise they inhabit.

"But that you see is the very problem, for just as there is no decay, there is no discord of any kind. For the animals that means no predators or dearth of foodstuffs, and, for the inhabitants, no rancour nor competition; neither is there disease or ageing. All are at peace with one another in perpetual loving kindness and never-ending youth. The place you find yourself in is completely flawless."

"But how then can you take issue with it as it seems you do, for is this not what all hope to find in the heaven that at their end awaits them?" said Selina. "I can see no fault, only wondrous delight that such as this exists; a heaven on earth rather than just a possibility after death, should your deeds merit it.

"But how did this place come to be and how did those present arrive and make it their home?"

He raised his shoulders and spread his hands.

"By all accounts the weaver of the Tapestry was exceptionally gifted, and it was almost certainly commissioned by one of the lords of the manor, though I cannot be sure how long ago that might be, but being on such a grand scale, with just the one weaver, it must have been nigh on a lifetime's work. And maybe it was that very fact which caused a powerful imbuing of his life force to be woven into its fabric. That which he created was indeed thus caused to take on a life of its own, but there was also, maybe right from the beginning, something other alongside and quite separate that charged it. Some powerful force or magicking that also compelled it, but was not benign, of this I am certain, though I know not who was the magician or the witch that cast the spell, only that I was caught and snared within it and remain thus."

Selina could hardly deny that spellbinding might well be a factor to consider when all she was bearing witness to was exceedingly uncommon in all regards, but her enquiry was tentative as she put it to him.

"How long have you been thus ensnared and how did such a happening come about?"

He frowned in concentration as he sought to give her answer.

"How long is hard to tell, for night and day here are not measured in the same way, and there is no change of season, nor indeed change of any kind to mark the passage of time. Each day is exactly like the one that went before in every respect. There is therefore no sense of progress, of moving forward, only of repetition. And as nothing fades or dies, there is neither new growth nor fulfilment. The beautiful flowers will never complete their cycles and make seed. The cubs and other young animals will not grow to maturity, and none here will have fresh experiences that will grant them wisdom and understanding. They will remain forever untried, untroubled and childishly happy in their ignorance.

"I do believe that I have been in this place a considerable time, years perhaps rather than months, but I cannot be sure. As to how I came to be here in the first place, that I can tell you easily enough. There is no mystery there.

"I am a troubadour, and in my performing I travelled from place to place singing, reciting, storytelling and relaying news from region to region. And in the presenting of my art, I was welcomed in every grand house the length and breadth of the land. Hungry to learn of all that transpired in other realms I was given of the finest they had to offer till they had wrung every last crumb of detail from me. But when that was done, they loved as much to listen to the old romantic ballads of tragedy and heroic deeds, of love found and lost, and found again, of treachery and sorcery, sacrifice and saintliness. There was an insatiable appetite for my wares and I lived like a lord till the one fateful day when it all came to a bitter end.

"It was All Saints' Eve and in the Great Hall downstairs all were still gathered around the table after feasting and partaking liberally of the fine wines, mead and other rich brews. I had finished my part and laid aside my mandore whereupon to the rousing chords of other musicians, those gathered took lustily to the dancing, leaving me free at last to do as I would.

"Being set apart from and above the other players, my status earned me a bedchamber for my repose rather than the usual communal sharing in the hall or side rooms, and I went up to it, glad to be done with having to play the part as well as the instrument. It was indeed this same room that you now occupy, and in the many fine houses I have been lodged, none other could compare in terms of splendour. The candles had been lit and silver bowls of irresistibly exquisite sweetmeats were on offer, but, and here we have it, it was the Tapestry above all else that held me in thrall. I must sit before it and study it, enraptured by such a vision of idyllic existence. The more I gazed, the more I found it impossible to tear my eyes away from all I beheld, but then I had absolutely no wish to do so, wanting only to lose myself in it to the forgetting of all else. The candlelight, with its wavering gleam, made it seem as if rather than a still representation as with all like images, there was movement, and the more I watched in fascination, the more pronounced the artifice became, till it was no longer an illusion but the true fact of the matter, and without doubt the woven web came to life before my eyes.

"The floor level of the chamber and the ground level in the animated Tapestry being on the same plane, I had only to walk forwards to enter into that other place. At the moment of crossing from one to the other, my eyes closed of themselves, then, when they opened, I found that, beyond belief, I was in paradise.

"There I was welcomed by the inhabitants as unquestioningly and as willingly as they embraced the animals, they seemed neither surprised nor curious as to my sudden appearance, and to my delight drew me unreservedly into their activities, and I danced and sang with those whose youth and beauty were entirely perfect and without blemish.

"I had come with my mandore still slung about my shoulder, for of long habit I never let it beyond my grasp. It is my livelihood and my treasured possession, and I guard it constantly lest harm befall it. Making a show then of tuning it, I struck my habitual pose and began to regale my hosts with the most beguiling of my melodies. Choosing those that had earned me my reputation, I was confident that they could not but charm, delight and deeply move them, as was ever the way with all who listened. But it was not so. They smiled and applauded politely but otherwise took no special note. Somewhat abashed, I left my instrument beside a tree, certain that here at least it would come to no harm whilst I further explored this enchanted place.

"Leaving the dancers then to join the waders in the crystal waters of the brook, it was here by chance that I learned that I must leave before sun up. Seeking to know more of this realm and its inhabitants, I spoke with one handsome youth playing with an otter cub, asking him where everyone went at nightfall. He told me there was no such thing as nightfall, but at a certain time each day, everything stopped and all became still. Then, as in sleep, they knew no more till that which had ceased began again and they resumed their happy pastimes. I asked him what might happen to me, who came from a different realm with different laws if I was still there when such a thing occurred. He was perplexed by what I said, for he could not envision any place or thing other than that which he knew and inhabited. Although he was able to acknowledge that I was clearly other than the rest, he said he knew not what might befall me, but maybe if I stayed I would become as one of them and be governed by their rules, such as they were.

"I gleaned from this scant information that his 'certain time each day' was without doubt our sunrise, for their day was our night and in living separately we were in reverse to each other. And although they did indeed live, it was no more than an animation of what was portrayed in the Tapestry. None had past or future, just an ever-enduring perpetual present that of its nature lacked any form of variation. The weaver had created a masterpiece that portrayed powerfully his own vision of perfection, but perfection being the ultimate ideal could go no further. Nothing can be made more perfect, so there they were, perfectly beautiful, perfectly content and perfectly innocent of all the experiences of our imperfect world. They endured no suffering, knowing neither fear nor distress of any kind. For it cannot exist in a perfect realm. And so, in their serenity they knew nothing of extremes, not just of the harsh and cruel, but also of the exquisite, of the rapture that attends intense and passionate response to art or to a beloved person. Thus, they could only respond gently and mildly to my music, for this was the limit of their capacity for feeling.

"By now, uncertain how much time had passed and if it had a different length or stretch in the Tapestry world than our own, I made my way back to the place where I had entered in, hoping the return journey could be as easily done as the other way. Looking in the direction from whence I had come, I saw that all ahead was rendered blurred and indistinct. Nor could I discern the bedchamber, but, knowing it must be there, close but unseen, I closed my eyes and strode forward. A sensation akin to encountering a sudden cold spot in an otherwise warm clime, and of stretching and yielding accompanied the crossing between domains. 'Twas no more than that, and on opening my eyes I found myself safely returned to my own world.

"Knowing not what hour it was, I betook myself to the top of the stairs whereupon I heard the lively noise of revelry still issuing up from below. The morrow being the Sabbath, with no roistering permitted to encroach upon its sanctity, I was thus informed that the o'clock must still be short of midnight.

"Returning to my chamber, I took to my bed to ponder upon the wondrous things to which I had borne witness. There, lying back on my pillows relaying to myself all that had passed, sleep overtook me, till of a sudden I came to myself in remembrance of the fact that in that marvellous place I had left behind my mandore, leaning against a tree. I struggled into my senses and my clothes in clumsy haste, for I must rush to reclaim it before the chance was gone and it was irretrievably lost to me forever. If like all I must depart at break of day, who knew when I might come this way again. Thus, I made my second unfortunate excursion to the Tapestry world but this time, God help me, I did not get back before the curfew.

"Nor would any find my disappearance aught to remark upon, for it would be assumed that I had made an early departure with other places to travel to that must be attained before nightfall. None then would seek for me or have any cognisance of that which had befallen me. And so, to my utter despair it proved to be, until this blessed day when you come bringing me hope that liberation might be at hand."

Selina, now more comprehending of his situation and with her sympathies therefore engaged, asked, "How was it possible for you to see me if you are confined and restrained within this separate realm that has an impregnable screen?"

He ran his fingers distractedly through his perfect curls, leaving them none the less undisturbed by such assault.

"I have the sense that much time has passed since I fell foul of the law that keeps me ever prisoner here, and, during this sentence that I unwillingly serve, I have surmised that few others, if any, have taken lodging in this bedchamber before yourself. Maybe then, there was no previous chance for testing as to what might be possible.

"But I have a faith too that reassures me that ardent prayer has the power to unbind the snares of even the most tenacious spellbinding conjured by evildoers. And also, by God's good grace, certain people are born into the world endowed with some gift or quality of being that renders them impervious to such malign sorcery. I think you might be such a one, for I saw you surrounded by light. I had no apprehension of your situation, nor have I ever been able to see beyond the limits that confine me here, but you I beheld clearly shining like an angel in the darkness and thought you must indeed be such, sent as the answer to my prayers."

Selina, disturbed by such accolade, nevertheless did not argue that he was mistaken, lest he lose heart when he had barely attained it. Rather, she affirmed that she would do all that was in her power to aid him, and she sat with him by the brook to plan what would best serve his cause.

"I must first know your name then discover if the chatelaine has knowledge of you and when you were last here. As she has served in her position for many a long year she might well know of you if your reputation earned you a recognition and regard that necessarily heralded your coming with good remembrance. Also, I shall seek to discover all that is known regarding the making of the Tapestry; if there were indeed others involved in its construction apart from the weaver himself, and if there are notions of sorcery attending it."

She regaled him then too with the story of her own past and of her coming to reside in the manor, for it was clear that there was common cause between them. Both were in a form of entrapment that denied them the freedom to choose their own way, and for each there was much that was unknown and uncertain. How to ascertain also whether there be good or bad intent behind that which had befallen them and whom could be trusted.

He gave his name as Tristram Swayne, but said although he had not encountered the chatelaine directly in overseeing the preparation of his bedchamber, she might well recall his name and renown. Lady Isabella he had heard spoken of, but she was not in evidence during the festivities. And he had seen it as of little moment, surrounded as he was by so many other titled personages, lavish in both attention and tributes.

Selina said that given the way of things with so much in doubt, all enquiry must be conducted in a way that would not arouse suspicion, for she could not be sure how her questioning might be interpreted. Though gently done, it would be attributed hopefully to no more than a natural curiosity regarding her new domicile.

'Twas then that Tristram said he would make good his offer, and take her to have encounters with those who made the Tapestry their homeland. And in so doing he found in the enterprise a renewed pleasure in its sweet simplicity, her delight reigniting his own lapsed appreciation.

For as they approached those dancing, they willingly opened their ranks and drew them in, and Selina found herself at once bedecked with daisy chains, then, with her hands held fast, she was spun into the exhilaration of whirling movement. With mind and body in as much of a spin as her feet, she could not refrain from laughter, causing her companions to become equally obliged to join her in merriment, and, laughing too, whirled her about all the faster. Nor did she tire or become dizzied by the vigour of the dance, for here such limits were unknown and there be naught but perfect joy and unlimited capacity to experience it. Totally surrendered then as she was to the bliss of the moment, she also became entirely forgetful of the hour. Tristram halted her regretfully when it was time to depart, for he saw full well how loath she was to leave behind the delightful company that she had so long craved. But he assured her that the pain of parting could be easily remedied, for she could return on the following night and every night thereafter should she so desire. She affirmed fervently that this she would do, and would bring with her the telling of all she had learnt in her endeavours on the morrow.

He led her then to the place which formed the portal between the two worlds, but before he instructed her on how she should prepare herself, he said, "This day has been a blessed thing for me, for even if I must still wait some while yet to achieve my liberty, your coming and your promise of help has freed me from a misery that was as binding as the entrapment I must endure. I give thanks to you and for you, with a full heart, but I also entreat you that you in no way put yourself in harm's way for my sake. Let caution be your watchword, with remembrance of the saying "Tis better to be safe than sorry." Best all be done at the pace of a snail rather than race to an end that brings only your undoing."

CHAPTER EIGHT

When Selina was returned again to her own bedchamber, it was to find that the full moon's silver sheen had been entirely obscured by blanketing cloud. Its lack giving the depth of night that particular intensity that signalled its final throes, for the darkest hour is ever just before the dawn.

And although she had not slept, her sojourn in the Tapestry world where all perpetually continued in uncompromised perfection, had of necessity bestowed these virtues upon herself. In a realm where neither weariness nor languor held sway, none had need of the restorative powers of sleep. They were required to cease activity and lose awareness in those times of imposed suspended animation, but in this they were stilled by the dictates of their domain, not by tiring of their joyous pursuits.

In total contrast to her previous drowning in a sleep so deep that she had felt bewitched, she was now so wide awake she knew it would be futile to expect further repose. But with so much having transpired and so much to ponder upon, she had need to have her wits about her in any case if she sought to make some sense of it all. This was no time for slumber, for however impossible it might sound or seem, there could be no doubting the fact that she had just spent all the hours of darkness conversing with a troubadour marooned in a Tapestry.

And had she not also danced and played with the beautiful creatures, both human and animal, that dwelt in that enchanted world? And was it not her avowed intention to do exactly the same thing in this night to come? She most certainly needed time to think on these exceptional things, with particular dwelling on the thought that she may return thence each and every night should she so desire, and she so definitely did. How could she not? She climbed into bed then, not to seek forgetting in sleep, but to dwell on all that had happened and what might happen next.

Of a sudden all the old bounds and limitations that had ruled her life over the last four years fell away, and were dispelled and dispersed like blown autumn leaves. For overnight everything had become its opposite, and the previous woeful lack and emptiness had been filled, and filled to the very brim and running over. She had been blessed with the coming of delightful companions, and of enjoying pursuits with them that had hitherto been but the stuff of dreams. Heaven on earth really could exist, and she had miraculously found it within the confines of her own chamber. And this secret and heavenly place that she had discovered, unlike all else here was not forbidden and locked against her, but was a realm to which she herself had ownership of the key, a key that none other might confiscate and consign to a chain about their waist. They would not and could not, for they knew naught of it.

But in the receiving of this boon she had now been called upon to discover how that key granting her entry could also be turned about in the lock to achieve the obverse, gifting the troubadour the freedom to leave. And mayhap this might also mean, not just the undoing of fastened ways in and out, but of the loosening of spellbinding too.

But who was she to volunteer for such a task? She knew naught of necromancy, even though Tristram Swayne would have it other, persuaded that she was a bright angel come in answer to his prayers. What she could and would do, though, was to glean all knowledge as best she may in hope of discovering that which would unbind the curse that held him. When he had overstayed the time permitted, he had activated a snare that caused his entrapment. But who was it that had set the snare and to what end? Whosoever they might be, the saving grace came in knowing that whenever a spell was cast, it always had a countermand if it could be discovered and brought to bear. And it was also said that good intent had greater power than malign in the ongoing battle between the opposing forces of light and dark.

That notion brought to mind the exclusion of the light in Lady Isabella's chamber. Was she perhaps also in thrall to some witchery, or could it be that she herself was the witch?

Her musings were stayed then by the almost imperceptible sound of the door being gently opened and Selina had realisation that, although the time was still just short of daybreak, her own ghostly visitor was come. Staying hushed and without motion so that it would appear she still slept, she watched through half-closed eyes, attentive as to what manner of person she would encounter.

Making her way carefully in the scant light, a girl of maybe no more than thirteen stole in with silent tread carrying a ewer. Lifting that which was already in place upon the chest, she replaced spent water with freshly drawn, taking care in so doing to make no sound as she set it down.

Her hair was entirely concealed by a white kerchief, and she wore a simple dress that in the restricted light appeared to be of grey or pale blue cloth with the sleeves bound by white cuffs. Wrapped about it, from waist to ankle, was a matching apron, and, with such attire as this clearly denoting her station, Selina appraising her was minded that she herself had expected to be thus clad and likewise in service to others.

How come that she should be so favoured and this girl not, for it seemed she was not in subjugation only by the mere whim of chance. But truly fate was ever thus capricious and fairness never a consideration. There had been nothing fair in the operating of the Pestilence, with the worthy more often than not taken and the unworthy spared.

Having set the clean water in its place, the maid next freed a fresh towel from the crook of her arm, and laid it alongside the ewer before stooping to lift yesterday's used item from the chair and along with it the worn shift. In a trice, Selina extended her hand and took firm grasp of the girl's wrist.

"I bid you good morrow! Though 'tis still more night than day, I am well pleased at any hour to make your acquaintance."

The girl let out a little squeal of affright, but did not struggle to reclaim her arm; instead she stood meekly in resignation as if she had been apprehended in some wrongdoing. Selina, swinging her legs free from the bedclothes, sat sideways on the bed and bade her nervous visitor sit with her.

"Please, be at your ease, and know that I am delighted to meet at last the benevolent person who has brought me all I have had need of. But this achieved so silently and secretly that till now I could have neither knowledge of you nor the pleasure of remedying that lack.

"Tell me then, was this part of your instruction, that you may not rouse me, for it seems I am not permitted to meet with any who serve here until such time as I am told I may. Though when that time shall come is not ascertained, so it may well be yet a distance off. Meanwhile I must hold myself in patience and converse only with the chatelaine and Lady Isabella at given times. Thus, when I said I was most pleased to meet you, I spoke nothing less than the truth, for indeed I am utterly weary of only my own company. Please tell me your name and your terms of employment and all other information you might wish, and you will be doing me a great service."

The girl, clearly ill at ease despite Selina's entreaty, sat down stiffly on the very end of the bed, and, head lowered, would not meet her gaze.

She spoke hesitantly.

"Mistress, my name is Flora. My duties are to attend to the bedchambers and whatever is required in the Great Hall. Mostly this is done when it is known that they will not be occupied.

"It is as you suppose, I have indeed been given instruction that I must not wake you but should leave you be, for I am also informed that your sleep will be of such a kind that rousing you would be difficult in any case."

She paused for a moment as if in consideration before she added in a low voice, "In this I am led to believe that should I do so, it might even cause you some harm.

"But I think engaging in such converse as this might also be unwise, when I have been advised to refrain. Though there is nothing that is exactly forbidden, all being implied rather than stated, even so none here would care to stray far away from what we are precisely bidden do."

After a short space of quiet, she added as if in afterthought, "We accept that Madame and others have greater understanding in how best we should be guided in our actions and conduct ourselves. We submit to their authority knowing we are safe in their wiser keeping."

Selina, alerted by this declaration of abject acquiescence, remained nevertheless unconvinced of its sincerity, for it was quoted as if learnt like catechism rather than uttered from conviction. She pressed Flora further.

"Tell me pray, do you live close by and how came you to have employ in the household? For how long have you served?"

"I came here a long while back as but a little child, along with my mother and my grandfather. I have no remembrance of any previous abode. My grandfather you already have knowledge of, for it was he that fetched you here. That is his employment, driving the wagons and carriages and tending to all the needs of the horses. It was this ability that marked him, and why it was that Madame sought him out and would have him come and join the settlement. He has ever had such a rare way of working with both draught and riding horses, and in doctoring them should they fall sick, that it has earned him great repute far and wide. My mother and I were granted our position here on the strength of it, for he would not come without us. She and I lack comparable skills, but my mother was given regular employ in the bakehouse, and myself too as soon as I was of age, doing whatever requires attention, for all who abide in the settlement are found work here in one way or another."

"Your grandfather then is Jacob. He was most kind to me, and I have great hope to meet with him again but as yet that has not proved possible. Please do convey that hope to him lest he think it was not my intent and I have forgotten my promise."

At this mention of Jacob, Flora did now raise her eyes and look directly at Selina and her rigid posture eased a little.

"My grandfather is ever mindful of you, and would have it that I must report back to him all that I have awareness of with regard to your wellbeing. He has an uncommonly tender heart for a labouring man, I think that is why the beasts will do anything for him where others fail. They seem to have an inner knowing that he will tend them in a way that comes from a true understanding of all their needs. But his concern embraces all living things. On learning that you meet with no one and must dwell here with none to comfort or support you in your new domain, he had me leave a posy of violets for you as token, hoping that you would comprehend its message and be cheered by it."

"I was indeed, for I interpreted it as such."

Flora got to her feet abruptly then in some agitation, saying she had much to do at this hour with many other duties to attend to and must take her leave at once lest she be missed and rebuked. Gathering the ewer and shift in her arms, she made hastily for the door.

Selina did not attempt to keep her but took pains to reassure her as she left that she would make no mention to anyone of their encounter. She added that she looked forward to seeing her on the morrow, and should she be awake of her own accord, to speaking with her again. She was minded to ask her just before she left, why it was supposed that she would sleep so deeply that she could not easily be roused.

Flora, pausing for a moment on the threshold, offered a surprisingly honest opinion, which was at odds with her previous display of unquestioning conformity.

"When I attend your room, both the sweetmeats and the candles I bring are prepared specially for your chamber and given to none other. I have noticed that they have a very particular aroma. Mayhap then the reason might be to do with them, though I cannot say for sure if this be the case or for what purpose if it is."

Then she was gone, leaving Selina in a turmoil. What Flora had just offered her as reason for her prodigious depth of sleep made her earlier understanding seem flawed and ill considered.

If the sweetmeats were concocted to enthral the observer and the candles gave off an intoxicating smoke for the same purpose, then, as Flora said, for what reason? Did whoever prepared them have knowledge then of the

Tapestry, and maybe wish to entrap her in the same fashion as the troubadour? And had he not likewise also remarked on both in his first enthralled beholding of it? If her belief that the discovery she had made was unknown to all but herself it would suggest that such reasoning be sadly amiss.

Yet surely this could have naught to do with Lady Isabella, for had she not said she had other need of her, one to do with her fulfilling a role that required a closeness and accord that would come only with time? And that she must listen assiduously to Abigail's revelations regarding the history of all that had gone before towards that end.

Abigail herself could not be seen as suspect, attending Lady Isabella with total devotion as she surely did. It was inconceivable that she would plot to serve her ill by doing aught that would be against her wishes.

To find answer it was plain she must discover who it was that prepared the sweetmeats and candles for her chamber. But she realised if she knew not whom it was that instructed them it would avail her little. All must remain in confusion till such facts were known. But she minded then her own advice to Tristram, that all should be done so as not to raise suspicion, lest those who had ill intent, whoever they might be, were alerted and sought to thwart her efforts.

Unable to be at ease, she left her bed, and, having cleansed herself with good usage of the freshly drawn water Flora had provided, donned the clean shift, before sitting back down on the bed's end to gaze afresh at the Tapestry till such hour as Abigail would come. She noted that the daisy chains that had hung about her neck before she departed the web were not in evidence. It would seem then that they could have no existence beyond their own domain and must stay within its confines.

The brightening of the coming new day gave enough clearness now to behold the image spread across the chamber's wall and she gazed intently with a different seeing.

Tristram, in the foreground, turned towards her and away from all else, seemed to have a different look and stance from that presented before. He was still apart from his companions, but surely now without that previous air of one lost and forlorn. In his facing forward there seemed instead an eagerness that indicated he was in pursuit of new direction rather than in desperate hope of deliverance.

His figure in the Tapestry was as firmly woven into the structure as was everything else when it had been fashioned long ago by the weaver, yet she could not doubt that some change had occurred. How come he was depicted in any case when it had been wrought before his entrapment? Those others who inhabited the tableau were also firmly anchored in the mesh of the web, yet had they not leapt into graceful agility with no seeming restraint? As she contemplated them now, despite being constructed of no more than silken threads and skilled hands, she had undoubtedly seen them gifted with life, and assuredly too she had talked and laughed with them. Her eye running over the imagery was stayed here and there by recognition of those in particular that she had disported herself with, yet presently here they were – no more than spun yarn laced into a patterning that deceived the eye into belief that it had reality.

Though he was part of it, that the troubadour was real enough she could not doubt. He had remembrance of all that had befallen him and his life before ensnarement, but these others, he had said, lacked such remembrance because they had no life other than the endless repetition of the moment shown. If this was so, then they were not real beings at all.

Should she discover the words or deed that would unwind the enchantment and free Tristram, what would happen to these others who existed within the Tapestry? Would the lives they led that had no real substance but seemed so joyous, cease to be? If they had come into being only through the casting of a spell, the undoing of the magic would necessarily undo them with it and they would be no more. Such thought disturbed and unsettled her. It was her intent to return to their world this very night and the anticipation of its coming entranced her as much as any other bewitching. But what was she returning to? A phantasmagoria that deceived the senses into accepting make-believe, portraying that illusion so beguilingly that you wholly and willingly embraced the deception.

She could find no idea of a solution to it all that brought her peace of mind, and, disturbed and fretful, she gave off from her perusal and lay back with closed eyes till Abigail should come to fetch her to her breakfast.

She had but a short span to wait before, like Flora, Abigail came with gentle entrance, lest she waken her before she was ready to be roused and thus cause her some confusion. Finding her in repose but wakeful, she confessed that she brought a newly sewn gown for today's wearing that she must first ensure be of good fit, but then added with resignation the truer reason for her early coming. Just as she ate but sparingly nowadays, her sleeping was likewise meagre and she was thus ready to rise earlier than most. Such behaviour she acknowledged might not be welcome to those of younger age and habit, and had Selina still slept she would have withdrawn till a more appropriate hour.

The trying on of the new attire was without problem, for it had been made according to her measurement and fitted without fault. Selina, roused from her previous despond by having its silken folds fall about her raised arms, could not but take delight in it. Unlike the ponderous weight and restriction of yesterday's garb, this was fashioned from a lighter material and was short of the floor by an inch or so. Also, it had a rich crimson hue that entranced the eye and was embellished only with silk binding at neck and sleeve. With such vibrancy of pigment and perfect fit, there was no call for additional ornament, though when she had dressed her hair into two looped braids, Abigail fastened a rope of opal beads around her neck, then, standing back, nodded in satisfaction, declaring her well presented. Unable to resist spinning about to enjoy the spread of the skirt, Selina happily agreed that such finery as it was styled to do turned her into the likeness of a princess.

Then as before, the chatelaine accompanied her to the hall and the table where a fragrant breakfast was laid out and waiting on her. Leaving her whilst she attended to her business in the kitchen, Abigail affirmed she would return in a while to conduct her to Madame, but to take her time at the repast for it was still the early hours and Lady Isabella would be some while yet before she was ready to receive callers.

Selina cast a sideways glance at the head of the table to check whether his Lordship's place was still laid anticipating

124

his return. It was. She would question Flora regarding this on the morrow. Mayhap she could relate more of the tale with regard to his absence and looked-for return. Although all inhabiting the settlement did as they were bid, according to Jacob such discipline did not curtail their speculation as to what might lie behind appearances.

But perhaps Abigail might reveal more of the truth in her narrating of the history of Lady Isabella and how things had come to pass. It would surely prove necessary if she was to have a fuller understanding of her patron as was mooted she must. Or then again, she could be informed by Madame herself in due course.

Alongside this endeavour, she had the separate task of gleaning whatever knowledge there was with regard to the troubadour in the quest for his deliverance. She had hope of taking him some small crumb of encouragement and comfort on her return this coming night. Perceiving her as his angelic saviour, he would expect no less. In which case she could but trust that the angels were watching over her too and girded for action should it be called for, and the courage passed to her from her parents would need to stand her in good stead, for who could doubt that there would be testing times ahead?

CHAPTER NINE

When Abigail was returned to the hall from the kitchen as before, she led her to the landing outside Lady Isabella's parlour, whereupon with a respectful tap at the door, calling out that they were come, they received acknowledgement and entered in.

All was as yesterday: the curtains more than half drawn and Madame in her chair with her back to the window. The only change was in her gown, for now she was robed in purple velvet with a heavy jewelled girdle worn low at the waist and her hands were encased in black lace gloves that mimicked the veiling obscuring her face.

As the chatelaine turned to close the door behind them, Lady Isabella raised a hand to stay her in the action, and with a gentle command dismissed her from the audience.

"Abigail, there is no need for you to wait on us. We are blessed with most clement weather so why not take yourself to the garden and have the pleasure of it till we have completed our discourse and Selina joins with you there."

Abigail was much taken aback. It was clear she had not

anticipated exemption and could not construe any reason or purpose that might be the cause. Her face registered both hurt and confusion, and Selina, dismayed to see her thus, made an involuntary move towards her, hand outstretched to touch her arm in offer of comfort. Clearly devoted to her mistress as she was, she could but interpret such action as a personal rejection and thus a most grievous slight. The resulting wound sustained, as was painfully evident, was disabling. In witnessing her discomfiture, Selina turned then to Lady Isabella with a look of entreaty, owning that she would welcome her presence. But on the moment, with a stoic effort, Abigail managed to regain some degree of composure, and with a stiff curtsey said no more than, "Madame." And presenting a brave face despite severely ruffled dignity, she let herself out with as much aplomb as she could muster.

Lady Isabella, remarking afterward on the incident, sounded a little contrite at the chatelaine's upset, though Selina, unable to see her features, could not tell to exactly what degree.

"Do not distress yourself with regard to Abi. I promise you I will make it up to her, but I do think it will be more productive if we have no third party. Two being company and three being one too many as they do say.

"But if enlightenment can only come at the cost of sacrifice, or the casting aside of old habits, then it was illuminating to see your response to her disquiet. You could say that I learnt something of value at her expense and could not have learnt it in any other way. What was demonstrated was that you are clearly a champion of the afflicted and would plead on their behalf, a reliable sign of a stout heart, and a virtue that will surely have its place in what is to come."

She paused then to invite her to be seated, indicating a chair some few feet distant. It had been positioned to benefit from a shaft of light that managed ingress, thus rendering her visible in the gloom, whilst at the same time ensuring Madame herself remained even more unseen. But if her face was screened by both veil and lack of light, her voice was crystal clear and, as she expanded on her reasoning, Selina again took heed that there was no note that would identify it as that of an older woman.

"Abigail, due to her long service and dedication to duty, would bring a cautionary influence to proceedings. It is clear she has taken to you, and from what I have just witnessed you reciprocate with like response, but her primary concern will ever be for myself and my wellbeing. She will therefore inevitably seek to exert some control and to slow progress to a pace she feels comfortable with. Her very presence would be brought to bear on us both, even should she utter not a word.

"My own mother dying in giving me birth, Abi is the nearest I have in experiencing maternal care and concern. And she having no child of her own invested all such potential nurture in attending me in my early years. Thus, we have a bond that inevitably exerts its pull, but there are times when the need to sever the binding ties of apron strings becomes necessary, lest those binds restrict our freedom of choice.

"Her cautionary stance would seek to hamper me, and were she present I would not wish to cause her upset by rejecting her wishes. It was the kinder thing to do as was done, so think me not careless with regard to her feelings. I am not, but I must command my own council, and sentiment can render us weakened if we surrender to it."

Selina, remaining silent as Abigail had instructed, wondered now in light of what Lady Isabella had told her if such discipline perhaps came more from the chatelaine than from Madame herself. But to avoid error, as with the priest, once more she held her tongue and would so continue until invited to do otherwise. She had not long to wait.

"Tell me, Selina, how do you find your new life and place of residence? What aspects please you and is there aught that does not? Please speak freely, for I would know your mind in this, and talk of the simpler things will pave the way towards the deeper concerns that must follow."

Invited to express her true feelings, Selina gladly grasped the opportunity to ask at least some of the questions that were clamouring constantly in her head. But she must tread carefully, for had she not considered that Lady Isabella might be as much in thrall to spellbinding as the troubadour or even herself be the witch?

In considered reply, she voiced the obvious, for it would be expected, but also because she did indeed seek such understanding.

"Why must all the doors be locked and myself forbidden to meet any who are in employ here? Though I have evidence of them all about me I cannot commune with them. As you are aware, my grandmother lived in isolation and thus so did I for the four years I dwelt with her. I had hoped never to repeat such style of living again."

By way of reply, Lady Isabella startled her with what

sounded very much like an oath, and her voice had a different and harsher tone when she gave answer,

"But four years and you think yourself ill-used! You know naught of isolation! Had you walked in my shoes and borne a lifetime of such privation, then you might own that you were on intimate terms with solitary confinement, and one that had but scant chance of change in the foreseeable future."

Then, recomposing herself from what she clearly regarded as a regrettable lapse of good manners, she continued, "There is nevertheless always the possibility of redemption, for me and for us both, slender but actual, and Selina you could be the redeemer that brings it all to pass.

"But I have gone ahead of myself. I had not meant to touch on such matters as yet. Maybe I should have retained Abigail after all to curb my waywardness. Let me then return to your very reasonable concerns regarding your status. As Abigail will have informed you, such exclusion is temporary but initially necessary.

"Despite our communal way of life, of all those who work and dwell in the settlement, none have had personal encounter with myself. There have been but two who owing allegiance to none or no one, meet with me, Abigail, of course, and the priest. None would dare to seek knowledge of me by questioning either source. The priest is bound by the sanctity of his code, and Abi would scorch them with fiery outrage should they try to coax her into any revelation. It is also a fact that, where she is concerned, most have respect and perhaps even some fearfulness in their dealings with her, for her guard is impenetrable and her loyalty formidable when it comes to withholding what is not for their ears or eyes. They err too on the side of caution, lest she feel obliged to report back to myself any hint of impropriety or unseemly prying.

"But you would be viewed in an entirely different light, being young and newly come amongst us. It could be assumed that in your eagerness to establish yourself with those already present, you might very possibly prove more amenable, and, in so being, more willing to divulge aspects of hitherto close-kept secrets.

"Indeed, you might, Selina, and though it would be understandable it would be disastrous. Thus, till you have become as seasoned as a battle-hardened soldier, it cannot be risked."

Selina could not but accept the caution, remembering the eagerness with which she had addressed Flora, and her carelessness in complaining about the restricted way of things regarding her movements and meeting with anyone other than the chatelaine and Madame. She had been unrestrained in expressing her concerns with no thought at all for discretion.

As Abigail had said, she must first prove her loyalty before she was gifted greater freedom. She could see her point. But alongside that, and just as pertinent, ran her own uncertainty as to exactly what she would be espousing. For being as yet unschooled in the way of things, she did not have enough knowledge to make an informed choice and 'twas a fact that loyalty must be proven on both sides. Meantime she could but bide her time. By way of giving reason for not pledging an immediate promise of fidelity, she offered, "My Lady, it is hard to swear allegiance to you when as yet I am not permitted to see your face. If I was thus privileged it would be possible then to decipher all the looks and moods writ upon it, for that which is portrayed outwardly in the features gives evidence of the soul within. And such portrayal is essential for us to witness if we are to know the measure of the person before us.

"It was given to me by my priest that you were a woman full of years and become frail and dependent, yet such telling is not borne out by the little I can countenance. All then is hard to make sense of and I know not what to think. May I be privy to knowing what is the cause behind your wearing of the veil and of the isolation you lament of so forcefully, but seemingly have no choice but to endure?"

Lady Isabella was quiet for a long moment, and when her voice was returned to her it came with a deep sigh that presaged much sorrow.

"Ah, yes indeed! How did I, who was taught by my father to face the world and never turn away from whatever challenges it might present, nevertheless end up skulking in the shadows like a leper? Mayhap you think I am indeed a leper? There are many tales spun around the cause of my withdrawal, all fanciful and none having aught to do with the fact of the matter, but I will tell you this much, there was neither accident nor disease at the heart of it. I am not grotesque as some gain pleasure in supposing."

Selina, stirred by such confession, was moved to ask if she was not disfigured what other reason could demand her total seclusion.

But at such request, Lady Isabella shook her head vigorously, and, clapping her gloved hands, declared, "Enough, enough! I will talk no more now on how or why

I was afflicted. Instead, I will give you answer to a question you have not asked but might well have done.

"The doors are locked and barred at night that none may enter into the house from the domestic quarters or elsewhere. And once Abigail has every key that has been given out returned to her keeping and counted in, when she herself has taken to her bed, then that is the time I reclaim my house and my liberty. Come the evening with all banished and none to behold me, I can at last shed the hated veil and walk the corridors and stride the Great Hall unencumbered by such blindfolding. I may gaze about me with clear sight and remember again the life that is gone and those who peopled it. The reacquainting that comes from walking the length and breadth of the old home in sweet remembrance brings salve to the grief of loss and regret. Likewise, in the shedding of the veiling that marks and punishes me as much as a scold's bridle, I am liberated from that cursed bondage too for as long as the night lasts. Its lack during that welcome span restores me to myself and saves me from lapsing into despond.

"I have my garden also of course, but that was more newly fashioned and has no resonance from the past to console me. It is pleasing and I am appreciative of it but 'tis not the same as the joy of traversing the manor and the memories and sensations that gladden my heart even while they torment me.

"As I cannot reveal myself, this is the only way I may have access to my domain, for in the hours of daylight the veil of itself would not be enough to protect me from curiosity and speculation.

"While it is ever the way for all in their dotage to pine

for their lost youth and the times that are gone, I assure you with me it is not just a maudlin hankering for previous times, but much more than that. For although the times have gone, as go they must, I am still firmly rooted in them, yet have not been able to follow where they went. I truly am stuck in the past, even though it no longer exists, thus in actuality I belong neither here nor there, though you will not divine the meaning of my words as yet.

"And what your priest advised you regarding me was not subterfuge. Though I am neither frail nor impaired, when you quote him as saying I am long widowed, implying that I am aged, you are not in truth amiss. Also, if there is presently foolish guessing regarding the necessity for the veil, at least it is harmless whilst none can see me. 'Twould be a different thing should I come before them in person, however well hid by black gauze. They would be in receipt of visual evidence that would inform their hitherto fanciful speculation, and that would not be without harm or risk.

"Thus, like the owl or the bat, I inhabit the hours of darkness when all others are insentient in their beds. It is why I start my day later than is usual even for the high born, and must take my rest when I should be up and engaging with the day's activities."

Selina, having heard this much, could not refrain from seeking further understanding with regard to Lady Isabella's widowhood and the place ever set for her husband. He, a man who despite being either dead or otherwise departed, was yet still expected to present himself for repast.

"My Lady, if your husband is long deceased, for who is the place set at table? Is it purely in honour and remembrance of him, though Abigail said when I enquired not to wait on him before starting my meal as he may be delayed, which made but little sense?"

Lady Isabella gave forth a sound that was both sigh and moan, and it stirred the veil in front of her face with its deliverance.

"You will have heard tell no doubt, that it is supposed that my husband is not dead at all but has deserted me because of my degradation. The setting of his place at table is by my order in craven hope that he will return to me to honour the vows he pledged at our betrothal. The fact that it flies in the face of my claim to widowhood is apparently brushed aside or explained away as the behaviour of a woman unhinged by such perfidy.

"I will enlighten you lest you have like suspicion. I am neither widowed nor deserted, but my husband is indeed gone from me. His going was not of his choosing and certainly not of mine, 'twas more like unto my father's abduction and thereunto there is a ransom still unpaid and owing. You could indeed call it a king's ransom, but the currency demanded is asked for in coinage we do not have and cannot attain, but I speak metaphorically. His deliverance cannot be bought with gold or any manner of precious metal, for the price is beyond such simple barter. 'Tis exchange of a different kind entirely and, because of that, the situation has remained ever in deadlock for none can see a way of resolving a riddle without any apparent solution."

Selina felt the hairs on the back of her neck rising, for she had understanding of what it was to which Lady Isabella was referring, though how that knowing came to her she could not say, save it was of uncommon kind and source.

And because of it she could not but exclaim, "Madame, was this aught to do with the Tapestry in my bedchamber?"

Lady Isabella turned towards her, and, though her own face was hid, it was clear she was studying Selina's.

"Child, how can you know that? Do you speak with some authority regarding the Tapestry?"

Selina then took stock of all that had transpired. Much had been revealed but however much she felt herself being drawn into that which Lady Isabella had confided in her, above such considerations she must hold fast to her own pledge to watch and wait. Till she knew who she could trust with certainty and who was the spellbinder, she must exercise care and caution. She answered then with such concerns well recognised, but also with nothing less than the truth, for indeed she could not give the source of her knowing.

"My Lady, I have no such authority, and cannot offer any cause as to why I should regale you with a referral to the Tapestry as having aught to do with the loss of your husband. It would seem the words came to me of themselves and were uttered before my mind could grasp what sense they made."

Lady Isabella cut short further apology with impatience and gave other reason for what had occurred.

"This knowing you speak of that comes entirely of itself, has about it the mark of a more penetrating perception than that which is arrived at from lengthy pondering. It is gifted to those with eyes focused on inner rather than on outer seeing – visionaries. And this assuredly is the very virtue that we now seek. Such clairvoyance perchance might see the way through the tangled, twisted labyrinth which confuses and defeats those who seek their way out. Wholly dependent on use of chart or compass, 'tis clear such paltry aids to navigation cannot suffice in this impasse. The answer to a conundrum cannot be found thus, for neither wit nor will, logic nor reason will avail aught and this I know to my cost."

Selina must seek further understanding. "If your husband is lost and cannot be found and returned to you, why is his place ever set at table?"

At that moment, Lady Isabella stood and turned about to face the window, and Selina, surprised by the unexpected action, nevertheless could now behold her stature. She was taller than was usual for a woman, slender and straight of back. Her frame defied the claims of advanced age as much as did her voice. It seemed she must rise in order to spread her arms for it was a necessary gesture in giving response.

"'Tis set there not in vain nor foolish hope, but because it must lay constant claim to his right to occupy his seat. On our marriage, he became lord of this manor and naught can be brought to bear to refute that claim. It makes declaration of the legitimacy of his incumbency and fixes him firmly where he belongs, here with me in this place, and such anchorage can be neither denied nor circumvented. It is the only thing that prevents him being forever lost and gone from me, my one stay against powers that would have it otherwise, thus it must ever be done."

Again, Selina defined the meaning behind Lady Isabella's words. This was a countermand that must stall the completion of a cast spell. It rendered it impotent, unable to proceed to its desired aim. But although its intent was thus frustrated, it was insufficient of itself to break the curse, whatever that might be, the result being a stalemate rather than a victory over malign forces. With this much understood, she must ask, "My Lady, if your husband is spellbound, who is it that holds him in thrall?"

Isabella returned to her seat then, and when she had settled herself gave answer.

"I will leave the telling of that to Abigail. Our discourse this day has wrought an understanding between us that I dare to trust bodes well for our future conferring. Let us give thanks for that and leave all in that favourable position. Go now instead, and hearken to that with which Abigail shall further enlighten you. We will meet tomorrow and make good use of all you learn in the encounter."

CHAPTER TEN

As she made her way back down the stairs and through the torchlit passage to the kitchen, Selina barely paused to listen at the door. Her head was already filled to bursting with all that she had learned, and at back of that was the promise of tonight's encounter with the sublime world of the Tapestry. She had more than enough to fully engage all her thoughts and senses, and in truth she realised she no longer felt herself a sorry dweller in the cast shadow of exclusion. Rather, she was now in haste to meet with Abigail and hear more of the story that was inevitably drawing her in, despite her self-admonishment to remain vigilant.

She found Abigail seated on the stone bench, hands resting in her lap full of keys. She had selected one which she turned about in her fingers as if it was a string of rosary beads, and indeed in such action she seemed so deep in contemplation that she did not witness Selina's coming, and started when she had awareness of her.

"Selina, you are come. How did you fare with my Lady? I must ask seeing that she forbade my participation even though I would not think to interrupt in any way."

Selina, anticipating such response, hastened to offer reassurance.

"Abigail, she confessed to me that 'twas not harshly done, but to save you from anxiety lest you feared she reveal too much too soon before I had proved myself worthy. She sought only to spare you from such distress."

Abigail answered with some resignation, but also with a degree of irritation.

"You have no need to explain my Lady's motives to me, I who have cared for her since the day of her birth and who know all her ways of thinking and being better than any. Think not to instruct me as to her reasons."

Selina apologised, begging her pardon for an attempt to offer comfort that had proved clumsy and ill considered. Nevertheless, she noted that Abigail, however well she insisted she knew Madame, had certainly not anticipated her exclusion and thus it had come as an unexpected and painful shock to her.

But, Selina mused, it must be a conceit to ever suppose that we know people so well that we can predict all their thoughts and deeds. Was it not in fact hard enough to know ourselves when we were ever prey to wayward emotion and action? Like the knowledge that Lady Isabella had spoken of, that came of itself, they inhabited us regardless of our will and overrode our considered choices.

Mayhap this was the very reason that we could be spellbound. At those times when we floundered in indecision or confusion, we were not in charge of ourselves, and in our susceptibility offered both invitation and a way in for the sorcerer's wily charm. And having no doubt a far more persuasive and compelling appeal than could be conjured by any itinerant mummer, it might prove nigh on irresistible.

Abigail accepted her apology with a good grace.

"Change is coming and necessarily so. Each day finds me more unfit for the duties that I must perform and I am weary of the burden. My devotion to my Lady cannot bring alteration to such fact, and should I not lay down my yoke willingly and soon, the choice of continuance will no longer be mine to make.

"I am nevertheless conscious that, although time is precious, there are dangers in haste for all must be done with care. Mistakes once made cannot then be unmade and better by far to lose an hour rather than a whole cause.

"You are destined to step into my shoes and take on the tasks that I have performed this long while since, but more than that will be asked of you as you must by now be aware. We will come to the revealing of such requirements in the continued telling of my Lady's woeful misadventures, so pay heed and I shall take up the tale from where 'twas left off."

But before Abigail was thus able, Selina must first press her for greater understanding with regard to her own part.

"Abigail, why was I chosen for this employ? How was such decision arrived at when so little could be known of my suitability beforehand? Since I am arrived, there is an unsaid but apparent acceptance that I was especially selected for this role. Have you not just owned to the fact? And if it is thus then whom was it that chose me, and by what authority?"

Abigail, still tracing the scrolled embellishing of the key in her hands, gave a nod in acceptance that the enquiry was pertinent and also that she would address the issue first.

"The knowledge of which you speak does not come by way of interview seeking to discover the merits or otherwise of a candidate, for such procedure is lengthy and the outcome not guaranteed. 'Tis a poor system when much is at stake. Hence it was not employed with regard to yourself. We sought instead the certainty that can only come by different but truer discernment.

"My Lady conferred with her priest. Although he is an instrument of the established church, which holds that all magic be the work of the Devil, he keeps his own council on such matters. Did not our Lord cast out evil spirits, he would argue, raise the dead back to life and violate the Sabbath when it was fitting? Thus, he could discover no wrongdoing should he engage in combat with spellbinders, and in that engagement seek liberation for such innocent souls as were entrapped and possessed by witchery.

"Being a spiritual man but endowed with the gift of far seeing, he set to descry all about in search of such a one as might assist in the quest. He sent forth a call to the angels that they would deliver us from evil, and it was shown to him then, in the way given to soothsayers, that he would find what he sought in your grandmother's dwelling. He beheld it in his mind's eye, and you therein, bereaved and homeless. And in that seeing he was made aware that you were the one that could undo the bind that held all till now, imprisoned and helpless. With due haste he persuaded your own priest that placement with Lady Isabella would be a blessing to all concerned and thus it was arranged with none to frustrate the outcome.

"Do not feel yourself used or sacrificed to a cause for which you did not volunteer. Instead have trust that this is your destiny, that it must be fulfilled and may not be avoided.

"Even so there can be no surety that all will turn out as is hoped, for the grip of the sorcerer is vice-like and 'twill be hard indeed to prise away the taloned claws from the captured prey. Accept your lot, but see it rather as challenge against the forces of the underworld, and should you win, with the necessary grace of God, great good shall come about by your hand.

"Now let us return to our tale of Madame, and as you listen you will be gifted with an ever-greater understanding – one that has as much to do with awakening to your role as it has to do with the hearing of what happened afterward."

Selina now gave Abigail the nod, indicating that she was settled enough in her own mind to give her full attention to the tale. Being also more alert to the idea that she herself had a vital part to play, no matter that it made but little sense, increased her want to hear all that there was to tell.

Abigail let go of her key then and took in a deep breath as if she were readying herself for total immersion into the past. Not as in remembrance and recall, but more as if she betook herself there in person as would a traveller or a pilgrim.

*

Lady Isabella had confessed to the envoy prince that but for consideration of all who were dependent upon them in the domain, there was naught that she would not surrender for her father's sake. Such a brave and bold statement it was, the truth of which was about to be put to the test for she must next prove such words were not idly spoken. The ransom demanded for her father's safe return was nothing less than a total giving of her very self.

The outlaw prince stated his terms in measured tones, his strange accent somehow giving greater emphasis to them as if such foreignness was peculiarly appropriate in spelling out the extreme price she must pay like unto a judge passing stern sentence.

"My Lady, there is but the one concession asked and your father will be restored to you and no harm done further. The cost of life that regrettably attended the affray is harm enough, and it is this consideration above all else that has dictated the cost of his release. Before I state those terms agreed by my family and the forum of statesmen who considered and advised on this matter, I must first acquaint you with the relevant facts that led us to the result of those deliberations.

"There are many such as we, who have come to the shores of your country from diverse places, seeking to establish themselves here for all must depart their own homeland and place of birth for reasons of disease, deluge, persecution or other calamity. It must also be owned that there are some who come amongst you for no other reason than to pillage and lay waste, with scant regard for the native populace, and 'tis these marauders that are a scourge on both other incomers and the indigenous people alike.

"But many of these latter who are the victims of their murderous attacks have unfortunately thereafter a tendency to see all incomers in the same light, even though we are as much at their mercy as are they. Thus, my own people living in quiet settlements learning the language and ways of their hosts are nevertheless frequently set upon and persecuted, not just by such outlaws but also by the local men with whom they have no quarrel.

"For it is alas also the way of things that such men are in bondage to petty small lords and have no choice but to obey their demands, despite any reluctance and misgivings they might have of their own. Such a one was the lord who called upon your father to take up arms to defend him from so-called ferocious brigands.

"Let me tell you the truth of that engagement. That particular lord had a liking to go out hunting our people as they blamelessly gathered kindling or foraged for the pot. He justified such barbarity as like unto the necessary extermination of vermin, and indeed whether they be man, woman or child, they were pursued, caught and dispatched with as little mercy as that shown to rodents. But such meagre slaughter was soon not enough to sate his bloodlust, and thus he led a raid at dead of night upon an outlying settlement with no defence. Setting the dwellings afire whilst all were abed, those who ran forth from the flames were ruthlessly put to the sword. Nearly all perished.

"Such a deed could not be left unavenged. That which had been done to us must be visited upon the cowardly perpetrators if we would stop their evil deeds for good and all, lest one more innocent life be lost. And 'tis true no quarter would have been given and no man spared in that affray, for our blood was up and we were in no mood to strike with anything less than our full strength and fury. And had your father not come we would have prevailed and meted out to them the rough justice that they had earned. But even in the heat of battle with righteous anger fuelling our sword arms, no woman or child would have had need to fear us for 'tis not we who are the barbarians.

"When your father and his followers came fresh and ready to preserve an ally, we, who were weary from the conflict, knew we could no longer prevail for the odds were now reversed and against us. To avoid prodigious slaughter, we needed to withdraw and so 'twas done, but we went not in total defeat, for we took your father with us as hostage. This deed bringing us assurance that there would be no reprisal, nor counter attack, whilst we held him prisoner.

"The offensive had been bloody, both parties stout in the belief that right was on their side. Indeed, many could not cease from the fight even when 'twas time to retreat, for so intense was their sense of grievance they would not give way and lay down sword nor axe. But when it was at last known by all that your father was taken and his life at stake, then there came an uneasy peace. Those on your side had prevailed and seen us off, but rather than them going home as conquering heroes, the upper hand was yet with us, for we had them backed helpless into a corner as long as we held their lord, your father, in our power.

"Now, during the deliberations in the four days that have followed, your father was brought to the forum and bid be fully involved, and thus he became conversant with all the facts as I have just laid them before yourself. Without doubt he is a fine and noble man, and he had no prior knowledge of the wretched deeds wrought by the man who had called upon him for succour, for all his vile acts were done in clandestine manner. So, in this, although he be entirely without blame, he was nevertheless moved to make recompense for our ill usage by one of his kinsmen, and to protect us from any further such outrage.

"It became clear to all as we considered the situation that in order for that to come to pass, an allegiance must be forged between us that would ensure our safekeeping under his patronage, come what may. And we would likewise play our part in a mutual swearing of the brotherhood of chivalry and knighthood. Within the days of our discourse, your father learned much of our culture and history and found within them a deal that stirred him mightily to good regard and appreciation. He saw that we were not the primitives generally supposed; indeed, such reduction could not be further from the truth. In recognition it was agreed by all there gathered that the surest and most binding treaty be of course the allegiance and commitment of marriage. And thus, for the sake of ensuring my people's safety, and having guarantee that no other petty lord may ever again visit such persecution upon us, it was agreed that you and I should enter into wedlock should you be willing. I have pledged my word and agreed to such contract for 'twould provide the surety we must have in our continuance here. In joining with your father, the greatest of the local lords, we would together become an unassailable union. My personal considerations are of no matter beside this boon."

Isabella recoiled, stunned. It could not surely be the case that her father, who had ever cherished her, would put the cause of these alien people with their unknowably strange ways and unchristian customs before her. That he had consented to her usage in barter, reducing her to no more than a tool in trade, was impossible to countenance.

There must be some misunderstanding, as was more than likely in an exchange taking place in disparate languages.

"I must speak with my father," was her only rejoinder. She could indeed say no more, for she was aghast at what was proposed. What words were there to be spoken in response to the unspeakable?

The prince in contrast seemed in complete control of himself. True he had been granted more time to address himself to the situation, but, more than that, it would seem he did not question that this must be done. He would sacrifice himself to the greater good. Yet he answered her with gentleness.

"Of course, each one must have their say and agree only if they believe 'tis the best outcome when all has been considered. That you are allowed a space to think your own thoughts first. I shall leave you now and return at sun up on the morrow to convey you to your father."

But the span of one night was not enough to make her more sensible to what was being asked of her. She felt no time would suffice to reconcile her to such request.

Yes, it was the way of things that marriages were arranged for the advantage of dynasties, often with scant, if any, regard for the two people so contracted. It was also true that as the solitary heir she had no choice but to marry, but that all in good time, with the knowledge that her father would give due consideration to her wishes, and she would not be excluded from the choice of partner.

This prince, with his odd clothes and odd accent, his ignoble small horse and his undoubted strangeness, in all respects had neither domain lineage nor coat of arms to bring entitlement to any such offer.

He had a dignity and bearing that singled him out as of noble birth, but of what matter was that when he no longer had a land of his own where such title held sway, nor castle, manor nor estate? With none such, what dowry could he offer that might persuade her father to see him as an asset rather than an obvious non-contender? There must be some other cause that she was not yet privy to that had held sway. Mayhap all was not revealed and some other plot was afoot. Till everything was known, she could not think further on the matter. She must await her reconciliation with her father, and that at least she could contemplate with unreserved joy, for above all else she now had evidence that he lived and she would see him on the morrow.

As he had given his word, the sun was hardly risen above the surrounding treetops when the prince was come again. He came at brisk pace, leading another horse like the one he rode, and this he said would be for her use as part of the way was difficult with no easy passage. These robust mounts by their nature were sure-footed and used to such terrain, their frames and sturdy legs not given to the loss of balance or damage likely in breeds with more delicate fetlock or pastern.

As she was obliged to do, she asked that he take some breakfast with her before they set out. She had no knowing of how far he had come, but supposed it was some considerable way, thus it was a necessity as much as a courtesy. She herself had but little appetite, and she had hope that he would decline and that they would make haste to wherever her father might be detained. But he said with a small bow that it would please him to break bread with her.

Seated at the long table in the Great Hall, a substantial

repast was speedily brought and set before them, with some retainers remaining and taking up position at a distance. There they were ready to be called upon should aught be found amiss or wanting in the fare, for who knew what this ill-garbed, wild man normally took for his meat.

But before he partook of anything, he surprised Isabella by bending his head and touching his brow and heart whilst murmuring a few words in his own tongue. His accent, so foreign to her ears which were used to her own language, sounded poetic and expressive when uttering those of his own in what was clearly a grace and thanksgiving for the food he had been given. She bestirred herself to do likewise to demonstrate 'twas also her own custom, though in truth she often enough did not honour the tradition should she be alone at table.

Urging him then to eat freely of the victuals provided, and to give notice of anything he wanted that was not offered, she raised her eyes to look at him directly from her place opposite. She would seek full knowledge of who and what he was that she might have awareness to her advantage in all that would come to pass when they reached his abode.

Even in such simple movements as he must make in reaching for the platters and flagons, all he did was accomplished, with a style and grace that would have marked him out as an athlete, or maybe a skilled swordsman had that been his weapon. And there could be no doubt that such ease was in no way hampered by the soft leathern clothes which clad his limbs. Yet clearly from those facts with which he had regaled her regarding the affray, he was as much at home in battle as in honouring either his spiritual practices or the rituals of courtly behaviour. She must also own his appearance again compelled her attention, for like the language he spoke that was like none other she had heard, his stature, fair hair and eyes so blue that they seemed as if lit from within, were likewise particularly uncommon. 'Twas his unusual and different presentation that caused her to want to keep looking longer that could be normally considered proper; that, and of course the need to become acquainted with all she might glean by such detection so as to get the measure of him. Thus, she assured herself.

Aware of her appraisal, he smiled a little and suggested she might wish to know his name as much as his title, seeing that they must spend time in each other's company for some while hence. He made no mention now of the marriage contract, and for this she gave thanks, having no wish to speak of it further till she had conferred with her father.

"My name is Aelianus, one most likely new and strange to your ears as of course is all else about myself and my people. It might then be easier should you call me Allan, a name familiar to you and one as is used by others of your realm for their convenience. I take no offence at such exchange."

Isabella was more than a little vexed by the assumption that she would be unable to get her tongue around his name, and the resultant feeling of thus being patronised by someone making allowances for their host's inferior intellectual abilities. Nevertheless, she answered with due courtesy, though not without the need to reassert her rank and authority.

"If you plan to dwell amongst us permanently, 'twould suit you the better to take on and be known by a name befitting that choice, Aelianus, thus for all our sakes henceforth you shall be known as Allan."

He nodded acceptance of her advice, though again she felt his respect came not without a hint of amusement, and she was aware of how pompous she had sounded to her embarrassment. Such ill ease was immediately followed by further vexation that he was so easily able to wrong-foot her.

She then asked quickly, to mask her disquiet, how long she might be away, for she would need to inform those who must be in receipt of such knowing that they be able to prepare for her absence and subsequent return.

"It is not easy to give measured terms to all that we must put in consideration at discourse, and 'twill not be speedily done with so much to settle. Perhaps a further four days might suffice, though should that be insufficient an envoy would be sent to bring news of how things fared. How think you on this, might it be acceptable?"

She was aware, he being the one in control of how things were conducted, that he had no need to make pretence of asking her approval, yet it was well done and she was minded to respond in kind.

"I, who have not been privy to all that has passed in the four days that have gone before, must bow to your informed judgement in this regard. But if you will excuse me, I will go now and inform the chatelaine and the elders of that which you have presented, then when 'tis done and you have finished at table I would be glad to start on our journey, for I am with great impatience to see my father."

"And I can assure you he is of equal urgency to see yourself."

Then, with a pointed look at her elaborate gown, he added, "Might I suggest you wear serviceable garments that will not cause distress should they be snagged or grimed upon the route, as there are many narrow and thorny passes to be traversed. Finery would become caught and snarled, a fact that must slow progress, which I am sure you would not wish."

When all such necessities were attended to, they set out, Isabella having given strict instruction that none must follow. She would take no risk that might put her father's life in danger, therefore even though both were of noble birth they journeyed forth with neither retinue nor standard bearer, and being modestly clad looked no more than two simple souls going about their business.

Chapter Eleven

When they were returned to the hall and sitting together for the midday meal, even though she was impatient to press Abigail for answers to the many questions raised in response to her telling, first Selina must regale the chatelaine with all that had passed between Lady Isabella and herself. For she was of good intent to offer solace following her dismissal from the exchange, and in recounting all that had been said in full detail, 'twould indeed be as if she had herself attended.

Alas, it did not have quite the soothing affect she had foreseen. Mayhap 'twas even salt to the wound, as with boasting of a merry time you had enjoyed at an event to which they had not been invited. Like unto Isabella and the prince, it seemed she could not get it right, for had she not already this day made clumsy attempt at reparation?

Abigail, however, understanding her purpose, made no comment on the disclosure, but rather, giving a long-suffering sigh, turned the subject instead to sounder matter. She was ready, she said, to respond to her enquiries for she anticipated many. Selina needed no further prompting.

"The first thing I must ask is with regard to the prince and the marriage contract that was the ransom price for her father's deliverance. Was he, or is he even yet, the husband for whom the place here at table is faithfully set?"

The chatelaine shook her head.

"You are getting ahead of what has been revealed and that cannot be let happen, for 'twould only confuse both the telling and the listening. Your wanting of greater understanding must pertain only to those things which have thus far been presented."

Selina, frustrated by the rebuke but with reluctant acceptance, lost no time in voicing her next question.

"Lady Isabella says she must remain in isolation, for the veil of itself would not be sufficient to save her from an inspection that must be too dangerous to permit. And I, having audience with her, must be likewise withdrawn from the society of others lest I reveal such facts as would jeopardise her safety.

"The only thing that I can glean from such statement is that those things which make no sense and puzzle me would be wont to confuse others in like manner.

"Namely, of what age is she, for she does not have the look or the way of an old woman?

"And you also, Abigail, how old are you and at what age did you become nursemaid to Madame? These happenings that you tell of, when was it that they came to pass?"

The chatelaine nodded in acceptance of this enquiry and, it being in order, she shifted and resettled herself upon the bench. For it seemed she was anticipating some length of time as being necessary to give considered response, and she must first see to her comfort.

"With regard then to when, and in what manner I became nursemaid to Madame, 'twas when I was of much the same age as are you now.

"At the time, it was impressed upon me by my parents that I had need to find either employ or intended husband, for it was time for me to leave home and make my own fortune and future. There being scant room available for myself and all my siblings, as the firstborn I needs must be also the first to fly the nest.

"But having no committed swain 'twas clear I must find employment, and it so happened that I heard tell of the sad misfortune of Madame's mother, and knew her father would be in need of help in raising his motherless child. And so, I boldly betook myself to the manor and there pleaded that I was in all respect ideal for the task. Well versed in all aspects of child minding, being the eldest of many, the newborn infant would be entirely safe in my care.

"Madame's father, though sorely grieved, had made it his business, as he must, to find at once a wet nurse. He had engaged a woman of good repute who had lost her own child in a similar sorry fashion, but she could not commit to the full care needed for she had duties to her other small children.

"Thus, he brought me into the hall, and there questioned me for some long while that he might get the measure of me. Then, when it seemed he was satisfied, he took me to the crib where the infant Isabella lay, recently fed but yet awake. Her eyes, though newly wrought and making but little sense of all she beheld, seemed to lock onto mine as

I stood close by her, and I do swear at the very moment our gaze fastened, both knew we had a sacred contract. Nor was my Lord insensitive to such exchange, and thereupon at that moment all was sealed and has remained ever thus.

"'Twill take no great wracking of your mind to count the years that have passed since then, for if I was fifteen years of age and am now nine and seventy, 'twas four and sixty years ago when I came to the manor. The events of which I have just told were eight and forty years ago."

Selina stayed her there, for she must have certainty that she had heard right.

"Should this indeed be the case, and I do not doubt you that 'tis so, then Lady Isabella is sixty-four years of age. And, Abigail, of the forty-eight years since those scenes with regard to the prince were enacted, has Madame been ever hidden from the view of others? And in this imprisonment has she also been devoid of contact with any soul other than the priest and yourself?"

The chatelaine, setting down her knife which had seen but little usage, was for a spell both very still and very quiet, but when she raised her eyes from her platter to gaze fully upon Selina 'twas a different matter. The power of the look she fastened upon her was very like that which she had spoken of between herself and the infant Isabella, and such power was projected from her crow black eyes that Selina felt its intensity as if 'twere charged with some extraordinary force. For it demonstrated in its fixation her total allegiance to Isabella, and was proof that in such unrestrained devotion, she suffered fully all her sorrows and hurts as much, or even more than did Madame herself. And it was clear also that she would demand and expect no less from Selina.

"My Lady's withdrawing needs must be for most of that length of time, and, as you will countenance, 'twas no easy affliction to bear, for none by their nature choose to live apart in such a way unless they are by choice a hermit."

Selina had an understanding then of Madame's contempt when making a comparison with her own four years in isolation. It was indeed a paltry thing as against a span approaching fifty years, but she needed to question further regarding this spread of time.

"'Tis established then that Lady Isabella is of sixty-four years, but, Abigail, even though her face is hidden from view by the veil, that which can be seen gives no evidence of such an age. Rather one would suppose 'twas the form of a young woman presented before you. Is this not so, and if it is then in what strange manner is such a thing accomplished?"

"All I will allow at the moment is a retelling of that which my Lady revealed to you when she owned that she dwelt in the past. For in her confession she placed no blame on cloying sentiment or nostalgic yearning, but spoke only of that which is based entirely on the fact of the matter. But tomorrow you have my word that our tale will move forward and embrace all that must be told to make good sense from seeming nonsense. Let that then be sufficient for the time being. Is there aught else that exercises your mind?"

"Abigail, I was given to ask Lady Isabella if the disappearance of her husband had aught to do with the Tapestry in my bedchamber. I do not know where such a notion came from. It seemed to be born of its own intent, having no origin in my own mind that I could see. Will you tell me what you know of its making and for what purpose it was fashioned, for 'tis a wondrous thing, and like none other that adorn the walls here in the hall, nor doubtless elsewhere in other halls in other manors."

Abigail, who had picked up her knife again, lay it down once more without reluctance.

"The Tapestry is indeed a rare and special thing, but it was not in fact commissioned by any who have had governance in this domain. It had been specially wrought at some goodly time past for kin of the prince, and they, holding it in high regard, brought it with them from their own distant homeland.

"When all had been arranged and made sure in the contract of allegiance drawn up after the deliberations, it was to be given as a sign and seal of conjoining – a wedding gift – that being the most valuable thing that they owned, proved their fidelity. Thus it came to us and was hung in the chamber that had been allocated for the wedded couple.

"We heard tell that it had been fashioned over many years by a weaver of such fabled skill that he had imbued all depicted in it with true being, though few dared voice such heresy aloud, for all knew that only God has the power to create life. But then again, the prince and his countrymen, coming from some other place had mayhap other gods and other customs that were tolerant of these ideas. However, we had need to quash any disquiet here regarding heathen or devilish practices before they began, and so such differences were not noised abroad, and thus 'twas generally assumed that the weaver of the Tapestry had been a man of our own country and none here denied it.

"Its history before its coming to the manor was wont to have those in receipt of such knowledge, treat it with the same respect as might have been given to a holy relic, but it was its most recent history that should have alerted us had we only been in receipt of it. For this was indeed of unholy kind. Here was no grail from the Last Supper, but rather that which could be better likened to a poisoned chalice."

Selina, now in some dread at what had been revealed, pressed for further understanding.

"If I have been given lodging in the finest chamber, the one prepared for Isabella and the prince, furnished as it is with a Tapestry that now sounds more cursed than blessed, then clearly 'twas done for a purpose. What purpose, and why have I not been alerted earlier if 'tis such as you describe?"

"All in good time. The revealing of those things which will give you a full understanding must be first appreciated and completely understood. Mayhap you already have some apprehension of the Tapestry's enchanting qualities. Being as you are the one chosen as instrument to undo the spellbinding, it would be likely."

Selina persisted without any lessening of zeal, for if she was intent on revisiting the world of the Tapestry this coming night, she must acquaint herself with as much knowledge of its enthralling powers as was possible.

"If, though, it is indeed of unholy nature, am I not in some danger being in its proximity? I have found myself falling into a strange torpor if I engage in a lengthy inspection of it, and it becomes most difficult to break my gaze. 'Tis like being mesmerised."

Abigail looked alarmed at her revelation. Clearly she had not expected such a response.

"Do not let the beam of your eye become entwined with its emanations as yet. 'Tis not time till you have been instructed as to how it must be done, and tomorrow and the morrow after we will prepare you for your engagement, till then 'tis best to turn from it and give your attention to other pursuits."

Selina refused to let the matter rest there.

"Who other than myself has had lodging in the bedchamber where it hangs? Have any in the forty-eight years we have spoken of fallen foul of its enticements in any way?"

Abigail, now looking ill at ease and clearly in two minds whether to reply, spoke cautiously, tentatively calculating as she went how much was safe to divulge.

"There is one for certain and mayhap another, though of that we can have no surety."

Selina understood that in the second instance she referred to Tristram, and it was given to her to know that the other lost soul was Lady Isabella's husband.

"Is it not Madame's husband that you speak of when you tell of the one who was most assuredly ensnared?"

Abigail, now much unsettled, called an end to further discussion, but Selina could not yet allow cessation for she must glean all possible information, for Tristram's sake as well as her own.

"Will you not then just disclose who the other might be? Was it a guest or person of rank here to have discourse with the lord?"

The chatelaine seemed of a sudden to weaken in her resistance and consented to answer, for it would seem that even if it was against her will and better judgement, she was equally disturbed should she avoid replying.

"This was a more recent happening and it was at the

161

last grand revelry held here for a special purpose. All were given to understand that it was to celebrate All Souls' Night in honour of the deceased lord, my Lady's father, and all the dead. She did not attend, of course, for she could not, but she made a good excuse and all of status came gladly and there was feasting, and music and dancing that lasted the day long and into the night.

"Amongst those who were invited for the purpose of diverting all assembled was a young troubadour, much renowned and feted for his gift to enthrall all who gave ear to his story telling and his playing of the mandore. The sweet strains he brought forth from the plucked strings were so beguiling they caused many to swoon, thus he was much sought after, his fame going before him like a herald.

"But beyond such considerations 'twas also given that he was of unusual temperament as many so richly blessed have tendency to be. It was entirely for these reasons, and none other, that the whole entertainment had been arranged, for 'twas hoped that, being endowed with a special way of being, he might prove to be another like unto yourself who could undo the spellbinding. Thus, he was given your chamber in which to spend the night, for 'tis at night that witchery walks abroad and comes into its own.

"But when first light dawned and all who had spent the night were bestirring themselves and making ready to depart, his chamber was found already empty. Thus, he had either made very early start, as was likely enough if he had far to travel, or he had become ensnared in the Tapestry's web.

"And if the latter was the case, then he had fared no better than my Lady's husband, whom it had been hoped full well he might deliver, but we know not which it was."

Selina, aware that Abigail had softened in her stance and was thus more forthcoming, seized the moment lest she speedily change her mind and refuse further telling.

"In what manner was it supposed that the troubadour might rescue Madame's husband if he had been given no schooling on how 'twas to be done, and you do say that it was a recent befalling. When did all this come about?"

"'Twas two years back, but other than that I will not say, for I have already said more than was my intent. Sufficient for this day, now eat of the fare provided before it chills and forfeits its savour."

*

Gathering crumbs and other morsels from the table into a kerchief, Selina betook herself from the hall back to the garden, and there sat once more to think on all that she had learned. But before she began her reverie she scattered the offerings she had brought for the birds upon the table that had been provided for their fare. For her request had hardly been mooted than 'twas done, and they showed no reticence in attending. Their busy comings and goings with pause to splash for a short spell in the shallow bowl installed alongside granted her much pleasure, as did their ease in her company.

Many birds, however small, were garnered for the pot and were therefore ill at ease in close proximity with humankind; not so here. Perhaps Madame in providing adequate provision for all had forbidden it, wishing neither harm nor persecution of the denizens of the heavens. For like herself, birds being the only companions she could guarantee, they would be cherished, and with their vibrant carolling an additional joy when little other music was on offer 'twas most surely likely.

She shook out the last few crumbs still caught in the folds of the kerchief, then sat back down on the bench that since the morning had become warmed by the strength of the midday sun. The stone was somehow made to feel softer and more giving in its warming, like a cold heart that could be turned from hardness back to pulsing life by an encounter with the sweetness engendered by loving kindness.

And, thinking on love, she was minded of the fierce look that Abigail had bestowed upon her at table when she spoke of Lady Isabella's plight. The chatelaine was well disposed towards herself, of that there was no doubt, but that good regard could in no way to be compared to the fervid devotion she had seen writ plain on her countenance concerning Madame. Such passion was indeed as she herself had declared it, more a sacred trust than a contract of employment, one entailing sixty-four years of selfless service. For was it not a fact that she had sacrificed her own life like a nun entering the convent, when she had turned her back on worldly pleasures and her own self-fulfilment to answer what she saw as a more powerful calling?

And regarding sacrifice, had not Tristram's life likewise been given and lost to Isabella's cause, forfeited with little evidence of concern or regret? The lost husband was sought with earnest endeavour, but the lost troubadour would seem to arouse no similarly ardent seeking. And was not she herself of no more than equivalent value on the scale of merit?

It could be seen as having a comparison with the prince and the marriage contract, for he too had put aside his own intent in the interest of the greater good. But though it appeared the same with regard to themselves, 'twas not, for, unlike the prince, they had not in full knowledge volunteered as willing victims, but rather been taken more as sacrificial lambs.

Mayhap she would not be as lightly sacrificed as Tristram, but rather be fully schooled in all that would avail her in what was to come. For the outcome was of vital importance to Lady Isabella if she must put all faith and hope in the belief she was the only one capable of breaking the spellbinding.

Thus, she would be ever well cared for, not for her own sake but rather as the instrument in realising that goal. 'Twas a dismal thought, but then again it might yet be that a deeper attachment between them would be forged with the passing of days, for they were still but newly met. The possibility brought her some respite from such gloomy thoughts.

As she considered all she had learnt this day, she had an awareness that, as yet, she knew not who it was that prepared the sweetmeats and candles, nor for what purpose, for there seemed a confusion in intent. They might ensnare your gaze that you may not look away, or they may have you lapse into sleep as deep as that of a hibernating dormouse.

Neither had she any notion who the spellbinder might be, supposing they were one and the same. And in her engagement with such sorcery was there an armour with which she might gird herself to ensure protection from the dark arts and witchery? She vowed come Sunday she would detain the priest, for he was well versed in the ways of alchemy according to Isabella, and she would ask him to provide her with some holy talisman or symbol that he might bless and charge with Divine power. And this would be her shield and preserve her from evil.

But, she reminded herself then of her own pledge before she set out upon the journey here with Jacob. Her life with her grandmother had not been of her own choosing and she had vowed then not to be in subjugation to another in any future circumstance. 'Twould not be impossible to refuse such demands being made of her without her consent. Had she not affirmed that should she be cast back into some semblance of that which went before, she would run away? Mayhap Flora and Jacob might be instrumental in providing help in such an endeavour but it could surely be done.

Alas she realised, should she settle on this scheme as the way forward, it would of necessity entail abandonment of Tristram. And how could she make this her choice when he saw her as his angel and liberator, and just as did Madame, he placed all his trust in her intervention? He was firm in his belief that it was only she who could save him, and mayhap he was right. In any case she knew she would not, and could not, forsake him.

Nevertheless, when she returned to her chamber after supper, she applied herself to the fashioning of her jester's costume with much energy so that it would be ready if needed. And thus, she occupied herself till the coming of the witching hour when 'twas time to step again into the Tapestry's beguiling world, but as she cut and stitched, she lit but one candle and partook of no sweetmeat.

CHAPTER TWELVE

As the light of day faded and the single candle achieved but little recompense against the encroaching gloom, despite having eschewed the sweetmeats, Selina found it increasingly hard to keep eyelids, drooping with weariness, from closing. Seated on the end of the bed, her gaze fixed on the Tapestry, her body pleaded with her to lie back and submit to slumber. And this she knew was not the swooning response to witchery, but a full, natural tiredness that required repose. Yet she must resist the enticement of her downy coverlets lest she be unconscious when the Tapestry came into animation. 'Twould not do for her to be unavailable when so much depended on her presence, and she could not have certainty that the moon would rouse her as before. Resolutely then, she stood up and paced the length of the room to maintain alertness till the Tapestry started to change.

She felt that moment atmospherically before the manifest event; a change in temperature coupled with a charged tension in the chamber, and a compulsive need to take in her breath as she might before some challenge or feat of daring. Then of a sudden there it was; in a trice going from inert depiction to living tableau; complete with sound and smell it was come again, just as previously. And presented here, there could be no doubting, was an actual vibrant world, sure and certain in its own reality, and undeniably now very much getting on with its own business.

Tristram was soon apparent, come to the forefront and peering anxiously ahead as if his eyes were not yet able to pierce what was before him. But she could see him full well and she was not tardy in closing the gap between them. And as she came closer it seemed she came into his field of vision and he beheld her and called her name with relief and joy.

Closing her eyes, she stepped through the taut membrane that stretched between them and it gave easily before her. Then, there she was with little ado, at his side just as she had been yesterday. He straightway seized her hands as if to thwart any twist of fate that might snatch her back from whence she came.

His fair companions also came at once to claim her, decked with flowery garlands about heads and necks. They held out their hands as they smilingly insisted that she come join with them in revelry. Greeting those she had encountered most particularly on her previous visit, she promised to join them in but a short while. Yet even as she did so, she became aware that they seemed not to respond to her in recognition, nor recall the name she had given them only the night before. Seeing her confusion, Tristram enlightened her further in the way of things in the Tapestry world.

"You will discover that names are an unknown concept to them, for they have none of their own nor any need of them. They are as happy with one companion as with another in their sporting, so there is none in particular that they must call out to. They see you and would have you join with them, for all are welcome and none excluded but they retain no remembrance of you, nor the fact that you were amongst them but yesterday. For here, each day is born afresh devoid of past, and at the end of its span it dies, leaving no trace of what occurred to inform the morrow.

"They have life and certainly awareness of pleasure, and they are ever kind and gentle for they present perfectly the weaver's intent when he created them to inhabit his paradise. Thus, they are as he fashioned them to be, and in the intensity of his absorption he produced a masterpiece and infused it with his own life force. So 'tis as if these he brought into being are indeed his offspring. And the children he begat inherited life and movement and beauty, but he could not bequeath them a soul, for though he be in a sense their father, he is not God the Father. And lacking soul, they have no more real substance than an image in a looking glass. They are naught but the weaver's reflection. 'Tis why in the midst of many I am yet isolated, for they are no more than exquisite empty vessels."

But then he led her away from their sweet entreaties till he had attained a distance that was enough apart from their activity to offer a chance of uninterrupted discourse. For it was evident that he was in urgent need of such.

"Did you have any success in your endeavours? Has aught come to your attention as might at last bring me hope of deliverance?"

Selina divulged at once all she had learnt.

"Since your arrival here, you were deliberately chosen

to inhabit the chamber and be drawn into the Tapestry for 'twas thought that you had some rare quality that would serve the intent of Lady Isabella.

"'Tis not yet clear, but it does seem that perhaps by some trickery or bewitching that her husband was likewise drawn into the web, becoming lost in it and lost to her? Though she ever waits on him, he has not come back. She has also sought to discover the spell breaker that will release him from the curse. Your entrapment availed her nothing.

"So now I too am being prepared to follow after you, in hope that I can find in this place a man who has been lost without trace this long time since. I know not how it was supposed that you should find him if you were given no foretelling of such purpose. Is it possible that he inhabits some part of this place that you have not visited or know not of? The woods and mountains seem at a goodly distance. Do any go there?"

He shook his head.

"Of course, I betook myself to them in the early days when I thought I might find a way out should I scale the mountains. But 'twas futile, for when you stand before them you have awareness that they have no further side. There is only that which the weaver made and his creation does not extend beyond what is shown. The woods too are only there to be backdrop to the essential, the Eden in the foreground. It would not seem possible that had any other person been lost here in the same manner as myself we would not have had awareness of each other at once, being clearly of a separate nature."

Selina gave consideration to that fact.

"The lost husband had some misadventure a long time before your own, so surely much that we cannot fathom might have taken place in that time. The spellbinding and sorcery being capable of transforming fact and appearance could have turned him into a shape or form that now makes it impossible to recognise who he truly is. Mayhap like a witch inhabiting the body of her familiar, be it cat or other beast, he has been magicked into the anatomy and being of one of the animals that dwell in this place."

Tristram frowned, loath to contemplate such dire possibility.

"I know not what evil thing might be made happen where witchery is concerned, but surely it cannot entirely wipe clean the knowing of who we are, even should we be cast into some alien creature's body."

"I know not either, but tomorrow I am to begin my instruction on the part I must play to undo the curse, discover the whereabouts of Madame's husband and return him to her. What I learn to deliver him must suffice to free you also, so place your trust in that and forebear from further supposing, for 'twill avail you no satisfaction. Instead now let us go and join with the others, but beforehand, if you have your mandore yet with you, will you not regale me with evidence of your art? 'Twould please me very well."

The troubadour looked startled by her request, for none had begged him play for such a stretch of time that he had forgotten entirely such an entreaty. Yet when he had remembrance he was most willing and eager to demonstrate to her the ability that had earned him his repute.

He fetched the instrument from its resting place against an apple tree, and, putting the baldric over his shoulder, ran his fingers across the strings, gently plucking a few soft chords. Then looking at her he smiled and confided, "The lute, mandolin, mandore or theorbo, having at least six and twenty strings, are not only famously difficult to play, they are fiendishly difficult to tune. But here, all things remaining in ever perfect state, my mandore never goes out of tune, nor does it break a string. And neither do I lose my prowess, even should I fail to practise, as I hope to demonstrate."

Thereupon, after executing an elaborate bow, he bid her be seated on the soft sward whilst he serenaded her with his famed repertoire. Leaning his back against the apple tree, he gave himself over entirely then to the music, firstly with his fingertips and then with the addition of his voice and Selina must own she had never before heard music that she liked so well nor that stirred her so deeply. It was indeed as Abigail had described. Many of the others round about came to join them and listen, but they stayed only a short span. For much of what they heard was too plaintive for dancing, thus they dispersed to where other minstrels were playing lighter and merrier airs that suited them and their needs the better.

When Tristram at last put aside his mandore, he came and sat down beside her on the grass. He said nothing and she knew full well that he waited on her opinion, and to tease him a little she withheld her praise for a short space before giving his performance its due.

"I see now, or rather hear, why you were feted and so well regarded. 'Tis a sorrow and a waste that such a gift is but little appreciated here. I hope it brings some recompense if I admit that 'tis the loveliest thing I ever gave audience to."

His face reflected completely his pleasure at her praise, and thus it pleased her all the more that she was able to afford him some joy in the midst of his despair. But then she grasped his hand and insisted that he come with her, join the others and dance, that the good regard that had been established between them would not be lost.

And he needed no second bidding, and was happy to dance to the tunes of other fiddles and citterns notwithstanding that they were of different standard. 'Twas clear that in having her as a partner rather than a facsimile being, however appealing, was a hugely different thing. Selina likewise, parched from lack of companionship and merriment, gladly lost herself again in the joy of such fulfilment, and, forsaking all other partners, who minded not at all, they danced together till Tristram stayed her at last with regret, for 'twas time to leave.

But before she stepped out of the web and returned to her chamber, he needed reassurance that she would return to him again in the coming night, and at that moment it became known to her that he spoke not with regard only to her role in his liberation, but for her own sake too. Her heart stirred, she promised then that she would come each night without fail till he was free.

Returned to her bedchamber, the vibrancy that ever prevailed in the Tapestry fell from her, and she was visited again by the fatigue that for the duration she had left behind. It would seem that her humanity had its own needs and they must also be honoured, for even though the Tapestry imbued its visitors with a transcendent energy, it could not always totally override mortal frailty. With no reason now to resist, she climbed into her sumptuous silken bed, and, curling up, was lost to the conscious world in no time at all.

*

She woke to the rousing call of a blackbird in full-throated voice alongside her chamber window, and realised that it was of later hour than usual. Flora had come and gone without disturbing her, and she rued the fact that she had missed her, and with it the chance to learn more about her and the life she led, for had she not anticipated such a life for herself? But quickly bestirring herself, she prepared instead for Abigail's coming.

The dress left for her on this day was of patterned blue silk, trimmed about neck and hem with a fine band of miniver, and it seemed her preferences had been taken into account, for the length was again an inch short of the floor and the weight easily borne. She had hardly finished twining her hair about her head when the chatelaine came to take her to her breakfast.

Leaving her at table before she went about her business in the kitchen, Abigail first asked how well she had slept. Selina, sensitive to the fact that it was other than mere polite enquiry, perceived 'twas a probing for any hint that she might have acquired knowledge of the Tapestry. But abiding by her pledge of caution, she answered truthfully nevertheless, that she had slept very well and for longer duration than hitherto. The answer was accepted, and, apparently satisfied, Abigail left her to her viands.

Visited by remembrance of all that had befallen the night before, she found she was of good appetite, and, reaching towards the spread of fare, there discovered beside the dishes a posy of primroses in a pewter goblet. The gift and all that it conveyed in its presentation meant that as before she had need to take it in hand and inhale the perfume in gladness. That Jacob and Flora gave evidence of their constancy in such thought and care was a most encouraging thing, and it both warmed and strengthened her, causing her to regret afresh that she had slept through Flora's coming.

As she tore apart the fresh-baked bread, releasing its wholesome fragrance, she added alongside some dried fruits and soft cheese to her platter. But then, before she could commence with her meal, of a sudden she must stop, becoming aware that all about her was a strange excitement that chilled the air.

It was very like the charge that occurred the moment before the Tapestry was enlivened, but, as she was stayed in apprehension, she recognised that there was also a semblance in it of the way of things before a thunderstorm; of great power gathered in concentration and poised before tumultuous release.

What was this? For 'twas definitely something, a harbinger of impending calamity, a portent or ill omen that presaged an ominous event about to unfold? Whatever it was, it was far too tangible to doubt its authenticity. And what had become clear was that it was she who was the aim of its intent.

Then, without further signal, came a cyclone of spiralling energy that whirled round about her so that she was in that moment transfixed, enwrapped in its central eye by a suffocating but formless presence; one that sought as if to draw forth and steal not just her breath, but also the very spirit from her body.

Yet upon that self-same moment, it was as if in peaking to full intensity it was caused to split and sunder, and then to spill its force like a volcano or the propelled ball from a cannon. And in that expulsion, the air was at once cleansed and made sweet and good again, as is the case after the thunderstorm has abated. Emptied of lightning charge and the threatening roil and roar that cleaves the heavens, all is washed clean and baptised by immersion in a font of rainwater.

The torn bread still in her hand, Selina had no need to ask now what it was that had paid her an uninvited and unwelcome visit, for its repellent attentions had sparked within herself that which was ever there, but as yet had never been called forth into usage. And with its awakening had come knowledge, a knowing complete and fully formed, devoid of uncertainties.

Without doubt she had just had an encounter with the spellbinder who had come to test her and ascertain of what mettle she was made, but she too now had their measure, and though their sorcery be an awesome thing, it had lost its power in direct confrontation. For in its seeking to snarl and possess her, it had itself been dispossessed, the power expelled out of it causing it to burst asunder like Judas in the Potter's field.

This was the first skirmish, no more maybe than a speculative foray, but the lines had been drawn and the battle begun. And though as yet she knew not who the spellbinder might be, she had met with their capabilities and did not doubt that they were formidable or that she had seen but a fraction of their arsenal. Yet she was not afraid, for though she had done nothing of herself to combat them, had they not been decisively disarmed and she had certainty of what she must do?

First, she must speak with the priest and have his council, his talisman and his blessing. And she would next spend her time alone in the garden to sit in contemplation and entreat all in the world of spirit, be they angels or the great archangels like Michael who wielded light like a sword in combat with dark forces.

For the outcome of this conflict was nothing less than the liberation of entrapped souls whose spirits had languished helplessly in enforced bondage, and she was in need of the highest powers she could call on. Her regard for Tristram, though but newly confessed, she knew would also be a powerful thing in any joust with witch or wizard.

But she had no vainglorious conceit that good shall ever vanquish evil or light overcome darkness. Was not the church endowed with a plenitude of saints and martyrs proving 'twas not so? What was certain however was that she was come into realisation of her latent gift, an ability born straightway into full maturity without the need of schooling. It was akin to Arthur, who knew not who or what he was till he drew the sword from the stone. His kingship thrust upon him, ripened instantly by the need of a beleaguered kingdom in search of an anointed one to lead the people out of subjugation.

Her own calling sprang forth likewise on encounter with the spellbinder's visitation, an immediate reflexive retaliation in the face of evil. It had been her awakening and her initiation, and like Arthur she would not faint nor retreat from such encounters as must come. For Tristram's sake, she must seek out her own Excalibur for she would have need of a mighty sword and a shield too, even should she have Michael at her side, for who knew what calibre of demonic soldiery stood alongside the spellbinder?

This day there would be further revelation from both Lady Isabella and Abigail, and maybe by the end of it she would know all there was to know, and thereafter with the telling done, action must follow.

As she waited on Abigail to take her to Madame, Selina bit into the torn bread in her hand. She was still of good appetite and her hunger, it would seem to her, gave evidence of a readiness to engage in whatever was to come. Like the prince, she would have a righteous cause to spur her on. He triumphed, though astride an ignobly small steed, for both man and horse had an unusual style that overcame the conventional with the unorthodox. Maybe this should be her own tactic: surprise and confuse by never doing what was expected.

Chapter Thirteen

When Abigail was returned from her business in the kitchen ready to escort Selina to her meeting with Madame, Selina said naught regarding what had occurred in her absence. For what had previously been adopted as a chosen response was now confirmed as correct behaviour. Henceforth, she had no doubt she may put her trust in her instincts.

On attaining Lady Isabella's parlour, the chatelaine knocked respectfully, calling out on this occasion, "My Lady, Selina is here," determinedly excluding herself from participation before such indignity was thrust upon her. With invitation to enter forthcoming, she opened the door, and, after ushering Selina hastily inside, closed it decisively upon her.

On entry into the chamber, Selina, fully expectant of further experience of the pall of gloom that results from drawn curtains, found 'twas not as she anticipated. For rather than such a state as caused her discomfort, before her eyes were able to adjust to the difference from without to within, she discovered that the curtains were pulled tight back and restrained by tasselled ropes. And she beheld Lady Isabella sitting in the full light of the window.

She gestured to Selina to be seated. Now both were subject to the sun's brightness rather than herself alone.

And in that uncompromising exposure, Lady Isabella revealed herself, despite wearing the veil, as by no means of a great number of years. The fitted gown she wore enrobed a figure that had the slender lissomness that comes only with youth, and her hands, devoid of gloves, were without distortion or blemish.

Selina had awareness then that this day was the turning point; the pivotal moment when restraint was abandoned and everything revealed.

That the spellbinder also chose this same time to make him or herself known lay emphasis to the fact; thus she waited on Madame for revelation.

"I must confer with you now in complete earnestness, for of a sudden the time has come to make an attempt on our endeavour. This moment is not of our choosing, but is born from the agitation of the spellbinder, though indeed one day is as good as any other in such an engagement.

"The priest has said 'tis your presence in the house that has propelled things rapidly into action, for your very being here has stirred up the stagnant state of impasse that has held sway these long and dolorous years. Now the sleeping malevolence has had clamorous awakening. Aware of portentous change 'tis fully aroused and enflamed by the opportunities that such change might permit. The stalemate that has persisted to the sorcerer's chagrin and frustration has at last the possibility of resolution, and with it their will achieved.

"I might well have hoped for a little longer to inform and instruct you, but alas that is not now possible. What I have done though is to call on the priest, and he, being a minister of the church and vested with its authority, will prepare you for all you must encounter. We know not what that might be in unholy engagement, but can only trust that with best intent, good may prevail.

"Like the spellbinder, I too have waited for this moment, not knowing when, or indeed if, it would ever come, and 'tis now at last upon us, likewise bringing an end to my languishing in helpless inability to advance my cause. All will be decided one way or the other, yet I find, in the promise of completion, I am now uncertain in my want to allow it. For where there is chance of deliverance there is ever hope, but should we lose in the encounter, then all is lost, including hope. We are left in the finality with nothing at all, and a life stripped bare of either meaning or purpose.

"And in this embroiling of extreme and opposite goals with a decisive conclusion for one side only, it is you that will take my place as surrogate. And I can but submit to the fact that it must be so, for I am not endowed with the necessary virtues for such an encounter, and ignorant therefore on how to conduct myself. So, I must place my trust entirely in you, and the priest's perception in declaring you as the one chosen for the task. I pray most sincerely that he is not mistaken, for all our sakes.

"Before this day is done, whatever the outcome, I will shed at last the veil and you shall see me before you. But not yet; things must be done in proper order that there is no fissure in our defences as we confront the adversary.

"But come now and I will take you to confer with the priest; he is waiting on you. From thence you will speak again with Abigail. There is much to do and all must be concluded before nightfall."

Selina had said not a word all this while, nor had she wish or need to; 'twas plain enough.

Lady Isabella, with all due haste, stepped past her to the door, indicating that she follow where she would lead. She turned into the corridor that adjoined her own living quarters, and paced its length till she attained the last chamber, and here she rapped at the door but entered straightway, without waiting for leave.

The space within had been shaped and furnished as a private chapel; a raised platform at the far end was fitted in all respects to function as an altar. Upon it was a white damask-draped table bearing a gold crucifix, two large, ornate candlesticks with lighted candles, and incense burners scenting the air with sandalwood, sage and frankincense. The wall behind bore a tempura triptych depicting the Madonna and Child, Christ on the cross, and the Resurrection. Beneath it, fixed to the wall, was a small cupboard with glass window glowing red to let it be known that the Divine was present. An altar rail ran across the width of the area to the front with a red velvet kneeler before it. There were several pews on either side of the main body of the chamber, and set into the wall close by the door was a stone basin filled with holy water. Half a score of candles set upon ledges round about gave soft illumination and added their own warm scent of beeswax to the ambience. There being but three lancet windows, the candlelight was necessary, but also served to give a sense of sanctity.

Standing before the altar, his back towards them, was the priest, a man of considerable height, his grey hair tonsured as a monk. He appeared to be deep in prayer, but turned as they entered and gave them his undivided attention. His focus initially on both quickly became centred entirely on Selina, and she felt that concentrated gaze as a gimlet searching into the heart and soul of her. 'Twould be a hard thing to deceive such penetrating scrutiny had she anything she would wish to conceal.

Having delivered her into the priest's custody, Isabella wasted no time in unnecessary introductions or explanations, instead she merely nodded at the priest and informed Selina, "I will wait on you when you have finished the midday meal and your conferring with Abigail. I offer you neither advice nor caution on all that rests upon your shoulders, for what is to come is beyond my capabilities of intervention or contribution. Take all your instruction from the minister here and ever remember you were born into this role."

With such terse message delivered, she turned abruptly on her heel and left, pausing only to dip her middle finger into the basin of blessed water by the door and mark the sign of the cross on her forehead. Then she was gone, and Selina turned fully towards the priest, ready to hearken to all he said in order to prepare herself for that which lay ahead.

He came away from the altar, leaving the little gate in the altar rail ajar as he took up position in the first pew and invited her to be seated opposite. Unlike her own priest, this man, despite his gifts of clairvoyance and otherworldliness, was of considerable physical presence, looking more like a yeoman than a man of the cloth. She found his sturdy bulk reassuring, as such bodily strength is wont to do, for even should the fight be supernatural rather than natural, he looked like a doughty fellow to have on your side.

Before she seated herself in the pew he had indicated, Selina made certain to bow before the altar and make the sign of the cross on forehead, heart and shoulders. She honoured the ritual not just because of the presence of the clergyman, but to fulfil an insistent need of her own to do all as it was laid down according to holy law. In countermanding the spells and charms cast by sorcery, she knew all the observances must be immaculately performed if they were to have their full strength and potency in overcoming their opposite. The priest seemed to be of like mind, for he was robed in the full regalia donned only for high mass. His opening remark, however, was surprisingly with regard to her family rather than to do with the task in hand.

"First, I would inform you, Selina, that I have had discourse with your priest who sought me out to have reassurance of your wellbeing.

"With regard to your orphanage, upon learning more of your origins, I made it my business to discover how your two brothers Edward and Daniel were faring and so betook myself to your place of birth, and there, upon enquiry, I was soon able to encounter and have exchange with them." Selina, unprepared for this sudden and wholly unexpected turn of events, and at such a moment as this, was thrown into a state of confused emotion. None here had thought to ask her if she missed Edward and Daniel, nor offered to seek knowledge of their wellbeing. Rather it had been only her parents and her grandmother who had been noted, and that entirely because of their demise, a fact that was lauded for it signified that they could not interfere with what was planned for her.

The very mention of their names, which she had but scarcely heard spoken aloud since being forcibly separated from them, brought scalding tears to her eyes and an uncontrollable tremor to her voice.

"Father, pray tell me, how did you find them?"

"I am most happy to inform you that both are thriving. Your elder brother, Edward, is betrothed to his guild master's daughter, his future and wellbeing thus assured, and Daniel too does very well though not as expected. Finding he had hitherto undiscovered talent for the making of fine jewellery, he changed his apprenticeship, and this is now his employ, with his work most well regarded and sought after by noble patrons. His success has enabled him to set up his own workshop and dwelling place.

"They are fine young men of whom your parents would be most proud. They were much pleased to learn that you are well and living in the grand manner. It is their sincere hope that they meet with you 'ere long."

Selina let her head drop down, so that it was but the top of it that she presented to the priest, for she needed to hide an overwhelming unsettling in repose. With regard to such news, it was not possible for her to control her unbounded joy, nor her intense longing to see her brothers and be in their company again. The feelings thus invoked were too powerful to display before anyone, so she covered her face with her hands.

The priest waited on her, and, when she had regained her composure, she said naught but, "Thank you." And again, "Thank you."

Then when she raised her head, he continued.

"We must proceed now to that which lies before you. It is a formidable task, but though you have no previous knowledge of dealings with witchery, there is no doubt that 'tis you that is singled out to take on the challenge. I saw it plain, laid out before me in my own discernment. If you are the elect it cannot be that you will be left unsupported, but still we must pray earnestly for your deliverance and that of Lady Isabella and her benighted husband."

But before he proceeded further, and, quite other than her restraint with the chatelaine, Selina had the need to tell him of her encounter at breakfast with the spellbinder. And with that meeting, the coming into awareness of a dormant knowledge that dwelt within her, an ability that sprang into life of its own volition, primed and ready to engage. It seemed it was part of an ancient wisdom that had ever existed to combat evil in all its different forms and manifestations. It would appear that those who were enrolled into the service of this order had no knowing of it till an event or situation activated it, whereupon it presented itself in its full power, working with and through its delegates.

In the encounter at breakfast it broke the intent of the spellbinder with nothing more than its formidable presence. Selina had not been called upon to do anything of herself other than be the instrument through which it operated.

She also knew that she must call upon those other dwellers in the spirit world to come attend her in whatever she would encounter; to be behind her, before her and alongside her that she presented no unprotected aspect. Her other defence would be the priest's blessing and a talisman that she might wear on a chain around her neck resting against her heart, that a token would reflect strength and courage into her centre of being. Thus, she would be made both stout hearted and pure in heart – virtues essential to the mission.

The priest regarded her then with respect and thanksgiving, his trust in his own perception vindicated.

"I see there is little I can offer you by way of advice and preparation, for, as you say, others greater than I have imbued you with full instruction. I have already blessed and charged a simple gold cross on a chain for you to wear, and if you come to the altar rail now you shall receive it and I will give you benediction. The full revelation of the bewitching of Lady Isabella and her husband I must leave to herself and the chatelaine to disclose at their discretion, but all else I do now believe will be made known to you as and when you have need of it."

He betook himself then to stand before the altar, bidding Selina kneel at the rail in waiting. There, taking up the cross and chain already set out on the altar cloth, he proffered them towards the images of Christ and the Madonna, making silent entreaty for Selina's sake. Then, when 'twas done, he came to her at the rail and placed the chain over her head, and as it fell about her neck the weight of the cross was enough of itself to drop down and take up perfect position against her heart, and in its so doing she felt it swell and beat the stronger. The priest next laid his hands lightly on her head and made intercession for her safe keeping. And again, Selina felt the spoken words change their nature, turning themselves into a stream of infusing light by the mystery of invoked alchemy.

When she took her leave of him to go and seek out Abigail, he made a solemn vow that he would spend the night in the chapel in vigil. It being but a short distance from her own chamber and the Tapestry, his spiritual proximity must contribute to her safekeeping.

She came then into the garden. So much had happened of a sudden that a complete change in her way of perception was called for. For in a trice she had gone from apprentice to master, though her new-found skills had not had chance to prove themselves by testing. But if of herself she was callow and untried, she knew the power that had manifested at table was ancient, eternal and all-knowing, and, without doubt, so too was its opposite, and where one presented so must the other. 'Twas ever the way of it – the game of chess played out for the winning of a soul.

Newly informed of what had come to pass, Abigail was waiting on her, looking intently towards the place where she would first have sight of her coming. Her manner, when Selina was seated beside her, was stripped of all superficial niceties and preamble, rather it was a demonstration of her urgent and desperate concern for her lady. And in that moment, Selina, in witnessing such display, knew with certainty that she herself would be sacrificed without a second thought if it proved necessary. Had not Tristram been as lightly regarded, and it was why her instincts cautioned her in her dealings with the chatelaine. Those instincts now moved her to raise her hand to touch briefly and lightly on the gold cross, and in so doing she had reassurance that it shielded her with a protection as strong as a breastplate.

She was not standing alone without support, and she gave thanks for the priest and his unbiased dedication to doing the right thing. Confident then in her preparedness, she let her hands drop to rest in her lap whilst she waited for Abigail to begin.

CHAPTER FOURTEEN

The journey to the prince's abode, where my Lady's father was held in ransom, was of a day's length. And during that span, as they proceeded with due caution where difficult terrain demanded it, or with ease where the horses were left to find their own path, they of necessity must converse.

Allan soon acquired awareness that Isabella had no need of his attendance on her where the way be testing, for she discovered exhilaration in the intelligence and willingness of her new steed. And so, trusting her mount and her own skill, she did not feel obliged to select the safest way, but rather instead dared venture a more direct if more hazardous route. It was something her father would have encouraged, and she found need to demonstrate to Allan the fact that he had raised her so.

However, when they were not required to watch the way, at a steady pace alongside each other they fell easily enough into discourse, and this without any sense of obligation to adopt the stiff formality of required etiquette, 'Twas no doubt because they were without attendants and in neutral territory where neither held sway. Also, the gentle warmth of a fine spring day must of itself affect the spirits.

Isabella was curious to know how Allan had managed to come at such an early hour if the journey was of a day's riding.

"Did you dare to journey overnight with an extra horse?"

"It would be a foolish man who would attempt such an undertaking, and I do not tempt providence with ill-considered endeavours. No, 'twas not difficult to avoid any unnecessary hazard. I simply betook myself to the monastery that is nigh unto your manor. And there I rested the night before and the night after our meeting, with stabling for the horses also forthcoming."

Isabella could not conceal her amazement.

"You took lodging in a Christian abbey with the brothers? Can this be possible? Is there not a conflict of faith?"

He laughed.

"A conflict on which side? I respect and honour all faiths that are likewise tolerant, and, being able to provide good contribution for my keep, did not abuse the hospitality that I was graciously given."

Isabella did not pursue the topic of comparative faiths, for although she was curious to know more, now was not the time, with more pressing issues to address.

"Tell me of your family. How many are there who came with you from your own country and how long since was such a happening?"

"I am an only child born to my parents in their later life. My grandparents are all deceased, but my widowed aunt, my mother's sister, came with us, and a goodly number of members of our extended family also accompanied us. Other than our kin, we brought with us any of those who had been in service to us or dwelt within our bounds and wished to make the journey.

"We must leave, for a great cold had overtaken our homeland, far more extreme than a normal winter would visit upon us, though we knew not why. And it would not abate, nor the endless darkness that defeated the sun. Because of it we must either starve along with our livestock, or seek a new country. Many chose to stay, maybe hoping that the sun would return 'ere long, or because they were old and such upheaval too hard a task. Those leaving dispersed to diverse places, to lands and peoples that they had had regular encounter with through trade perhaps, or in other forms of exchange. Scholars and those who study the sciences and apothecary travel widely to extend their knowledge, and we were in receipt therefore of good awareness regarding many other lands and cultures.

"We are of a particular race, and in all lands we can find those of our kind that have gone ahead of us and settled where they felt an affinity. Thus, we were neither ignorant nor isolated, gaining wisdom from forerunners who instructed us as to adaptation and accommodation regarding this, our host nation. Even so, 'tis never a simple matter to be a foreigner in a strange land, and as I related to you previously, suspicion and hostility are all too likely a response should it be suspected that we bite the hand that feeds us.

"Upon considered debate with your father, he came swiftly to the conclusion that we make a valuable contribution in our intermingling, and come the second and third generation, we will be fully integrated and combined with no apparent separation between us. And is this not the way of it? A nation is an amalgam of diverse peoples who have come and been absorbed till you cannot see the seam that joins them, and the whole is enriched by addition. But we at present, being here but a hand's span of years, lack enough time to qualify as accepted and established. And till we do, we must suffer the pains of both transplant and suspicion."

Isabella, hearing once more how her father held his captors in high regard, pressed for further understanding of how this had come about. And with none at watch to restrain her, and the freedom that a large open space encourages, her questioning was more unhindered than would normally have been the case.

"You have it that my father is most well disposed towards you, and so persuaded of your virtue and good intent that, though 'tis hard for me to countenance, he has committed to a betrothal between us. In all his actions my father does nothing that is not well considered. He proceeds only after much examining and is never impetuous. It certainly cannot be that he would make such a generous gesture purely as recompense for your ill usage by a villainous neighbour. And all has been so swiftly done, 'tis not his style. Pray instruct me further, for I cannot believe that there is not more to it than you suggest."

Allan slowed his mount to a gentle amble before giving reply.

"Yes, I believe there is more, but I have not made mention of it for I thought it best to let your father speak directly to you regarding the matter. But I assure you it has naught to do with the terms of his release, 'tis a separate thing entirely."

It was not possible of course for Isabella to let the story rest half told.

"Do not think to leave it there for now, for I must have further knowledge of whatever it is that affects his judgement to such a degree."

Allan smiled at her insistence. It would seem she had forgotten the fact that her father was still held in ransom and were she wise she would do naught to goad his captors, nevertheless he was disposed to humour her. Her boldness and certainty in manner, as in her riding, evoked in him an admiration and good regard. Thus, he expanded on the issue as she wished.

"Your father has, during his imprisonment, been treated with no less respect than had he been an honoured guest. He was not cast into a cell and denied all freedom. No, it has been quite other. He has been constantly in our company, dining with us and having prodigious discussion on a variety of matters. And in such exchanges he has spent many hours conferring with my aunt, most undoubtedly to their mutual pleasure. Both having lost spouses, mayhap they share a reciprocal understanding, but whatever it be that draws each to the other, it seems no slight matter. For though they are but newly met it is clear that it cannot be lightly dismissed as mere dalliance. Besides, both are of an age when such conduct would be regarded as unseemly, but be that as it may, what might appear as most unlikely in all respects and circumstances obviously is not, for we have the evidence before us."

Isabella was shocked afresh by such disclosure. Not only had her father agreed to surrender her as a peace offering as if she were no more than an article of trade, but now it would appear, he intended to add himself to the bargain. Was there to be no limit to his generosity? Had he taken leave of his senses? She could not recognise the father she saw riding out so gloriously to do battle as having aught to do with this apparently obsequious lickspittle.

But then she must admonish herself with a reminder that he was in ransom and not his own man, and just as she had owned that there was nothing she would not barter for his sake, who knew what demands had been made upon him likewise? Shame on her that she so quickly betrayed him in a wayward mind, rather than trust in a lifetime's certainty that all he did was ever exemplary. Thus, she held her tongue and made no comment on Allan's disclosure. She would do as he suggested and wait to hear tell of the matter directly from her father's lips. Instead she changed the subject entirely by asking a question that had indeed taken up residence in that wayward mind's considerations.

"Might I ask if it be that all your people, the race you describe as spread abroad in other lands, have the very fair hair, tallness of stature and blue eyes that you present and which mark you out?"

Allan, somewhat disconcerted that she had so abruptly dropped the subject that she demanded he expound on, must draw his own conclusions as to the reason, but made no remark. Instead he answered her most recent request for enlightenment.

"There will always be some within a clan or other grouping that do not conform for one reason or another, but our defining characteristics are those which you describe." He then added with a little shrug of the shoulders and a smile, "Mayhap with long, dark winters and fleeting summers, like plants we grow tall and pale, reaching for the sun."

Isabella surprised herself then by giving a response that had she but allowed more time and consideration, she would have been aware was inappropriate.

"Unlike the plants, 'tis plain it does you no harm."

Allan, equally surprised by an entirely unexpected if accidental compliment, turned his gaze upon her with raised eyebrows, whereupon in embarrassment she could but mimic his gesture, and, shrugging her shoulders, she pulled a face that acknowledged her mistake. Regarding each other thus for a long moment in such attitude, Allan then threw back his head and gave himself up to unrestrained and delighted laughter. It was irresistibly infectious and Isabella found she had no choice but to mimic him yet again.

And in that moment, it seemed all caution and wariness drained out of them, dissolved and washed away by the warmth of mirth. Much as his description of the alien in a strange land, they had achieved acceptance of each other in recognising that their similarities might be more in operation than their differences, even given the circumstances.

When they continued on their way, the conversation had a different tone, and for the duration of the journey they were as any two who found much pleasure in each other's company. That they were tantalisingly aware that this too was the beginning of a different and separate journey that they had not expected to take, made it seem all the more like a gift from the gods, his and hers. Maybe one of his gods was Eros, who was accused of causing mayhem by shooting arrows into disparate and wholly unlikely candidates purely for his own amusement. They could be defined as such, yet the epithet did not quite fit. They rode side by side, and, though neither said aught to acknowledge the change, both were aware that the other knew, and this too was part of a dawning astonishment.

When in the mid evening they were come to their destination, they were in no way the same two people as started out – the span of time making far more than a day's difference.

But though 'twas that day's end, there was still plenty enough light left for Isabella to see the place to which they had come, and it was in no way what she had expected.

Though it was indeed mainly of wooden construction, as she had supposed, there was naught presented here that was either rough-hewn or primitive. The approach to the impressive dwelling was restricted and guarded by a massive drawbridge that straddled a deep-dug moat, and, as they approached, having been seen and acknowledged by guards, the bridge was lowered to grant them entry. Then, once they had crossed its formidable width, they were faced by huge doors, far weightier and more impenetrable than those of her own manor's portals, that yielded only to those with licence. You could not easily imagine them giving way to battering rams, and axes would but barely scratch the surface of the studded and hard-seasoned timber.

The steep, pitched roof that covered all was not tiled, but thatched in reed and extended far enough forward to form protective eaves over entrance and surrounds. The window shutters being constructed like the rest, in robust fashion, nevertheless bore deeply engraved carvings. These were of a most complicated patterning, an interweaving of plants, animals and birds contained in formalised depiction.

All was of one storey only, but clearly the design allowed it to expand as and when it was needed and 'twas already extensive.

The interior was set out much as her own manor, the Great Hall being the immediate chamber. It was furnished in exceptional and impressive style. The central table noticeably being not of boards and trestles but of solid wood with carved legs that supported its considerable length. And to the end of the hall was a raised platform bearing a separate table which presided over those assembled below. This was reserved for family members and any of status who were in residence or visiting. The walls, like most others such, were indeed hung with tapestries, but also they supported ancient standards, intricately carved panels and fine paintings depicting scenes from their mythology and their faith.

Isabella had a realisation then that all her assumptions, and those of her peers, were false, founded on ignorance and preconception. Here was a refined and beautiful settlement, isolated and well-fortified for no other reason than it must be. While misconception and persecution be as likely to be their receipt as hospitality, they need be able to defend themselves. Had she not herself as quickly jumped to the conclusion that his horse, his hairstyle and his garb marked Allan out as inferior? If she had claimed her father did nothing without due consideration, being never impetuous, clearly that was not her stance and she was ashamed to admit to it as being so.

But there was no more time for such reflection, for, advised of their arrival, his parents came at once to greet them, whilst retainers set about laying up the tables. As Allan had told, they were of more years than one might have supposed, more like grandparents than parents, but their garments, unlike their son's, were of conventional style, as might be worn by those of status anywhere in the land.

They received Isabella graciously, as if she were a guest and of equal standing to themselves, enquiring as to the journey with no mention of the true circumstance, and she, discomforted by her prejudice, was wont to respond in the same vein without immediate demand to see her father.

After the greeting, she was conducted to a fine chamber to refresh herself, but she did not tarry long for she was in great anticipation of their meeting, and when she was returned to the hall, the fare being ready to be served, all took to their seats. She was positioned at the top table alongside Allan, and, as she sat down, 'twas then that her father came into the hall and her heart leapt at the sight of him.

He looked exceeding well – no prisoner's pallor, nor hint of any secret persecution he might have endured. But he came not alone; alongside him was a woman of striking appearance, and their closeness, nigh unto contact, made plain declaration that they were in a relationship other than that of hostess and guest.

He came at once to his daughter, first bowing to Allan's mother and father in respect and deference for he must remember his place as captive. With a restraint therefore governing his actions, he did not embrace her, but rather took hold of her hands, and, bending his head, kissed them. She too kissed the hands that held her own with thanksgiving, for though it be less than a week since he was gone from her, with such trials as had been endured it seemed he had been absent an eternity.

When her father released her hands and stepped back, the woman who had accompanied him to table, Allan's aunt, stepped forward, and, with a slight bow of her head, introduced herself. She was clearly kin with her height, long, flaxen, braided hair and blue eyes, yet despite such obvious likeness, there was an otherness about her that would mark out a distinct disparity.

Though having a similar number of years as her father, and being thus in midlife, she somehow defied such definition, and had you not known beforehand 'twould have been no easy task to determine her age. It was not a simple matter of appearing younger than was the fact, but rather that she seemed neither young nor old, but in some way ageless. Her features too and her expression betrayed no exterior hint of who or what she was, being more akin to a mask, unmarked by outward display and nigh impossible to get beyond. Yet at the same time, 'twas without doubt that she was most compellingly attractive, and in whatever company she might find herself she would ever command attention. Her posture and serenely contained stillness somehow magnetic, she could never be ignored. Her name was Sibylla.

The look she bestowed upon Isabella was both concentrated and impenetrable, and she had no idea if it was an extreme study of a restrained manner, or if the woman presenting herself was devoid of warm feeling in general or to herself in particular. But his aunt demonstrated no change in demeanour as she greeted Allan and took her place beside him, so 'twas more general than particular, Isabella supposed, till she witnessed a markedly different response to her father seated on her other side. From impassive to vibrant, she changed in the moment, and his own countenance as he gazed upon her was lit with an intensity such as she had never before encountered. Here was an aspect of her father that had obviously previously existed, but had till now remained unseen and unknown to her, and Isabella found the new awareness a difficult and uncomfortable thing to accommodate. Separated from her by the space of two people, 'twas clear she would have no meaningful exchange with him till after the repast, but then, any form of serious business was never done at table in any case.

Seated between Allan and his mother, Isabella felt herself very much in subject to this family and dynasty of which she knew so little, and such little as she thought she knew now turned on its head. With newly aroused regard towards Allan, itself also a confusing if enchanting factor, she was at a loss on how to evaluate the situation or conduct herself accordingly.

Allan's mother seemed likewise uneasy in the uncertain nature of that in which she found herself, and, having no previous experience of such, lacked any rules or guidance to which she could turn. She was therefore subdued and said but little and that only to her husband, leaving Allan to attend on the ambiguous nature of their guests. For the hostage now seemed to be in suit to her sister, and his daughter was to be betrothed to her only child, and there was naught she might do to make it other.

Allan found no hardship in taking on the duty of host in his mother's stead, and in his attention gave no hint of being in the dominant position and Isabella and her father at the mercy of those who entertained them. He was more than happy to fulfil his requirements by conversing solely with Isabella, for while his aunt was also turned entirely away from him in conferring exclusively with the hostage, they found themselves likewise contained within their own company.

First, he would put her mind at rest as to how things must be conducted. This evening would be given to hospitality and naught brought to bear on such matters of contention as might exist, nor the terms of the ransom, for this would be left till the morrow after breakfast.

Isabella asked who would attend at this determining, for had not agreement already been reached between his father and her own as to the price of his freedom?

"In principle 'tis so, but we are of ourselves a peace-loving people, fierce only in the defence and protection of those things that are precious or sacred to us, and must therefore be preserved at all cost. Thus, I assure you, it would be wholly against such beliefs to achieve our ends by force rather than persuasion. I have already, as I informed you, been thus persuaded, my own intent gladly offered in barter if it achieve safety and stability for all. For there can never again be a repeat of the burning and slaughter of the innocent as was the cause of our battling. And with an allegiance sealed between us, there is guarantee that indeed there never shall.

"But in my willing acceptance I do confess it be not now what I had supposed, but rather has another possibility.

Might it not indeed be seen more as an unexpected gift come disguised as sacrifice?"

Isabella could but look at him in incredulity. She had not expected him to state his mind so swiftly nor so straightforwardly, and that which was but newly stirred within herself responded in gladness that he had already the courage to speak so plain. It gave her the want to mimic him yet again, but even so she managed to say but little, determined to instead mimic her father, reflecting the care and caution he exercised in all he did that error be forestalled.

Allan, sensitive to her need for holding back till she be fully informed, was in no wise daunted, rather he applauded the good sense she demonstrated. 'Twas a virtue he admired and also sought to practise.

By unspoken but mutual accord, they left further discourse on the subject till the morrow, and Isabella returned to her want to know more of his faith and what manner of church they built for the worship of what manner of god.

"*We believe not in a personal god in whose image we are made like yourselves, but rather in a spirit that is without form but manifests in all created things; animals, trees and all that exist in the world are come into being because of it and could not continue for a moment without it. In that sense, all things are equal, for all things having been created and ever nurtured by the Great Spirit, whom you might in that manner call the Father, makes us brethren and none more important than another. Thus, if we use animals and wood from the trees we revere, and all such things as we have need of, it is done with the awareness that whatever we take, we must ask permission first and afterward must give back that which is equal to what we have received."*

Isabella was amazed and much intrigued by such regard for not only the beasts but all existence. This was not the normal way of it with her own faith. For with the belief that man was given the right to name the animals in Genesis, came the assumption that he was at the same time given dominion over them and might use them as he chose. And with the understanding that dumb creatures were lacking a soul, a disregard for their welfare and creature comforts was deemed justifiable for they were of but little concern. Yet there were many who, regardless of such teaching, responded with a recognition and tenderness for all other forms of life that sprang from the heart, in much the same way as Allan described and she must acknowledge 'twas a sweeter way of seeing things.

The 'barbarian' continued to astound her, and each additional piece of information expanded her esteem. It came as no surprise then that her father had found much to admire, enough indeed to agree to commit to an act of union between the domains forged by the indissoluble joining in matrimony.

Like Allan, her own stance regarding such a contract had changed markedly, and that which had seemed irreconcilably at odds with her wishes was no longer seen in the same light. The one factor that did concern her above all else, however, was Allan's aunt, Sibylla. That she would have a role in whatever was agreed tomorrow she did not doubt, having borne witness to her father's regard for her, and also that the role would be considerable. What filled her with disquiet was an instinctive awareness that Aunt

Sibylla was not what she appeared to be, a respectable widow with a reciprocal response that echoed her father's. She was something else entirely, of that Selina was sure, and whatever it be it did not bode well for either her father or herself.

CHAPTER FIFTEEN

The next morning, when breakfast was done and the remains cleared away, the hall emptied save for a few retainers and the guards ever on duty at the entrances. Then it was that Allan's father, Bardolph, summoned them to be seated that they attend to the business in hand – the ransom settlement. He bade them assemble in the lower hall where they might sit opposite each other, the better to have honest exchange.

Bardolph, with Allan on his right hand, faced across from Isabella and her father, these four being the essential participants. Allan's mother and his aunt sat a little apart, next to Allan. They would be attendant but non-contributing lest called upon, or if mayhap they had aught they must speak on of themselves. That they were included here was unique and would not have been considered beyond these walls. Likewise, there was a council of elder statesmen to solicit should the deliberations require their steerage, though Isabella doubted the value of such input if they resembled those who sought influence in her own domicile. Beside such fact there was naught here of a prodigious nature that required skilled minds to unravel. 'Twas simple enough. Initially all that was needed was her yea or nay.

Allan had come to breakfast dressed in the conventional garments befitting a young man of his status, the soft leathers eschewed. His hair was also released from its restraints and framed his face in gentler manner. Thus presented, he changed from strange and unknown to recognised and known, and he looked exceedingly good. And because of the new guise, Isabella felt 'twas more as if she was meeting him for the first time, and was wont therefore to spend time in fresh regard.

At breakfast, when she had enquired of him the reason for such readjustment of apparel, he said 'twas comparable to the chameleon changing colour.

"When we are come into your country, we must adopt the dress and customs we find here. If it be our intention to stay and be accepted and assimilated, then we must not look at odds with local traits by presenting ourselves as decidedly other. It is only in times of conflict that we revert to what we know and make plain our difference. Thus, I restrain my hair that it does not hinder my vision, and dress in the garb that gives me ease of movement and freedom from any restriction that would hamper my ability. At other times too, while taking my leisure, I would prefer to don familiar habit for it feels natural and comfortable to me. Such garments as you choose to wear have much to do with presentation and declaration of status. They are very fine and arresting but they are styled for appearance not for ease I think."

Isabella must agree and was not sorry that she had donned simpler dress at his suggestion for the journey and what must follow, for she was well aware that it was herself that would be central to resolution regarding the ransom settlement, Allan having already concurred. Plain clothes were best suited to plain speaking, and she intended only the honest truth.

She had not spoken privately to her father as she had hoped. For he, though being granted much freedom, was still under curfew at nightfall and must retire under watch to his chamber. All exchange between them this morning would therefore now be in the public domain, and she could not ask of him what was his true mind.

Bardolph stood to address them both. Unlike his wife, who presented an unease born of confusion, he had a natural dignity and bearing that would be in evidence in any situation. Though aged now, and with the physical strength of former years gone from him, he yet commanded a respect that honoured a different strength come in its stead, a wisdom born of maturity that leant itself to diplomacy and a regard for one's adversaries that enabled compromise in resolution. For despite the fact that he be in the dominant position, he would use such power only as a last resort. He addressed them then not as victor, but as advocate.

"We are gathered to bring end to conflict, and in so doing to put aside distrust and doubt in acceptance, that together we be stronger in accord. United we are become a force for good that will ensure the safety and protection of our separate peoples, and that union must make of us one people with no division between us. There shall be in such conjoining a recognition that the sole distinction is regarding those of good intent against those who intend harm.

"Our aim is to establish a lasting peace in which all thrive when there is nothing to impede the establishment of secure settlements nor hinder progress. We shall achieve the prosperity and content that is our common goal. Towards that end, let us then indeed make ploughshares rather than swords. And we being now in full awareness that enmity has come between us through misunderstanding only, can be reconciled and allied from this time forth."

He looked then directly at Isabella.

"To this end my only son, Aelianus, has pledged himself to the commitment of marriage, that from such union the peace and prosperity we seek be established and it will be the seal that guarantee it. Your father has concurred in principle, least it be entirely against your will." He looked then towards Isabella's father in invitation to him to expound further on that fact and then sat down to allow it.

Her father rose to his feet and turned towards her, and like Bardolph he addressed himself entirely to his daughter.

"You are my one and only child, and therefore that which is most precious to me, yet my residency here these last days has persuaded me that that which Bardolph has laid out before you is an excellent thing for us all. With dangers abounding without, and rumours afoot of lawless invaders striking where they will, there is strength in numbers. But 'tis more than that alone. I am also persuaded by the art and culture that I have encountered, and the learned discourse in which it has been my privilege to engage, for they are unsurpassed. I came as hostage taken in battle, and am now captive in an entirely different and unexpected way."

Here he glanced briefly but significantly towards Sibylla, indicating that she was very much a part of that captivation.

"That you may make your decision advisedly 'twould make best sense for us to stay for the span of several days that you become fully conversant with Aelianus and all that you would be embracing, for then and only then can you appreciate what is being required of you."

But before Isabella could make reply, Sibylla raised her hand in indication that she had wish to speak, and in respect of her seniority Bardolph permitted it. She remained seated as a gesture of humility, but her voice was firm and without any hint of uncertainty.

"There is another and more obvious solution that would require no self-abnegation from these two young people. For however willing they be, such action could but bring them loss of future choice. And should they submit, however noble the cause, they must suffer the consequence hereafter.

"That cause can be served perfectly well by another but equal uniting. 'Tis clear I think that Isabella's father, Alfred, lord of his domain, and I are in high regard, one for the other. Should we be the ones who take the vows that unite both ourselves and the two realms 'twould achieve the same end without any need for sacrifice, rather it would be reason for a two-fold celebration."

A silence greeted a declaration that none had anticipated and were thus unprepared for, but Bardolph responded somewhat warily by enquiring of Isabella's father what his mind was in regard to such a proposal.

Looking at him, Isabella saw at once that he was as stunned by Sibylla's statement as were all others. 'Twas plain she had spoken without conferring with him beforehand, and it could only be supposed that in so doing had intended to force his hand. Mayhap she had been so certain of his enthralment that she had confidence that he must concur without need to question the issue. If that was the case, she was to discover her error, for he gave an immediate and unequivocal answer to Bardolph, and it was other than she had expected.

"I cannot, nor have I ever even given thought to remarriage. My daughter, Isabella, is my true heir and already all I have is hers. Should she choose to marry Aelianus, and I think they be most well matched, then the children they may have are her own heirs in waiting. But should I remarry, and, though it be less likely, 'tis not impossible that there be issue from that union, then these would become my inheritors in her stead, especially be they male. Such event must then be the cause of her disinheritance. Upon my death she would have no claim on that which is presently rightfully hers, indeed she would have no legality at all, thus becoming dependent on the charity of those who succeed her. Such possibility I can never countenance and so 'twill never come to pass."

Having emphatically delivered such crushing statement of refusal to Sibylla's offer, in recompense Alfred then professed, "This does not for a moment deny my most high regard for the Lady Sibylla, which has been a wonder and a delight to me and of inestimable value. 'Tis a joy that I hope will continue, despite there being no possibility of a marriage contract. And regarding such, it is my sincere hope that Aelianus and Isabella will find themselves so well suited that 'tis love that joins them together rather than the obligation of duty."

If Sibylla had been thwarted in her ambition she gave no outward hint of it, nor the stark truth that, impervious to her wiles, his unwavering and unassailable devotion to his daughter was of a strength that she had severely underestimated. Instead, the mask of her face registered only gentle acquiescence as she bowed to his declaration, whilst also graciously accepting the acknowledgement of his regard.

She nodded then to Bardolph, as though to own that she had offered her own self to take the place of his son, but such selfless gesture having been spurned, there was naught else she could do.

Isabella, having listened to the exchange, was gladdened to hear her father's response, not only for her own sake but also for his. She felt sure the woman's sole intent was to worm her way into her father's affections and thus become mistress of the manor. For should she and Allan marry as was hoped, she would continue in future in no better place than that which was her present lot, powerlessly living on sufferance as a relative. Such docile position would not sit well when she had seen a more favourable option and would have her way.

Isabella herself then gave answer, and though she was a woman and of tender years, she stood to say her piece like the men.

"When it was first mooted that the price of my father's freedom was the forfeiting of my own, I knew not how to reconcile myself to a such price. Yet I had owned that there was nothing I would refrain from for his sake and I will not retract that declaration. For love if it be true does not suffer limitation, nor draw back should the cost be all that you have.

"When I beheld him yesterday eve come into the hall safe and well, I knew such joy as filled me to overflowing, and in that moment I pledged that I would do whatever was required and gladly, if it return him home to me.

"I would confess also that the price that had seemed

so onerous, a necessary but most hard bargain be now not what it was. The more I know of Aelianus the more this is the fact, and 'twill not be hard to spend such time as has been advised in gaining further knowledge, for I am already more than half persuaded."

She looked directly across the table then at Allan, and he returned her gaze with unwavering steadfastness. In that moment both knew full well, her persuasion was not calculated in half measures and neither was he in two minds. He rose to his feet then, and, taking her hand most tenderly in his own, he kissed the back of it, then turning it over, kissed the palm in clear demonstration that here was more than a mere chivalrous gesture. And those gathered in witness knew that the reason for their gathering was without doubt accomplished, and Bardolph must at once call upon the retainers that they bring the best wine to honour and celebrate this joyful outcome.

*

"And thus, all proceeded apace, with the wedding planned and preparations speedily begun. It seemed there could be nothing capable of spoiling such a perfect happening as had come about."

Abigail sighed heavily in remembrance.

*

With hindsight, of course, we know that Sibylla would not allow her chance for advancement to slip away from her that easily. But what we did not know then was that she had gifts other than the female charms and wiles she had employed in seduction, for should they not suffice she had within her arsenal enchantments of a very different kind. Allan and Isabella were all that stood in her way and with them removed from the picture then the way was clear for her intention. She would override any residual resistance from Alfred by the brewing of a love potion, for being already under her spell 't would take but small additional impelling to push him past all denying or ability to resist.

When she heard tell that the Tapestry was to be the prime gift and that it would adorn the bridal chamber, 'twas made most easy for her to fulfil her purpose. Already imbued with its own thrall, she had but to harness that magic and bend it to her will. True, the weaver be dead and thus it was no longer empowered by the continued investment of his life force, which meant eventually, over time, it must die with him. But in the meantime, she could use its benign manifestation to her own intent, turning what was his invitation to such ones as had the gift of special apprehension to visit his paradise without harm, into a one way only excursion ending in permanent containment. Thus, in the reverse warping of the weaver's promise of safe return, she would have them lost and imprisoned in the Tapestry for all time, and when its life force be finally spent, theirs must likewise be terminated with it, and none the wiser as to where they were nor what had become of them.

And in his grief and distress, then Alfred must surely turn to her for support. She being all that he had, he would have great need of her in compensation for that which he had lost, and being in dread that he might lose her also must thereupon pledge himself in total commitment. And thus was her reasoning.

Therefore, whilst the Tapestry was still hanging in close proximity, she corrupted its own wholesome magic, imbuing it instead with a totally malign influence. Then when that was achieved, she brewed a concoction to bemuse the senses, putting some portion into sweetmeats and some into candle wax, that should the one not be called into use, then the other would suffice. And in this wise her snare was set.

When the wedding day was come it was a most joyous occasion, for was there not much to celebrate? Isabella and Allan being still in a bemusing of delight that, beside a treaty of peace and alliance between their two domains, somehow beyond expectation they had also been gifted a most happy personal outcome. And in bearing witness to it, none assembled there could attend their nuptials without full-heartedly wishing them good fortune, long life and happiness.

If only it had been so, for most surely it should have been.

The gathering and feasting were held here in Isabella's manor, and the celebrations continued till end of day. In such a stretch of time, Sibylla had no difficulty in placing sweetmeats and candles in their chamber and ensuring her curse on the Tapestry be in full sway.

*

At this moment in the telling, Abigail paused to utter her own curse.

"And may she suffer in Hell for all time for what she did, lest God should forgive her, for I never shall."

*

My Lady and Allan, on entering their chamber, when 'twas time for them to withdraw were almost at once enraptured by the effluvia permeating the air from the many candles. Then, behold! Before them was the Tapestry come to life and irresistibly bidding them enter in. Already light-headed from the unfolding of the day's events, then the more so by the intoxication of the candle smoke, they were helplessly bewitched beyond resistance and could but comply. Alas, 'twas indeed inevitable, and as soon as they had crossed the divide between the two realms, their fate was sealed.

Yet despite Sibylla's evil attempt to incarcerate them forever with no possibility of return, she had miscalculated the inherent magic of the Tapestry itself. Because 'twas sweet, she supposed it was less potent. In just such a manner she had miscalculated the power of Alfred's devotion to his daughter. Blinded by greed and ambition she was made careless, and thus she overestimated the extent of her own sorcery, whilst undervaluing that of pure love and goodness. Because of such a fatal error, her evil purpose was only half achieved and it happened thus.

When Isabella and Allan found themselves in such a divine place as an earthly paradise, at first they must experience naught but delight and have no wish but to stay for some long while. It seemed to them that in some wondrous way they had unlocked the enchantment of the Tapestry, though they know not how. But supposed it was because 'twas a wedding gift and 'twas fashioned for that purpose, with love being the turnkey that activated it? But such an innocent idea was soon shown of vain surmise when, in seeking the way back, it could not be found. And try as they might they could but wander ever in circles, discovering no clue as to how they might depart.

Whilst Allan questioned those who peopled that world, it was to no avail, for they could not comprehend that there was another world to which he had need to return. Meanwhile, Isabella pondered on such as she knew of spellbinding.

If the Tapestry was a good and blessed thing as had always been believed, then it would not have them enter in only to entrap them. There was most surely a way out that would be as easy to attain as the way in, yet somehow that portal had been hid that they should not attain it. Why and by whom? Answer came hard on the heels of the question and she knew who 'twas – Sibylla of a surety. There was no doubt in her mind that it was so and also that she was a witch. With this certainty Isabella had remembrance that knowledge of itself was power and such knowing as she needed came readily now from her mind's prompting to inform her what was required. It was to discover the magic, command or ritual that would unlock the doorway that should never have been hard fastened.

She called Allan to her then and told him of her apprehension that their containment was the result of a spell cast by Sibylla, with their release being dependent on finding the countermand. 'Twas not hard for him to accept such presentiments, for he had long suspected she was not what she would have you believe.

He suggested that could they but recognise some small detail or aspect of the place whereby they came in, mayhap if they then called upon the weaver by name, imploring him to open the way out, it could be that he would hear them. Or, if not himself, then the enchantment that operated the existence of what he had created might respond, their entrapment being wholly counter to his intent. Therefore, even though he be dead, it might yet be possible to operate the release mechanism that was subject to his governance.

They had come into this realm in such an excitement that they had paid but scant heed to their immediate surrounds, rather looking towards that which was before them, 'twas then no easy task to find remembrance of what had been but barely noticed. Yet in diligent searching they were met with the success of recognition, for Isabella beheld an arch made from a bower of scented blossom and 'twas the fragrance that stirred the knowledge that she had been this way previously. This assuredly then was the entrance portal and most likely the way in would also be the way back out.

Those two then stood together within the bower, and Allan called out the weaver's name, Lucius, in a loud and emphatic tone imploring him to respond to them in their distress and let them return to their own home and their own lives. The Tapestry was his wedding gift to them. Let it then in no wise cause them ill on this, the blessed day of their marriage. Another had overcast her evil spell with intent to seal them forever within his Garden of Eden. Surely he could not permit such foul deed to hold sway and contaminate the perfection of his creation.

This invocation he called out in loud tones and with much passion in his delivery. Isabella, grasping tight onto his hand and feeling the power of it charge through her own self, was stirred to belief that it could not fail to elicit response. And 'twas so.

The ground in that serene and gentle place was of a sudden subject to a violent agitation that increased in magnitude till 'twas so fierce that neither could keep their balance. Then it happened that the very earth on which they stood heaved up in tumult beneath their feet, and in its so doing, Isabella was pitched headlong forward whilst Allan was flung backward and both with such ferocious force that they had no control over its impulsion nor choice in outcome. Isabella felt their hands being torn apart, and 'twas then that she lost consciousness.

On coming to herself, she discovered she was lying on the carpeted floor of her bedchamber. She looked about her then as she struggled to her feet in expectation of finding Allan close by, but he was not there, nor anywhere, though she dashed about without and within the chamber, calling his name and seeking to find him.

In this wise was he lost to her and has never been found, nor has a way back into the Tapestry been discovered that he might be sought and rescued. These many long years it has been thus, the two opposing forces locked in impasse causing the one to be freed and the other to be held.

The troubadour mayhap did broach the spellbinding, though this we can never know for sure. Certainly, we never had a chance to question him and ask if he found any trace of Allan or if the way into the Tapestry be accessible to others.

The priest in his clairvoyance believes it is, and that you are the one given the gift, and therefore the obligation to do it. This night shall see if his faith and trust in what was revealed to him has true merit, and if there is aught you can conjure up from within yourself that shall be a match for Sibylla's sorcery.

Chapter Sixteen

Abigail had finished her telling then, with the instruction that all else from henceforth must come direct from Madame. She had relayed as much as was in her remit, playing her own part out to its conclusion. With this final declaration delivered, she had struggled to her feet, seeming to have become, in but a moment, increasingly old and infirm. 'Twould appear as if she had maintained herself hitherto purely by the strength of purpose required to complete her allotted task then afterward, when 'twas done, the strength went out of her.

As they made their way from the garden to the hall for the midday meal, she had need to hold on tight to Selina's arm, and Selina, aware of the quaking tremors transmitted through the grip of her fingers, was taken aback at such a sudden display of frailty. Mayhap it also evidenced that she was in fear and trembling lest the night's outcome go against them. For 'twas assuredly a hard thing for her to have faith that such as she was a fit opponent to encounter a sorceress, nor could Selina reassure her for she knew not herself.

Neither were of good appetite, but Selina ate her way doggedly through a goodly portion of the fare, determined to do everything in her power to be best prepared for what must come. Physical strength and endurance might be needed as much as the spiritual and psychic power that she must call on, and 'twould make better sense to eat well now rather than later.

Her own frugal meal quickly over and done, Abigail rose unsteadily to her feet, and, holding fast to the table's edge, delivered her final speech to Selina before she retired to her chamber.

"What befalls this night is beyond my failing powers to influence. For whatever comes to pass 'twill be entirely a battle of wills between yourself and Sibylla. The priest will pray for you and so indeed shall I, for my Lady's very life depends on it, but that is all I can do and it seems too little. Nor do I know how so many years of persistent enthralment might be undone and resolution found. 'Tis nigh on fifty years since Madame had sight of her husband. What will be the way of him should he be found? God alone knows."

Shaking her head in bewilderment, she said no more then, but, turning away from the table and Selina, she crossed towards the stairs with a gait not unakin to a sailor's on a storm-tossed deck. Yet, Selina did not move to assist her, knowing she would not welcome it, having urgent need to be apart from her. When she had attained her goal with her hand safe home on the banister rail, then Selina withdrew her watchful gaze and gave her attention instead to her own challenges.

In all that the chatelaine had told, she had awareness that there was much that was of similar nature between herself and Lady Isabella, and with regard to their encounters with the Tapestry. Was that in some way ordained? An essential concomitant?

Both had been subject to newly awakened feelings, be it to either Tristram or Allan, and both were likewise in urgent endeavour, seeking how they might release them from entrapment within the Tapestry.

Each also had comprehension that the breaking of the spell cast was in finding its opposite, the countermand. Allan had part found it in his beseeching of the weaver to deliver them from evil by calling upon him by name, which was Lucius.

She had heard tell that there was a power in names and their utterance. The saints could be alerted when summoned by name, and the archangels too, like Michael or Raphael. Though it had not been enough of itself to call out to Lucius, 'twould seem it was half the battle. What might be the other half?

Upon her encounter with the sorceress at breakfast, there had sprung forth in retaliation a source of knowing and power that she had been unaware was latent within her, but it had proved to be a match for Sibylla's. Would this be the way of it in the next and conclusive engagement? When the need arose would the power within her rise too in answer? It must surely be, for what could she possibly achieve of her own capabilities against a force as dark and venomous as Sibylla in her full fury?

And like the weaver who be long gone from this world, as also was Isabella's father, had not she too expired? Though such fact, as was evidenced by Lucius, was clearly not the end of it, for he still wielded an authority that could function from beyond the grave. And Christianity itself was founded on such premise.

She was alerted then by the sound of rapid footsteps approaching, and, looking towards the source, saw in astonishment Lady Isabella coming towards her, veil blowing almost away from her face by the draught she herself created in her haste. She wasted no time in preamble nor explanation as to why she had forsaken her chamber, but went straight to the reason for her coming.

"Selina, there is no time to waste sitting idly over the dinner table. Let us go at once upstairs where I may give you your instruction for the coming night. Then you must prepare yourself in whatever way you see fit and in such manner as the spirit moves you."

She turned about rapidly and retraced her steps in a rapid motion that was the opposite of the chatelaine's. Following on behind, Selina saw no trace of advanced age here, rather again the quick and easy suppleness of youth that belied that she was of four and sixty years.

When they had attained her chamber, she found the curtains were pulled hard back and the sunlight illuminated every corner in unrestrained brilliance, as if 'twere an act of deliberate defiance. And as Isabella strode across the room to her chair, she sat down in it in a most abrupt manner, whilst at that same moment wrenching the veil from her face in an emphatic gesture. She flung it from her in such way as made clear 'twould never be in use hereafter, then she looked at Selina in invitation for her to respond to what she had done.

Selina, at last given the freedom to look fully upon Lady Isabella's face, did so, and in the doing found, as was suspected, that the features revealed were not in any wise those of an elderly woman. Rather she gazed at someone of but few years beyond her own age. Her face, exceedingly pale from years of being denied access to light, made the contrast of her dark eyes and brows all the greater in comparison. Jacob had said she had been famed for her beauty and 'twas rightly so, for she was even yet, despite her travails, most fair to behold. How could such a thing be?

Isabella enlightened her.

"When I was expelled out of the Tapestry, from that day forth I have remained as then I was. The Tapestry's endowment of incorruptibility somehow followed me back into this, our very corrupt world. Thus, I have lived these many years since that happening in suspension. As I told you afore, I am therefore indeed locked in the past, but I cannot return there, though not from want of trying. It is sealed against me now, and Allan is also sealed within, and thus we are helpless to attain each other till such seal be broken. I had no knowing of how that may be accomplished till it was given to the priest to find an answer.

"He is an exceptional man, not in any wise like his forebear. The previous minister was a man of no great faith or degree of stature in any virtue. He was remarkable only in his profound lack of a sense of vocation. He retired two years back from a role for which he was totally unsuited and in no way entitled. The present incumbent come to take his place, as you have witnessed, is in all aspects a very different churchman. He is truly and rightly ordained. Having no fear of witchery, he does not recoil from such engagements for he sees it as part of his calling. 'Twere not for him this enthralment could not be resolved but must ever continue with no end in sight. Now you are come on his recognition, but neither he, nor I, nor any other, can know with certainty if you will prove to be a match for Sibylla. On the face of it 'twould not seem likely, but there being no other option we must put our trust in you in fervent hope that you have more to you than would appear.

"My life, blighted by the sorceress, has forced me to live apart from all about me for fear they have awareness that I have not aged. I have worn the hated veil that even the old priest should not know the truth hid beneath, and I have ever set Allan's place at table in certainty that such things must be done to thwart Sibylla's evil will.

"She is old now, yet still alive I do believe, and undiminished. And though her ambitions can never be fulfilled, she seems the more determined that neither shall we find the joy which was our promise.

"When on my wedding night I was heard calling for Allan in a great distress and despair, his parents and my father were come to me at once. But then they likewise found themselves in the same helpless position as was I, of being in desperate need of solution but with no knowing of what they might do to bring it about. It ever remaining thus, no doubt contributed mightily to Allan's parents' deaths soon after. With their only son lost to them in such a manner, so also was their purpose and will to live. For 'twas for his sake that they do all that they do, and take up residence in a country that was far from their own true homeland. And my own dear father must continue in agony. Forced to bear continual witness to my undoing, he went thereafter into steep decline, becoming but a shadow of the man he had been, for 'tis a truth that a man of action cannot countenance inaction in the face of great need. But because he had no present and visible adversary to battle, it must forever cause him a great and terrible fretting.

"Sibylla, on seeing the outcome of her scheming was gone badly amiss, and fearing for her life, vanished as completely as did Allan, and has likewise not been seen since. There are rumours that she is disguised as a nun and hid within convent walls; a blasphemous thing if it is true.

"But the sense of her intent ever haunts me in continual merciless potency, so I cannot suppose her dead, though I do most sincerely wish it. But such apprehension of her keeps me vigilant, inspiring me to ever do everything I know that might spite her will, though I am oft piteously weary of such an endeavour over these long and fruitless years.

"Before we proceed to preparations for the coming night, I bid you now ask of me what you will in any wise, for there are no prohibitions remaining."

Selina had listened throughout with no wish to stem the flow of Isabella's outpouring, but knew there were some things she must have answered in order to be fully informed. No remaining areas of doubt or uncertainty could be left, for they might weaken her ability. She had had innate certainty that all the rites of spiritual ritual must be immaculately performed, and Isabella too had experienced the same instinctive awareness. Now, to be without any unknowing was likewise a necessity, and thus must be addressed that there be naught done nor left undone as might in any way impair her quest.

"Abigail said that it was the tainted candles that Sibylla had fashioned that caused your undoing, for they overwhelmed your senses.

"The candles that nightly give me the illumination that I need and the sweetmeats that are left for my pleasure are also tainted, are they not? With the witch no longer close by, who could accomplish such a deed and for what reason?"

Isabella appeared to be made ill at ease by the question, and for a moment averted her eyes, unable to offer Selina her straightforward countenance. But she wavered for a brief spell only before giving answer.

"I must own, 'twas I. When Sibylla departed in great haste, she left behind the concoction that she had brewed, and 'twas this I made use of in like fashion. I had need to know at once if you were such a one as the priest posited and thus able to enter into the Tapestry's thrall. I said nothing of this to either Abigail or the priest, 'twas my own scheme entirely born out of an impatience that I could not control.

"But in that regard you have reported nothing to either Abi or myself of any encounter. Have you then as yet no experience at all of its magic? I know 'tis feasible that Sibylla, who has overlaid its enchantment with her own spellbinding, might well seek to keep you out that you do not interfere with her casting."

Selina herself was now likewise reluctant to offer straight answer, for though she needed full knowing for the quest's sake, she was also yet mindful not to reveal all her own knowledge, for fear that her safety might not be highly regarded. 'Twas Allan that mattered, and if her life had to be exchanged in return for his she did not doubt that it would be done. Fifty years of frustrated yearning by far outweighed their short span of being acquainted. Thus, she answered in truthful but circumspect manner.

"The candles at first had me mesmerised, that I was

compelled to look upon the Tapestry, but found in so doing, that I may not look away. 'Twas only when I managed, with great effort, to close my eyes, that I was thus able to break the thrall. Then instead in other wise, the aroma they give off caused me to fall into a most prodigious slumber. 'Twould seem therefore that the enchantment that came as result of inhaling the smoke, or mayhap from eating the sweetmeats, caused either the ability to see beyond normal vision, as if dreaming whilst yet awake, or if that effect was frustrated, then to cast you into the opposite, a fathomless and dreamless losing of one's senses.

"Thereafter I was most cautious and lit but one or two of the candles, though it did seem that the flickering of the flames be almost as bewitching as the fragrance. But not knowing if such enrapturing be a good or bad thing, I deemed it the wiser choice to leave well alone. Tonight, I shall not."

Selina changed the subject then that she avoid further enquiry, for her mind was set on not revealing that she was indeed well versed in the world of the Tapestry, including encounters with the errant troubadour to whom she now referred.

"Abigail acquainted me also with the fact that a musician was given residence in the chamber in hope that he might be such a one as could breech the barrier, enter therein and find and rescue Allan. But she also gave me to understand that, like your lost husband, he too disappeared, leaving naught but an empty room, though 'twas in no wise clear if he was also trapped, or had simply made early departure."

Isabella gave forth a deep sigh.

"Yes, 'tis true that a young man was thus lost as you

suggest, but in which manner we cannot say. We had great hope that he was such a one as are you, but we could not inform him of our intent lest he refuse and depart forthwith. Nor did we know how we might instruct him, having of ourselves no inkling of how it might be done, for 'twas before the coming of my present priest. I prepared the sweetmeats and the candles, but other than that, I had no knowledge of anything else that I might do to make my intent become fact. If he did indeed become entrapped in the Tapestry then he must surely have had an encounter with Allan, and mayhap even yet between them they will discover the way out of the web. That such happy event has not so far come about would have me believe that 'twas alas most likely that he had never entered in. At the day's end, fatigued after much performing, and no doubt with his senses dulled by wine, 'tis most likely he did naught but sleep soundly and make an early start next morning.

"But be that as it may, if there is nothing else that you must speak on, let us proceed now to that which is most urgent – your own encounter with the Tapestry.

"Sibylla clearly has awareness of your coming, and that you are the one whose mission it is to undo her binding and set Allan free. She has no direct nor personal knowledge of who you are but kens you by a change in the atmosphere that has penetrated the stagnation that formerly ever held sway in and about the manor. She will, without doubt, seek to prevent your entry into the Tapestry, or mayhap will let you in but not back out again, so you are doomed to stay alongside Allan should you find him. And should you gain entry, then indeed you surely must find him, for he remains trapped there since our wedding day.

"All these things I have surmised along with the priest for he has far greater knowledge regarding the ways of witches, and he has counselled me as to what she might do to forestall Allan's liberation and our reunion.

"I have had you daily dress in such apparel as I myself would wear, thus if she is scrying she must suffer confusion, for 'twould be hard to tell us apart. This night I have selected a garment for you to wear as is a favourite of mine, and therefore much associated with me. Then should she have awareness that you are making an attempt to broach the Tapestry, she may be tricked into belief that it is me.

"For I, having none of the occult powers that are gifted to you and the priest, she will not be alerted to the same degree of vigilance, nor be on her guard in full engagement. Rather she will suppose I have managed to enter in with some magical impulse learnt from you and will be delighted at further opportunity to entrap me and finally seal my fate as was her intent all along.

"In this wise you will have more safety and freedom to do as you will undetected. I shall join the priest and spend the night in silent vigil under the cloak of holy protection, and in such sanctuary remain unassailable and unseen.

"The priest says 'tis you alone who can thwart her will, and that we must withdraw, for our presence would only interfere with what you can and must do. 'Twould dilute and confuse its power should we put ourselves in the way. What we might do is pray, and that will be our role and contribution. I will remain now in my chamber until this evening when I repair to the chapel with the priest. Abi prefers to stay within her own room. You will not see another soul now till this be ended and you come to us with good news or bad, or do not come at all. I leave you then to your own devices. A simple meal will be left in the hall at the usual time should you wish it."

She went to the door then and held it open, indicating she would have Selina take her leave.

As she passed by her on the way out, Isabella did not reach out to touch either a hand or shoulder in solidarity as she might have done, but rather said simply, "May all that is good and holy attend you."

Then she closed the door behind her, leaving Selina from thence on utterly on her own with none alongside to give her strength or encouragement. Standing alone on the landing before the fastened door, she felt at that moment as bereft and abandoned as when her parents had died. A time when, despite being in the midst of bereavement, she had been parcelled off to her grandmother's dwelling as if she was no more than a nuisance to be got rid of in the easiest manner.

Now here she was, facing a witch who might do far worse than send her to a place devoid of human warmth. And there was not a one to guide or protect her, to insist she should not engage with such spellbinding lest she come off the worse. Neither mother nor father to refuse to permit their beloved daughter a confrontation that was both dangerous and foolhardy. She owned then that she had never felt more like the motherless child she was.

And though she was much caught up in the tragic befalling of Isabella and Allan, there was no doubt in her mind that she was no more to Isabella and Abigail and mayhap the priest too than an instrument that they could use. Their utter desperation, fired with the fervid hope that she might possibly be the one to deliver them, left no spare capacity to embrace concern for her own wellbeing. Had not Isabella just said that she may return with good news or bad or indeed not at all, yet they did not hold back on that account. 'Twas a desolate thing.

Once again, the notion to refuse a mission that might go badly wrong brought to mind her pledge to feel no obligation to remain in a place or situation that was not in her own best interests. She had been sent to her grandmother without consultation and from thence here in like manner. She owed no loyalty then to a placement that was arranged in no way for her own benefit and indeed might, for all she knew, be the death of her.

And now assuredly, with Isabella, the priest and the chatelaine all confined to their separate quarters till the morrow 'twould be the ideal time to seek departure. In the face of a danger that she must confront entirely on her own and which she did not know whether she would be overwhelmed by, why would she not?

Even as she rehearsed such a pledge in her mind, she knew 'twas folly, for whatever the consequences, the choice was already made. She would do this.

And 'twas not just for Tristram's sake alone, though that was much to do with it, neither was it a compelling entirely for the freeing of Isabella and Allan, despite that also being a powerful motive. 'Twas because there was none other could do this save herself alone. She knew it was so, for had she not felt the power surge through her in encounter with the spellbinder? Thus, it was inevitable, for you could not permit evil to thrive should you be the one that might stop it. It must be confronted and challenged and hopefully vanquished for no other reason than should you not 'twas as bad as giving it free rein. With the acknowledgement that, no matter the consequences, in this she had no choice other than acceptance, finally came calm and resolution.

She left the landing then and returned to the hall, and finding there that the table be not yet been cleared, gathered the scattered crumbs from the bread that lay about and other morsels of cheese and the like into her skirt to take to the birds for their midday dining. For she knew she would spend much of this time of waiting in the garden. Her own garden of old had been her sanctuary, now so too was this, and as blessed a place to be as any church.

Seated on the stone bench, she watched with pleasure and gratitude the birds which had come at once at sight of her. They filled their beaks with as much as was possible to fit therein, lest when they return from their nests 'twas all gone. And thus engaged, seemed in no wise tempted to first fill themselves with such wholesome fare. She marvelled then that sacrifice seemed to be so prevalent in all species. She and they offered themselves simply because they were compelled by instinct or impulse so to do. A moment's pause maybe to consider other options soon abandoned, an aberrant deviation from the inevitable. And yet, should their nestlings safely fledge, and should she, against all the odds, free both Tristram and Allan, would not that prove that unstinting commitment to a cause was our noblest impulse?

Nevertheless, she must admit, such brave stance was of little use in the circumstances; for if Allan could not first be found, how could he be rescued? In his own two-year sojourn in the Tapestry, Tristram had no awareness at all that he was also somewhere therein. And, as he had said, it did not seem possible that should he be, they would not have had encounter.

And if he was discovered, would he perhaps, as Abigail feared, no longer be able to find his feet in the world he had left behind? For whilst time in the Tapestry stood ever still, here things had moved on by near half a century. He must confront such news as his parents being long dead and nothing as it was. Isabella forced to live in isolation, and of those he had known full well, few still remaining thereabouts. For with her father's death, herself withdrawn and most departed, the manor no longer functioned as a thriving domain and 'twas just the working community left.

But such speculation was looking too far ahead, enough to think of finding him first and then the way out. And who knew what new thralls the sorceress had conjured that must be faced in addition to what was already operative? Aware that her supremacy was about to be challenged, she must certainly be prepared in readiness.

Selina raised her hand and grasped and held the gold cross for a moment, finding strength and certainty in what it represented. Whatever the Source of All be, she spoke to it now in simple terms of all that lay ahead of her, and what she had need of that her aim be accomplished. She besought the angels, the saints and Lucius to come to her assistance, and all those known and unknown in the spirit world as could help.

She stayed thus, lost in contemplation till the chapel bell, tolling five, announced day's end and called all back home from their labours. Her own were just about to begin.

Chapter Seventeen

Returned to the hall, Selina sat but a short span at table and partook of naught but water; to eat must of a certain dull her senses when she had need of unburdened clarity.

There was no posy by her setting this eve, and she had some small sorrow that it was missing for 'twould have seemed a good omen. But it minded her that she was on her own entirely in what lay before her, and 'twas the wiser thing not to forget the fact. Flora and Jacob had no notion that she was in such a situation as she was. Besides, looking for strength anywhere other than within herself could but weaken her now.

And what role Tristram might play could not be foreseen, and whether she would have need to watch over him as protector as well as look to herself. For he, perceiving her as having otherworldly endowments, might well continue to cast her in the role of guide and guardian angel. And he was a musician after all, not a knight or a soldier. Well as always, time alone would tell.

She left the table and the hall then, but first took from their holders the candles that were set about there, for she would not let Sibylla's tainted wares play any further part. And she had an inkling by dint of her own newfound inner wisdom that she would be able to enter into the Tapestry without need of recourse to witching aromas; it could be achieved by naught other than her own willing.

She ascended the stairs with a somewhat stolid tread till she attained the landing. Pausing there, she listened out for any sound, even though unsure if evidence of Isabella, Abigail or the priest close by would be reassuring. Though their prayers must be a good thing at least, she took comfort in that, there was naught to be heard from behind their chamber doors, neither cough nor footfall, all being as quiet as the grave – though please God that be not prophetic.

Entering her own chamber, if such it could be called, she closed the door behind her, wondering if those others listened out for sounds of herself as assiduously. With all dependent on her actions this night, they were surely obliged to hearken for any evidence of what transpired, however indirect.

She beheld at once Isabella's gown draped carefully over the back of the chair in readiness. 'Twas the purple velvet with girdle that fastened about the hips. She looked upon it, then immediately away, for, despite Isabella's reasoning, she knew beyond all doubt that she would not clothe herself in this garment. She had other plans.

The jester's costume was now finished enough to be worn. Though the seams were not bound and neatly presented, a fact as would have caused her grandmother consternation at such evidence of slipshod work, 'twas only apparent should you peer within. Without, all appeared in good order and was certainly most arresting to gaze upon, with the vivid colouring, sumptuous fabrics and striking patterning. As was her intention, it was a feast for the eye indeed and 'twas in this costume she would be arrayed this coming night, and, though it was subterfuge, such a disguise must also attract attention, thus she would be paradoxically hid in plain sight. And with the mask over her eyes and her hair tucked into the cap, none would perceive that it was she. Thus, she would pass unrecognised, and onlookers must indeed take presentation as fact and suppose 'twas a young fellow they have witness of.

Should Sibylla have the ability to see into the Tapestry, though she may have suspicions that Isabella would attempt such a ploy in hope to deceive her, she might not expect a less simple change of apparel, and with it also, gender.

There was something magical too in the fact that the costume was entirely her own work. From idea to design and construction, none other had a hand in it, nor knew of its existence. 'Twas a secret well-kept till this day.

She took up position then before the Tapestry, the backs of her legs pressed hard against the end of the bed to achieve best focus. Gazing upon it now before the witching hour was come, all looked innocent enough, no more than a tribute to the gift of art and design as made manifest in Lucius's creation. Yet before this coming night yielded to the morrow, 'twould see the struggle between the sorceress and herself played out to a finality. Like the affray 'tween Alfred and Allan, there would be no quarter given. But in this battle, there could afterward be no negotiation regarding the freeing of hostages, nor peace talks, nor bargaining of any kind, just a totality, all or nothing. There was no middle ground.

But her earlier despair was entirely vanquished now, and all that remained was a particular stillness, like a knight before the affray, who having spent the hours 'twixt dusk and dawn kneeling at the altar in prayer and contemplation, knows he is as prepared as is possible to be.

Nor could it be otherwise, for any weakness would be registered and made use of by the adversary. Sorcerers found entry into the soul's centre through the gateway of fear, and having once achieved access 'twas like the maggot in the apple, with all become rotten at the core.

Her armour against such invasion was the strength of her resolve and a stout heart that did not quail before any bedevilling witchery, however fearsome. Such brave stance would be tested soon enough, and again, only time would prove if it was more than mere vain rhetoric.

As the light began to fade, the twilight that came in its stead brought with it a shift in the chamber's atmosphere. The clear delineation between all that was in the space softened and blurred, as if their edges became less certain. 'Twas the time to prepare and Selina shed her gown and shift and took up the jester's costume.

The leggings were of good fit but not so tight that they betrayed that she was female, and also they had sufficient give should action be called for. The tunic, constructed with the same reasoning, ended at mid-thigh and was of looser fit, though not so much as to flap about in hindrance. The cap, with padded horns but devoid of bells, covered her head, closely keeping her hair well contained, and the mask, fashioned from cloth of gold, hid her face in entirety save for her mouth and chin. Holding her silver mirror up to have regard of the effect, she hardly recognised herself and was well satisfied that it was so.

That the jester was likewise known as the joker or trickster also gave her a pleasing sense of employing guile, for she was thus playing the spellbinder at her own game. Sibylla was the sly and devious one by nature of who she was, and would not suppose she ran any risk of encountering the same connivance.

Ready and dressed for that confrontation, she sat in waiting upon the bedside chair, having first folded Isabella's gown and stored it safely away in the chest, for it had no part to play in what was to come and be best hid. Having some while before the encroaching dark signalled that the time was upon them, she used it to her profit. She made a silent but urgent entreaty to Lucius that he bring all such power as he had to aid her endeavour to save Tristram and Allan, for their containment was against his good intent. 'Twas the evil will of a spellbinder, who, having caused great pain and despair, sought this night to seal her loathsome deeds by eternally binding innocent souls in the confines of his sublime work. She deliberately phrased her intersession in such words as Allan had used in his passion, for they had proved effective in undoing half the curse. Mayhap the remaining half of the spell-breaking might be forthcoming from those other great souls she also begged for deliverance.

Set on the chair in waiting, for heaven indeed only knew what, brought her remembrance of doing likewise at the door of her grandmother's dwelling before Jacob had come to fetch her here. As she did then, she had no knowing of what lay ahead of her, or what manner of trials she might be called upon to endure. But even though her dreams had forewarned her, she certainly had not supposed it be anything like this and if she saw then the truth of them, she must surely have fled away there and then.

But Isabella, Abigail and the priest were of one mind in their certainty – that there never was such a choice, only surety that this was her destiny. If that truly was the fact of the matter, then it would have been impossible to run away, or in any other wise frustrate or evade that which by spiritual decree had named her as the only candidate for the task. Like Isabella contemplating the marriage contract, she was more than half persuaded that it was so, for had she not felt the power come into her without her bidding? And Tristram too had beheld an aura about her that he believed marked her out as in league with the angels. Well maybe, but even if 'twas true, did it really matter in any case? For if there was something wicked wrought by ill wishing, and she mayhap could thwart its dire intent in any way, that was what mattered. You did it because you could, and if you could, then 'twas simple enough – you must.

The time between light, twilight and dark was of swift passing, for it was of the same duration as it took the sun to go from heaven to earth and below. And as it went to earth like a creature to its lair at end of day, alongside the sudden loss of light, a chill was come for it was still but early spring. Selina shivered a little in her jester's clouts, for they were of fine fabric, not intended for keeping out the cold. Mayhap too, the shiver that thrilled through her had a source other than the seasonal nightly drop in temperature. Perhaps it be an auger of the spellbinder drawing nigh.

She checked carefully that all be correct with cap and mask, and laid the gold cross outside the tunic against her heart, reassured by its solid weight; her talisman was no flimsy ornament. Then, certain all was in as good an order as possible, she stepped forward till she was again before the Tapestry. For though it was not yet come to life, she was in urgent need to test if she could gain entry without the candles' mesmerising thrall, and with naught to serve her save her own strength of purpose. Nevertheless, she had no choice other than to contain herself in waiting till the moment of its awakening came, for none could gain admittance before then.

She felt it as it happened, and at that self-same moment she asked again of Lucius that he allowed her entry for he knew her mission. She spoke but softly, having no wish to be heard by other than he, and was gifted straightaway with a strong and certain sense, that wherever he was, she indeed had his ear.

She strode forward then boldly, in no wise sure she would do anything other than have hard meeting with the chamber wall, but, closing her eyes for the brief moment necessary, lo, when she opened them she was through the divide and standing on the sward, and it had been most easily done.

There, however, she nearly did have collision with Tristram who was coming in urgent haste to meet her. He halted in confusion at sight of her for he knew not who she was. Thus, before she enlightened him, she was assured that her appearance was all she had hoped and intended.

In recounting the reason for her costume, she at once instructed him as to all that had taken place this day; that the witch Sibylla had awareness of her and her quest to release Allan from his long entrapment within the Tapestry. Thus, of a certainty, she would be in a fury that any dare try to unbind her casting, and she would do everything in her power to thwart such endeavour. 'Twas her avowed purpose to keep him locked within for all eternity, and Selina and Isabella with him, if by her sorcery she snared them too in their vain and foolish attempt to rescue him.

The confrontation would happen this night, and already she would be in no doubt, peering into her crystal ball or whatever else she used for such purpose, that she might discover where they were in the web and what they were doing that she could spellbind them.

Tristram, taken aback by all he heard, and in having sudden awareness that the situation was changed to such degree, asked in perplexity, "But he is not here, there can be little doubt regarding that. For had he been, as I have said, I most certainly would have had encounter with him."

Selina shook her head.

"He must be, for when by Lucius's will, Isabella was cast out of this place, in that same moment, by Sibylla's will, Allan was cast back in. And by her witchery she has kept him here these many long years. That you have had neither awareness nor knowledge of him means no more than that, and it is for us to find where he is as quickly as we may."

Tristram responded, still in confusion, "But even if that were in some wise possible, we still have to find out how he and I escape, for neither of us have any idea how it might be done. A fact painfully obvious since we are both still here."

"That you are here and unable to find release is not by Sibylla's will, for she has no interest in you nor what befalls you. Your entrapment is but an accident as far as she is concerned, and thus she will not be seeking to ascertain where you are nor in what wise engaged. This means you avoid detection in all you do, at first anyhow, and likewise, 'tis hoped with myself also, for she must look for a maid dressed as such, yet not like unto those others created by the weaver. And should her eye fall upon a jester, she be wont to think mayhap he must be fashioned by Lucius and pay no more heed."

Tristram was neither convinced nor reassured.

"But of what merit is it if we avoid her gaze, for it will be of no help in finding Allan, supposing he is still here after nigh on fifty years? Nor does it help us discover how we quit this place."

"What will help us in both matters is Lucius and the good angels who see all and from whom nothing can be hid. Let us entreat them now that they lead us first to that place where Allan has been erstwhile held, that we might attain him, and then to the secret portal through which we may depart."

She took firm hold of the troubadour's hand then that she might hearten him, for in so doing she hoped to likewise hearten herself. Again, she spoke in quiet tones lest others hear that had no business in so doing. She stated their need for answers to those two questions and that their call for aid would not go unheard but rather come speedily, and with it protection from a witch who was hell-bent on the opposite outcome.

The garlanded dancers and musicians surrounded them then as was their wont, for Selina was an arresting figure in her kaleidoscope of colours and could not escape their attention. So they, as ever, sweetly insisted that she join with them, and even though they were deceived into belief that she was a youth, it made no matter. For they, being without curiosity as to her identity and circumstance, had only the single wish, to sing and dance and take pleasure in all the delights of their paradise and pull herself and Tristram with them into joyous revelry.

Selina saw then there was an advantage in being in their midst, for 'twould render them as but part of the weaver's creation, whereas to stand forth alone as individuals must draw the penetrating gaze of the sorceress.

She cast her own penetrating gaze about her then, and alerted her senses to any prompting that might come from such sources as she had solicited. In once more asking to be shown where Allan could be found, answer came with her eye being unerringly directed towards the foothills, in particular to a place where the tree line ended and the woods gave way to the mountains. She marked the spot in her mind – 'twas alongside a silver spruce of greater height than those others round about it.

Turning then to Tristram, she told him that she had an apprehension that 'twas in that area they would find Allan, but he must ever argue the point.

"What would he be doing there by himself these long years? It is a truth that we have no need to eat in this place, though we can if we wish taste the abundant fruits that are ever in perfect ripeness and most delicious. But we do not hunger as such, for it is not necessary to sustain ourselves as in the other real world. Thus, wherever he was, Allan would not starve from want of food nor drink, nor suffer from any such lack. But what he would assuredly have great need of, like unto myself, be human contact. Lest it be in his case, that being withdrawn here such a great length of years, he has given up all hope and become as reclusive and hid away as a hermit. If 'twere thus, maybe he has become so changed he is no longer himself, and now has no wish to be found and liberated.

"For, when in the beginning I betook myself to the place you indicate, I found no sign or trace of any other person dwelling there, either like unto myself, or to the inhabitants of the Tapestry. There were but some few animals in evidence, those for which such habitat is natural to their species and therefore to their liking, but there were none other."

Selina again insisted, "Tis where we are bid go if my promptings are not amiss, but in any case we must start our search somewhere so let it be there. Now go fetch your mandore for we must entice our companions to accompany us at least part of the way that thus we be lost amongst them, and not made conspicuous by our actions or our singularity."

When Tristram returned with his instrument she bade him strike up as merry a tune as was in his repertoire. And when in compliance he had the instrument's baldric slung about his shoulder, at once he applied skilled and agile fingers to the strings, plucking from them effortlessly a riot of tumbling notes in glorious profusion. She asked of him then to make his way up towards the lower slopes of the woods. And as he stepped out in sprightly fashion, she grasped the hands of those on either side and had them join with her and dance to the compelling rhythm he brought forth, and with which he enticed them after him. All about them became caught up and beguiled by the lively air, and joined with them, drawn in train behind Tristram and his delightful game of 'Follow my leader'. Soon, therefore, a cheerful, laughing throng was wending its way up the gradually increasing incline till they reached the wood's edge.

'Twas here though that a strange happening was brought about, for it seemed they encountered an unseen, but nevertheless potent barrier that stayed them in their tracks. As they approached the trees, all, like unto a shoal of fish or a flock of birds, turned about in complete accord and returned the way they came. Still in full merriment, they would take Selina and Tristram with them, but when the two refused to be so persuaded, they gently released their hands and danced away from them, leaving them where they were. Whereupon their own musicians picked up the melody that they might continue on in happy procession.

Clearly they belonged wholly in the Eden that had its setting round and about the stream in the lower reaches. The woods were no part of it, and they, being not in their element in such a strange place, must find it as alien as would a fish out of water. Of necessity therefore, they were compelled to return to their own domain where they were at ease.

Selina and Tristram watched them go for but a moment's span, before she pulled him quickly in amongst the trees that they be hid from sight. Though how well they might hide from Sibylla's crystal ball discerning, she could not tell. No doubt the closer they came to where Allan was, the more she would be alerted, for her focus would be bound to concentrate most particularly on that place. But Selina dared not slacken her own guard, because thus far the sorceress had not revealed her hand. Such lack of activity meant only that she bided her time.

And though they were hidden for now perhaps, they too must eventually show their own hand. For should they find Allan and discover in what manner he was held that they might undo his spellbinding, 'twould be only then they see what such action provoked. Of a surety it must bring her into manifestation, and at that moment they would encounter the witch face to face. There be no hiding then for she or they.

Selina had no Excalibur, and Tristram had but a mandore. And though he was adept at charming and enrapturing a willing audience, he was wont to find such sweet skill of little use in a contest employing harsher and more absolute extremes of bewitching.

But Selina was not without weaponry, nor was she powerless. She had her blessed talisman, and alongside her and at her back were all those she had sought in the spiritual realms to answer her call to arms. And added unto them, she had the intersession of the fervent prayers of those in the manor. She had Tristram, and, should they find him, Allan too. And he was as she had heard tell, skilled in the martial arts and fully aware of his aunt's treachery. Therefore, if indeed he was within the web, his faculties and fitness would be as keen as ever they were, for nothing here was anything less than perfect no matter how many years had passed. Though in what wise physical prowess might fare in combat with sorcery was uncertain, at least he was bound to be in as much full fury as was Sibylla. The suffering she had caused to his new wife, Isabella, his parents and Alfred must righteously enrage him, and the need for retaliation and recompense be every bit and more, as powerful a motivation as was her ill willing.

All these things Selina surely had, but just as she knew not what Allan might achieve by the strength of resolve alone, neither did she know what she herself was capable of. For as that resource in her had leapt forth only in response to confrontation, 'twas clear it lay dormant till it was needed, being meanwhile an unknown quantity. Nor did she have cognisance of what devious or demonic devices Sibylla could call forth in like manner.

'Twas the time to find out.

CHAPTER EIGHTEEN

Now left to themselves, Selina and Tristram set out in earnest on their mission. Employing caution and vigilance in equal measure, they entered into the dense woodland, which, though it was filled with stately trees of diverse kinds, was nevertheless in no wise dark. Rather it was infused with golden light, as if each leaf acted as a reflector to the perpetual sunlight above. Treading with care over chamomile and other sweet herbs as carpeted the ground, they avoided as best they could the making of any sound or the causing of any disturbance, lest they betrayed themselves. And as they journeyed towards that place she had been shown, they were also obliged to halt every few paces to look and listen for any sight or sound that would indicate a presence other than their own. In so doing, Selina strived to bring all her senses into acute awareness, that if aught be amiss it must immediately capture her attention. She found nothing to alert or alarm her, but 'twas not easy to have expectation of foul deeds in a place of such perfection.

Mayhap all of Sibylla's focus be centred precisely around the place where Allan was hidden away and she wasted neither time nor energy in watching elsewhere. Perhaps then 'twould only be when they came into her field of vision that she would strike. All the more reason then that they be not caught unaware, for to be dealt a crippling blow at the outset, even if 'twere not a mortal one, could leave them disabled and the quest likewise impaired or even rendered fruitless.

When they at last emerged safely from the wood at the top edge of the tree line, though Tristram was silent all the while, Selina still held up her hand in warning that he neither speak nor make any sound. She saw before her then the larch that was the given marker, and while they remained still hid under the canopy of golden leaves, she peered ahead that she might discern some further pointer as to where Allan might be.

At once her attention was drawn to a place behind the majestic larch where a rocky outcrop jutted out from the mountain's base, and within it, half concealed by trailing creeper, she could just make out the entrance to a cave. She knew of a certainty by the tingling shock at her nerve endings that they had found that for which they sought. There could be no doubt that Allan was therein.

Taking hold of Tristram's elbow, she pointed to the cave and whispered in his ear that this was their goal. But they must somehow attain it without arousing the witch's attention, though how such a thing might be done she did not know. However, Tristram signalled that he did.

Round and about of where they stood were many pretty little pebbles that had tumbled down from the mountain slopes. They lay about in colourful profusion beneath the primroses and on the moss that clothed the gnarled roots of the ancient trees. He proposed that should they gather some of their number and toss them well off to one side or another 'twould draw the witch's attention for long enough that they gain entry to the cave. Selina had great uncertainty that such was the case, but, there being no other plan that she could offer in its stead, agreed, and bent at once to pick up two handfuls, and in so doing gave herself no time to think further and change her mind.

They discharged their burden well away towards their left, and the polished stones produced a merry clatter as they came down upon their target. And at the very beginning of the sound they made, Selina and Tristram raced across the narrow divide that separated them from the cave mouth, stooped low and as noiselessly as possible in all haste. Selina was painfully aware even as she hurtled forth that the jester's costume, while it served well in concealing her identity, was hard to hide of itself, and with its vivid colouring was wont to stick out like a sore thumb.

Pulling aside the long strands of creeper that hung like a beaded curtain across the entrance they dived within, whereupon at once it fell back into place after them as if it had not been disturbed. There being no lack of head space within, they stood upright and turned about and the light that came from without was plenty enough to see all about them.

The cave floor was strewn with soft hay, which emitted a warm fragrance, and at the back 'twas piled high enough to suffice as a sleeping platform.

And thereupon, stretched out and soundly sleeping, lay a young man. He was dressed in very fine raiment, not in garb as would be donned for night-time repose. His hair was exceedingly fair, and round his neck was fastened an intricately carved gemstone on a leather thong. They had no doubt that they had found Allan, still arrayed in his wedding clothes and full fast asleep as he had been for nigh on fifty years.

Could he be woken, or was he so deep in torpor that he was indeed lost to the world?

Selina went to him and studied him close by. His breath came and went in easy rhythm, and, when she bent towards him, she could feel it warm upon her face. Here he lay undisturbed this great length of time, resting on his side with one hand tucked beneath his cheek and one knee raised in a position many adopt as they settle for the night. He did not stir. Tentatively, she touched his shoulder.

He startled then to such degree that she instinctively jumped backward, for he woke on the instant, and straightaway sat up and regarded both herself and Tristram behind her with surprise. Taking note of the jester costume and the mandore, he asked, "Are you players from the wedding party, and how come I to be here? Where is Isabella? Is this some game we all play but in which for some reason I have succumbed to sleep? Come, I must return to her at once."

Then he came fully to himself and let out a low moan.

"Ah! Now I do recall all that overtook us. We fell foul of Sibylla's witchery and her scheme to have us lost forever in the Tapestry. I called out to Lucius to set us free but I remember no more thereafter. 'Tis clear, is it not, that alongside being lost in the Tapestry, I have not had natural slumber, but further entrancement that rendered me helpless. And if I have been thus afflicted, what might have happened to Isabella? Are we both still trapped here in the Tapestry? For if she is also here, I must find her at once, lest she be in some grave peril wrought by the sorceress."

At which point he leapt from the bed of hay to his feet with all the agility and vigour he had before he fell into the witching swound those long years ago. For it seemed there was no mark or legacy of confusion in either mind or body.

Selina calmed him then, assuring him that Isabella was fine and well and in no danger.

Then she relayed in full detail all that had happened since their entrapment. And being such a long and sorry tale, it must surely cast him into a turmoil of shock and bewilderment – a condition it would seem at first he had fortuitously escaped.

But 'twas no false dawn, he was dumbstruck for hardly longer than it took to tell the story, then in every wise fully informed he was immediately ready to go forth with alacrity. Ablaze with zeal and charged with avowed intent, he swore at once an oath to dispatch the sorceress, for though she be kin she had sold her soul to the devil. Thus, the long years of enforced inactivity fell away from him in but a moment's space as easily as if they had never been, or mayhap being the very reason he now eschewed all patience.

Again, Selina calmed and warned him.

"I feel full sure by my own apprehension that the witch also be roused and wide awake, for she can tell by her crystal gazing that we have found you, and even now are with you, here in the cave. Of a certainty then, she will strike as soon as we come forth from here. I know not in what manner she will employ her witchcraft, but that 'twill be fearsome

I do not doubt, and we are in grave danger should we do anything reckless or foolhardy.

"Though it is hard, perhaps, for you to be advised and led by a female, I promise you, 'tis I who can best oppose her and match her in counter magic. I know this of a surety, so hearken to me at all times and do not act alone, impelled by your own urging."

Tristram nodded acceptance at once. Allan looked unconvinced but agreed in principle.

'Please, God,' she prayed. 'Grant that he does nothing that will confound us all.'

She went forward to the mouth of the cave then, that whilst being screened from view by the curtain of creeper, she may discover what transpired without. But as she came close to the entrance, she felt of a sudden that she had an encounter with a wall of ice so bitter cold that it froze her in the moment, and she became incapable of further movement.

Then, whilst Tristram and Allan were likewise rooted to the spot, came a tumultuous roaring, and the ground beneath their feet began a fierce trembling that grew ever more violent. For the sound accompanied a quaking that would seem to rattle their very bones, and when both reached an extreme that was nigh on unbearable to bodies or ears, then they also came to their climax. And the roof of the cave creaked and groaned and heaved and yawed like unto a barque being wrecked in a storm at sea. It was surely the case that the very mountain was coming apart, and in its splitting asunder must tumble down in great descent on top of them in an all-consuming avalanche. Indeed, 'twas like unto the end of the world.

But 'twas not, for at last it ceased and all was still and quiet again.

Selina, staggering a little as she struggled to regain her feet and her balance, knew full well what she would find when she looked out from the cave to see what had come to pass.

In fact, there was naught at all to be seen, for the view was entirely blocked. As much as Selina could tell, they were entirely trapped within by the great boulders that piled up in front and all around.

They were entombed. Sibylla had succeeded in burying them alive.

When Tristram and Allan also had their balance returned to them, they too came at once to see what havoc the witch had wrought, there to find she had done nothing less than bring the mountain down upon their heads. Now, like a corked bottle, they were sealed and tight-fastened in the cave.

Yet 'twas not dark – the cave was somehow filled with light.

Sibylla, it seemed, could corrupt the perfect peace and beauty of the Tapestry with her sorcery, overriding its tranquility with her own evil intent, but not totally. She was not able to extinguish the light which of its very essence be white, just as her defining mode and colour be dark. Thus, even yet, they were still well able to discern their situation.

Allan and Tristram both pushed and pulled at the boulders that pressed hard against the mouth of the cave, only to discover, of course, that it availed them nothing. The boulders were as immovable as Sibylla had intended, and all attempts to dislodge them pathetic in their futility. But they gave thanks that they had the light. That was good, for 'twould be a dire thing should they be not only entombed, but also in pitch blackness as would properly be the case.

Whilst Tristram and Allan searched about in the further reaches of the cave, lest there were other tunnels leading off that were a way out, Selina remained where she was. Stood at the blocked entrance, she was attentive to her own awakening, for she felt it stirring to life within her.

When the witch made her formidable ability manifest in the pitching of seismic bolts of thunder and lightning that caused the mountain to erupt, she could not fail to also activate the opposing powers. And those spiritual presences which Selina called upon spontaneously in the instant, were in complete accord with that which had ever dwelt within her – the ancient wisdom incubated till it be needed. Alerted now, it was roused like Allan into immediate preparedness after long dormancy.

With her first strike, the sorceress ignited the fuse that connected the two extremes of opposite intent. And once lit, the wick must burn on and cannot be extinguished till the spitting flame finally runs its course and turns either to the left or to the right in explosive conclusion. Now begun, it was unstoppable, and Selina had comprehension that in its happening she became more than herself. She was guided and directed by that which was beyond her conscious control, but nevertheless was so full well recognised and acknowledged that she surrendered willingly to its directive.

And thereupon, she felt some part of herself leave her body, as if it went out through the top of her head, and she found she was flying free over the mountains. Laid out below her she could see the whole of the land of the

Tapestry. She beheld the stream and all those who had followed after Tristram up the hill gathered there still in their never-ending and never-tiring merriment. And she saw the animals amongst them to their mutual pleasure. Then her eye was compelled to that higher place where there were but two animals who stood in watch over all. Majestic and magnificent in their dazzling white coats, the great stag, his head crowned with many branched antlers, and the stallion. But then she saw that the stallion was no horse, 'twas a unicorn – the long, spiralled horn that adorned its forehead was as dazzling as if 'twere made of pure diamond. Even though she was high above them, she could see they both were of great size and powerfully built, and she was in awe of such strength and beauty. But then they raised their heads and looked up and 'twas clear that they could see her, even though she could not see herself. And they bowed their heads in acknowledgement, but what did they acknowledge?

In answer she next saw that there was a figure beside them. Slight in contrast so that at first she was not aware of him, but it was he as stood in command of them. Elderly, he was wrapped in a dark blue cloak that had depictions of the moon and stars woven into its fabric. His hair worn long and as white as the mythic beasts, was parted in the centre and he had a beard of the same hue and length that also was parted in the middle. She knew he was Lucius. He beckoned her to come to him, and she descended till she alighted like a bird at his side.

Close to, she saw he was not tall, but in every wise stately and imposing. The many lines upon his face were clearly etched and the weave in the stuff of his cloak plain to see, and there were the intricate designs of astral symbols sewn in gold into the woollen cloth. He looked like unto Merlin, but despite the richness of detail she saw in front of her, she knew he was not truly present. Lucius had departed from this realm and any other of an earthly plane. He was a phantom, but none the less real for all that. And was she not such herself, for of a certainty her corporeal body remained back in the cave?

Lucius greeted her.

"'Tis a good and timely thing that you have come at last. Prince Allan's enthrallment has caused me much pain these long years of its duration. For though it happened in the Tapestry which was of my making, it seems I cannot remedy that which is against my will. This vile deed you alone can resolve, and though it is in no wise an easy task nor of assured outcome, it can be done if all goes aright.

"'Tis said, and rightly so, that hell hath no fury like a woman scorned, and such a one is Sibylla. Over the many years her stance has not softened, but rather like a usurer's interest, it has increased till it be impossible to meet the cost of all that she considers her due. Whatever she exacts in extortion can never be enough to satisfy her insatiable demands.

"For my part, what I can contribute to your redemptive quest is the qualities and purposes of these noble animals, the stag and the unicorn. I had them made to keep watch as sentries, for all domains, however perfect they be, have need of overseers to act as watchers and minders. They have formidable powers that mayhap they never need bring into use, but if that need does arise they are ready and they were well schooled in their employment. Though they were of gentle temperament as are all here, if called upon to be otherwise they have the brute force of the great beasts they are. I place them now under your control with the giving of the two bells that summon them – the gold calls on the stag, the silver on the unicorn."

He handed her then two small bells, their clappers bound about with soft padding that they remain silent when not needed. Selina put one in each pocket of her jester's tabard, and, as soon as 'twas done, she found herself rushing up and away at dizzying speed, faster than she could bear witness to, till, with a shock, she came back into the self she had left behind her in the cave.

And, strangely, it seemed no time at all had passed. Tristram and Allan were still at the back of the cave in search of an alternate way out, and she was before the entrance in the same pose that hitherto she undoubtedly had been.

She called them to her, and told them to look no further for the answer was found. They came as bid, puzzled and uncertain as to what she meant. She did not trouble herself to explain that she had just had a meeting with Lucius, for 'twould take unnecessary time, and time was limited and precious with all needing to be accomplished before dawn. And, as they had no knowing of what yet lay ahead, it must not be squandered but used judiciously that they have enough to spare.

"I have the ability to call on the help and strength we have need of. There being but the one entrance with no possibility of moving the boulders from this side, 'tis clear they can only be moved away by endeavour from the outside."

Allan and Tristram questioned then what help she could call on, for she seemed to talk in riddles.

For answer, she took from her pocket the golden bell and removed the padding that silenced it, then she shook it back and forth with due thoroughness that it gave forth its sound. But its chime was of low note and not the rousing tone she might have supposed. She was minded then that magic was, of its nature, secret and hidden, not like a trumpeting horn calling troops to the advance.

But before Tristram and Allan could demand explanation, the response to the bell's summons was at once plain for all to hear, and it informed them that deliverance was at hand.

For there was a loud racket without of rocks moving and shifting in vigorous manner, and the clash of what sounded like pikestaffs hitting against the solid boulders. 'Twas abundantly clear to the young men in their listening that rescue had come, but in what shape or form, if those others who dwelt here would not venture into the woods or beyond? Besides, such activity was not within their scope or apprehension. They knew naught of entrapment or ill will.

But soon enough they discovered the identity of their deliverer, for a gaping hole appeared in the piled boulders at the cave's entrance, which revealed not only the blue sky and yellow sun, but the massive antlers of the stag as he thrust them beneath the fallen rocks, tossing them aside as if they were no more than feather cushions. In less time than it took them to get over their amazement, the way was made clear that they might come out without hindrance.

His task completed, the stag stood before Selina in all quietness. She was his mistress now that she had the bell, and he waited on her to honour her wishes.

Standing in the entrance with Tristram and Allan close behind, like the stag she also waited and did not at once come forth. For first she must hearken to her inner promptings, that she sensed what the witch was presently doing, and whether 'twas safe to leave the cave. But assurance was given to her that all was calm within and without. Sibylla was not currently active. Mayhap she was licking her wounds, for her scheme had proved faulty and had achieved nothing. She may also need to rebuild her psychic energy before she was able to strike again, a fact that gave them temporary respite. Selina moved out freely then into open space. All was safe and well, for the moment anyway. Tristram and Allan followed after, full glad to be free of the cave's confines.

Selina approached the stag then. So huge he was, she reached not even to his shoulder. The great head above her was crowned with a broad spread of antlers that reached out so wide that they were like the branches of a mature oak, though they certainly were fashioned from harder stuff.

She told him with thanksgiving that he had given great service, and they owed him much, but now he may stand down and go back to his post alongside the unicorn. For, having freed them from entombment, he had done that which was required of him and he was no longer obliged to wait on them. Should he be needed again, she would summon him as hitherto.

He bowed his head in obedience, leaping away then as bidden down through the woods, dazzling in his brilliance, and with such sure-footed grace as denied his prodigious size. When he was gone, Selina wrapped the muffler around the bell's clapper and returned it to her pocket.

With Lucius's help, the first half of their mission was accomplished. They had found and liberated Allan. Now what remained was to discover how they could be liberated from the Tapestry, for the one be of no use without the other.

Chapter Nineteen

Following after the stag, Selina and Tristram, now accompanied by Allan, retraced footsteps that but a short while ago they trod in reverse. This time however they had no need to creep with stealth that they make no sound, for with Sibylla, like unto the stag, presently stood down, such caution was not required.

If it seemed the sorceress must withdraw for a span to rebuild her waning powers, restoring them back to full capacity, they knew it can be but a temporary respite. For having failed in her first attempt, in her next strike she surely intended to garner and unleash all the devilry that was in her power to conjure and project a maelstrom of dark matter into whatever shape or form she so chose. And if she was capable of moving mountains 'twould in no wise be a small endeavour. But for now, free from her malevolent attention, they made the most of her withdrawal, for it was essential to find with all due haste how Tristram and Allan might escape from the Tapestry.

They were all in agreement that the obvious place to seek

for the way out was the way in. That was beyond dispute with Selina having free passage in its usage, but not so Allan and Tristram. They were constrained by a binding that caused an impenetrable but invisible barrier to seal them tight within the web. Though 'twas not in like manner as they were sealed within the cave, for there the boulders that imprisoned them were mighty and clear to see, whereas the screen that held them prisoners in the Tapestry was not. No noble stag could toss that aside, for there was no tangible blockage with which to engage, and 'twould be akin to jousting with a waterfall. What they needed to discover was how it might be penetrated and a portal created that stayed open.

When they were come to the place where Tristram entered in and where he also first pulled Selina into the web, there they paused to take stock. They saw nearby the bower through which Isabella and Allan gained entry, so knew of a surety that the common portal be thereabouts, even though it forbade their leaving.

Part of the spell-breaking was gifted by Lucius and they had his good intention ever with them, but of itself it was not sufficient. For when Isabella was propelled out, though she grasped tight onto Allan's hand, she could not bring him with her and they were torn asunder. 'Twould not be possible then for Selina to try to do likewise, pulling two that were entrapped back into the world when one could not be brought.

She went to stand apart for a moment then, that she turned in on herself in seeking answer. Now was the time to test her new-born gifts and virtues and find what merit they had and how available they were.

And she was much encouraged, for response came forthwith as if 'twas there just waiting to be bidden. She had absolute certainty as to what must be done without need for lengthy pondering. She turned then to Tristram and instructed him, "Give me your mandore, Tristram."

Then she demanded of Allan, "And you, Allan, take the gemstone from around your neck and give it into my keeping."

Both did as they were bid, but needed assurance that it was absolutely necessary, for these things were precious to them above all else they owned. Tristram had his instrument close by him at all times, and Allan never ever took off his amulet, for it was sacred to him. Selina reassured them that it was precisely because they hold these objects in such high regard that it must be so. For they were as essential to them as life itself, and thus represented their owners to high degree. You could not envisage one without the other. Tristram would not be himself if he lacked his mandore, likewise Allan and his amulet, for he never was without it. Because of this close association, the artefacts could stand in proxy for their owners.

Selina would cross the divide as she may freely do, back into the bedchamber, and bear with her the mandore and the amulet. And by bringing them with her through the barrier, it would be confounded by such ploy. It was not programmed to recognise a representation, even though the depiction contained the true essence of the person it was part of.

Then, because these essential things could not be separated in any way from their owners, being indeed as integral to them as were their very body parts, the barrier would be cleaved. For if some bit of them came across the divide, the remainder must follow that they be made whole wherever they be.

Tristram and Allan comprehended at once her reasoning in the quest to undo Sibylla's binding, for it rang true.

She stepped forward then with the mandore's strap buckled tight and worn crosswise over breast and shoulder that it be secure. And the leather thong of Allan's amulet she tied in a triple knot about her wrist, for she was aware that it may only be worn at the neck of the person to whom it was consecrated.

But as she stood, poised on the threshold, about to cross the divide 'tween this world and the other, Sibylla gained knowledge of what she was about to do, construing her intention, and in a flash she was back from her sojourn. 'Twas vain supposing that she might not, for was not such purpose the very reason for her continued existence? And as she returned she came in full furious manifestation, coupled with a great outrage that they dare think they could evade her will. The very air about them was charged with the projection of her venom so that it almost crackled, and they felt it press upon them with such malignant force that again it rooted them to the spot. Then, on the instant, once more she demonstrated her power that they were in no doubt as to whom it was with which they contend.

She created out of nowhere a mighty whirlwind that came and lashed around Selina with centrifugal force, trying with great might to snatch the mandore and the amulet from her. Together, Tristram and Allan leaped immediately to her aid, and, seizing her arms, they pulled her to the ground, shielding her with their bodies that the hurricane be less able to tear at her. The barrier they created served to protect her from the worst of the tempest's ravaging. Also, she had both things secured so fast to her, that despite the storm they could not be prised away. Though it thrashed about her in savage fury, it spent its force to no avail. It seemed to have an ordained span, for soon enough it become just a spiralling eddy with little strength left, and then 'twas nothing at all, as if the breath was gone from it.

But, of course, though the storm abated, that was not the end of it. Indeed, 'twas as if it was but a foretaste of far worse to come.

For no sooner had the three of them struggled to their feet than their ears were assailed by a different roaring. The sorceress wasted no time in conjuring up further fearsome evidence of the power of witchery, for she was determined that they had pause for neither respite nor recovery. And this time 'twas neither storm nor eruption she visited upon them, for beyond doubt what they heard now was the full-throated howling of some ferocious, predatory beast.

As one they turned towards the source of the bloodcurdling sound that rent the air. And behold, a huge creature, its pelt the fiery colour of Hell's gate, was bearing down upon them. Though it had blood-red eyes blazing like hot coals, all they really had awareness of was the slavering jaws and massive tusk-like canines that filled the gaping maw.

'Twas like unto pictures they had seen of a sabre-toothed tiger, and, as it raced toward them in great loping bounds, it looked as if it was crazed with hunger.

Allan had no sword, nor did any have aught they might use as weapon to defend themselves. All Selina had was the bells that Lucius had given her, and this time she knew she had need of the silver one, and, drawing it forth from her pocket, she shook it vigorously, praying for immediate intervention.

And she had it. The very instant the chime rang forth, the unicorn was there, stood before them, direct in the path of the ravening beast.

But the tiger was in no wise halted by its appearance or its defiant stance. 'Twas as if it could not be diverted from its purpose by anything, however challenging; indeed, it seemed blind to all about it, save for Allan and Selina. Its eye fixedly upon them, it launched itself forward to attain and bring them down, then, once felled, to rend them with its terrible teeth and claws.

But the unicorn was also a powerful beast and it sprang at once into compulsive action, for it too had its instruction and imperative. It was to thwart evil and protect those in danger of its malice. Selina had called out in fear for her life and her entreaty must be honoured.

Like a mighty warhorse, it charged the beast as it came in a headlong rush. They met, as they must, head on. The clash as they came together was like unto battering rams, two wholly unrestrained driving forces with opposing purpose. Both were of prodigious strength and both were magical creatures. The tiger had teeth and claws as keen as the finest blade, and they were conjured by the witch to slaughter the prey in most cruel fashion. The unicorn was vested with qualities that must repel evil and protect good, and, in so doing, it would give no quarter.

Though the tiger was formidable, it was of primitive construct. It could accommodate but one command at a time, and that was the order to attack Allan and Selina. Thus, it had no concern with the unicorn, save to apprehend it as a temporary obstacle in its path. Regardless then, despite their shattering encounter, it speedily gathered its haunches beneath it to make a mighty leap that would carry it over and above the impediment that frustrated its passage. 'Twas a fatal error of judgement, for at the very zenith of its soaring pounce, the unicorn lowered its head then thrust up swift and sure with the blazing horn on its brow. In mid-flight, the horn drove deep into the tiger's heart. It was a fatal blow.

On the instant, the tiger disappeared as if it had never been, and the unicorn tossed its head vigorously and stamped its forefoot, before rearing up on its hind legs in triumphant display that it prevailed. Then, like unto the stag, it stood submissively before Selina that she command it should there be anything further she required.

But she had her wits elsewhere and there could be no space to give thanks for deliverance, for she knew from her inner wisdom that, bested twice, the witch must prevail in the next encounter. The third, by decree, would be her final chance before she too, like the tiger, lost her powers and must again withdraw.

With every sinew stretched taut, Selina now braced herself for confrontation with whatever diabolic creature or mayhem she summoned up next.

*

And Sibylla came then in her finality, fully aware that it would be all or nothing, and with no intention of embracing the latter.

But in her coming, this time she conjured up neither wild wind nor savage beast. She was done with subterfuge. She came undisguised. She came as what she was. She came as herself.

She manifested before them at a distance of nigh on eight ell, and she presented herself in guise as Allan had witness of when last he beheld her. Her gown was of an exceedingly dark shade of deepest red, akin to the tiger's pelt. Her fair hair was dressed in a single long braid that fell over her left shoulder, and in her right hand she held a rod that of a certainty was her wand. Without doubt, she was most comely to behold, but such beauty was assuredly no deeper than her skin, for the heart within was the very opposite. And if she was yet alive, in truth she must be aged, withered and weak of limb and vision. She conjured herself then as she was of yore, that she regain her power. But it was but an illusion, and as with all that be manufactured by spellbinding, it could exist for only a limited duration. Therefore, whatever she intended, she would strike swift and with all her might, for she had no choice to do aught else.

Round about her there pulsed an aura that had the appearance of dark smoke. It seemed to both emanate from her and at the same time sustain her in its midst. And though it seethed and roiled it stayed close by her, for Lucius's Eden constrained to some degree her ability to corrupt its innocence.

All these things Selina had awareness of. She knew it was paramount she stay out of her energy field, for 'twould disable her. Sibylla no doubt had other intent.

Then, with the rod held at the length of a straight arm, she pointed it at Allan as she walked towards them with measured tread. She kept her unwavering gaze ever on him and 'twas clear she intended him some grievous harm. Mayhap she planned to send him again into endless, fathomless sleep that he never ever would be able to find his way back to Isabella.

Allan saw plain her purpose, but though he had grave concern that should he do aught to evade her she might turn her wand on Selina or Tristram in his stead, he was driven by a compulsion beyond such considerations. The very sight of her in her concentrated intent to cast him back into the torpor he had just escaped caused a fury to rise in him as fierce as be witnessed in any wild animal. Therefore, forgetful of, or disregarding Selina's council, and, whatever the cost, at once he must rush forward to disarm her. Letting out his battle cry to affright her, for it put the fear of God in many, he must also roar out his determination to bring her scheming witchery to an end. For he had in mind the great harm she did to his parents, Isabella and her father. And so, he charged at her, with all the speed and might that a trained warrior be capable of, his aim being to snatch the wand from her grasp before she had chance to use it.

But Tristram saw immediately his purpose and could not stand by, for he perceived that only with the two of them acting together might they prevail. The witch would be unable to aim at both in the same moment. Thus, he too threw caution to the wind and himself into action, and together in unison they sprang at the sorceress.

But such action was reckless and as ill-considered as Selina had foreseen and counselled against. For before they could attain her or the wand, she brought it into use. Whirling it around and behind her at a pace almost too rapid to follow with the human eye, she cracked it like a whip before she deployed it. A jagged flash emanated from its tip, and when it reached them it exploded in fiery discharge as if 'twere born from a thunderstorm. And dividing thereupon into twain it became a streak of forked lightning, and the two tines struck Allan and Tristram simultaneously in the centre of their foreheads.

Both were thrown violently backward and lay motionless on the ground, senseless or dead Selina knew not which and had no chance to attend them.

For Sibylla turned her gaze and her full attention now on Selina, and 'twas just they two who were standing alone, pitched one against the other. The testing time had come and one shall prevail and one shall perish.

The unicorn could engage with anything that she conjured, but not with the witch herself. Therefore, having no role, he stood aside, and could but wait till again he be called into use.

But Selina had no need of intercession; no need of anything other than that which had already come to her, for she felt within herself the power rising. It was maturing into its fullness like a curled new leaf or bud that unfurls rapidly in the warmth of spring. It expanded and stretched as do all things as they wake from sleep into vigour. Like too a butterfly that emerges from the chrysalis, it was a different thing entirely from that which came before. She knew, whatever befell, she was as best prepared as was possible to be. She was ready and she was without fear, and being thus lacked the vulnerability of the faint-hearted.

Sibylla had felled Tristram and Allan, but presently held her ground before she made her attack on Selina. Though she had confidence in her own abilities, she bore in mind her previous errors and the fact that she could not afford further mistakes. Time was not on her side, but haste was likewise her enemy. She moved then with calculated precision that she achieve perfect effectiveness.

But as she drew nigh unto Selina, of a sudden she was visited by an unsettling disquiet and experienced a novel uncertainty.

She knew the colourful jester that stood by the unicorn was indeed Selina, yet something was not as it should be, but she knew not what. She extended her rod, testing the ether but did not bring it into use, for now the uncertainty was growing and she had considerable unease. She began then to circle round and about Selina that she get the measure of her before she struck.

Then, she was taken aback, for without warning the jester began to dance. Leaping nimbly from one foot to the other and with head nodding from side to side, he clapped his hands over his head in most lively manner.

She called the jester 'he' for it seemed 'twas surely a fellow. Yet she knew 'twas not. But the actions, though they were playful, were more masculine than feminine. She stopped in her tracks, suspicious and unsettled. She raised her wand threateningly as warning, but in response the jester danced the faster, till at dizzying speed the vivid colours of his costume seemed to blend together in dazzling, iridescent display. The effect was almost enough to blind her, and she was alarmed and retreated some several paces.

She needed to take her eye for the moment from the jester, for he seemed to have the ability to disrupt her powers and she must centre herself. Doubt and confusion would assuredly diminish her strength and it was already close to its allotted span. She must strike and soon, for she had not the luxury of extended time. Whereas, when she looked again at the prancing jester, he seemed to be gaining in energy and, with lively animation, was spinning like a top.

'Twas too much, though it was not done as she had planned, she was goaded into immediate action.

She gave forth then a fierce, high-pitched sound that surely was the blood-chilling screech a witch gave vent to as she cast her hex. And, turning full towards Selina, she raised her wand.

But even before she achieved the action, Selina, faster than seemed possible, at the same instant changed her ways. She ceased her spinning and stepped forward to take instead a motionless stance in a bright shaft of sunlight. And by thus presenting herself, exposed and unarmed, she seemed to invite the witch to do her worst.

And she did. She must.

The jester's teasing and taunting had much provoked her. She knew 'twas what jokers be wont to do by dint of who and what they were, but this impudent player was not such a one. Here, standing brazenly before her, was an upstart girl, little more than a child. And she dared think to confront a sorceress as was of supreme skill, without any sign of fear, whereas if she was wise she would be on her knees begging for mercy. Not that it would have been forthcoming, but 'twould have been gratifying. Her lack of awe and respect was a most grievous insult. She should pay the full price for her contempt. Thus, filled with rancour, her waning powers were boosted by the promise of sweet revenge, and, with a vigour born of malice, she stepped three paces forward that she was exactly opposite Selina and in perfect striking distance for her wand's span.

But Selina did not move defensively, as duelling swordsmen were wont to do, presenting her shoulder rather than her heart, nor did she in any other way try to put herself out of harm's way. She faced Sibylla square on, making no attempt to deflect or evade whatever she conjured.

In fact, it seemed she deliberately did the opposite. She took a further step forward, closing the gap between them, and positioned herself in the very centre of the shaft of sunlight that shone in undiluted brilliance between the branches. It emphasised the vividness of the rich fabrics she wore. She was as exquisitely arrayed as a bird of paradise, but 'twas the cloth of gold mask that caused Sibylla to almost falter as she prepared her wand for fatal delivery. The sun, rather than throw light upon her so she was an unmissable target, illuminated the mask to such degree that it shone as if it was forged from white heat and was unbearable to countenance. But even more than that, it presented her as endowed with a radiant face. And her whole self appeared to shimmer in its reflection. She looked like unto an angel. She glowed. And to Sibylla's horror, in her brightness she intimidated.

She knew she could wait no longer, lest her power be compromised and become insufficient to achieve her purpose. She must strike now.

At once, she stretched forth her arm to its full extent, and pointed the tip of the wand at Selina's heart. Then, having fixed her aim, as before, she whirled it around and behind her, releasing the charge with a report like unto the crack of a whip.

The stream of energy that burst like lightning from the rod streaked across the intervening space towards Selina, and, like the arrow unerringly finding its mark when dispelled by an expert bowman, it struck her heart. The witch's aim was true.

But, unlike Allan and Tristram, Selina did not fall.

'Twas the witch herself who fell.

For Selina took up her position in the sunlight for particular reason. The lightning that spewed forth from Sibylla's rod struck not her heart, but the cross the priest had given her. And in its golden shining it acted like unto a convex looking-glass that reflected the power back to its source, but with redoubled strength. That which she sent forth with murderous intent returned to her; intact but magnified. She perished indeed from a heart attack, but the sorceress was the author of her own destruction.

For a moment only, she lay upon the sward, slain by her own hand, but then like unto the tiger, she disappeared. She was a phantom after all, and, as did Selina, she returned to wherever her corporeal body presently was. But whatever place it resided, she would still be dead.

'Twas over then.

It was hard to have realisation that the witch was vanquished, her tyranny at an end and that all now was well. For nigh on fifty years her malice, spite and greed had ruled, and in their supremacy caused the destruction of the lives of the innocent. Now at last, thank the Lord, all the evil that she did was undone

And then, in thanksgiving or in exhaustion, she knew not which, Selina sank to her knees, and with gesture like unto Isabella casting aside her veil, she took off her jester's cap and mask and lay them down. Or maybe 'twas more like unto a knight unbuckling his sword after the affray. They had served their purpose and she had no further need of either. But, unlike Isabella who rejected the veil as a loathsome thing, she would ever keep them and hold them in good regard. They would be put away in the chest that her grandmother used for their storage, for if she did not give her a blessing before she died, she did leave her the remnants that proved to be her granddaughter's salvation. And then, while she was on her knees, she offered up a prayer for her grandmother. For though she knew not what she did, 'twas done just the same, and she blessed her with a full heart, rather than the other way around.

The unicorn came to her then, and, bending low his head that she may grasp his silken mane, he raised it up that he might bring her to her feet. She saw that Lucius now too was alongside, and he saluted her in acknowledgment of her victory. For he was full glad that his Eden was itself again, free from the witch's corruptive contamination, but above all that Allan would be liberated.

She told him she must go at once to Tristram and Allan to discover how they fared. But Lucius assured her that at the very moment the witch fell they were risen up. And the truth of such statement was made plain, for they appeared then, coming through the trees towards her.

Allan was upright, but walked with slow and careful tread like unto one subdued after surviving such heat of battle that 'twas almost his undoing.

Tristram stumbled in dazed fashion, as if he was not yet in command of his feet or his senses.

The very sight of him in such state turned her heart

sideways, and she was compelled to go to him, and, putting her arm tight around him, gave him her shoulder to lean on. And he was most glad so to do, even when he had recovered enough that he no longer had the need.

She turned to Lucius then.

"Are we now free to leave? With the witch dead and gone, there be no longer a need for special ploy to depart from the Tapestry?"

He bowed his head in agreement.

"The only rule still presently in governance is that should you stay beyond daybreak you will be caught and confined in the cessation of activity as are all others in the web. Then you will be bound to wait out the day till twilight comes again and releases you to go as you please."

Selina asked then the question that had vexed her previously.

"What will happen to the Tapestry now? If it has a limited life span and one day will lose its animation as it seems it must, what shall become of all who presently dwell therein?"

Lucius took a moment before he responded.

"All things have a natural span, and then depart this life and this planet to go to that which come thereafter.

"Those that have long dwelt in the Eden which I created are not ensouled, and therefore inherit no soul's journey that takes them forward to further evolution. They have not that entitlement nor possibility, or so one would suppose.

"But yet, because they have long continued in the life they have in the Tapestry, one that is wholly good and springs entirely from a simple impulse of loving kindness, over time they have developed some degree of awareness.

They are no longer mere depictions of an ideal state of being that has no reality. There has been a dawning awakening in all that dwells in the web. The germ of comprehension has been born, and however much it is, as yet, in its infancy it contains potential.

"The Creator and source of all that is will acknowledge and nurture such latent possibility, and grant it the right environment in which it may develop.

"And I too have been granted the knowledge that this will be a transposing of everything in its entirety that is in the Tapestry, whether it be a representation of the human, animal, vegetable or of the mineral kind. They all be as brethren this long while, and therefore have a kinship that cannot be separated out, and it shall be honoured and blessed in what is to come.

"For henceforth, they shall all be given birth in the kingdom of the Elementals, the realm of nature spirits and the domain of the faeries. This is the ideal opportunity and place for them to make the transition from facsimile to true manifestation. In this environment, they shall be gifted the seed spark that ignites the life force. And from thence they shall no longer have the appearance of living souls, but 'twill be the fact of the matter."

Selina asked then, "And the Tapestry? Does that mean it will cease its nightly animation?"

Lucius explained that it must be so and for good reason.

"As I wove my own dreams into its fabric 'twas never my intent to make it the magical thing it became. That happened of itself and those of like mind could enter into it both physically and spiritually, and that seemed to me a sweet and goodly thing. But then I discovered so too could the witch. Though she was not of like mind, she was in close converse with every form of magic and able to harness and exploit it to her own end.

"She turned my paradise, my Eden, into a place of entrapment, where the two lovers were torn asunder; one to perpetual torpor and one to endless anguish. Had the Tapestry not been fashioned, such wicked cruelty would not have been possible, and though Sibylla has been dispatched there is no guarantee that others of similar ill intent would not also seek to bend it to their will.

"But the time is also ripe for me to quit entirely this incarnation and set out on the journey that I have long delayed. Obligation to those I created and those who suffered by my hand held me back as they must. Now that all is well for all involved, I am free to depart.

"The Tapestry shall now revert to what it was ever meant to be, no more than a woven work of art that inspires admiration and stimulates the imagination. It will, with time, fade and degrade, for it is finite, but 'twas well made so 'twill last many a year till, like all that have an earthly span, it perishes from old age and decrepitude.

"Other weavers and other artists will come in my stead and create greater works, for it is ever thus that those who went before bequeath a legacy that stimulates fresh inspiration. One thing truly leads to another in an ever-developing continuum, for it seems art too has a life of its own that must evolve.

"When you go forth now from the Tapestry, I shall close down the portal that gives you right of way. None other shall have entry forthwith, and Allan and Tristram I think will not be sorry.

"Selina, I am ever in your debt for 'tis you who have freed us all. We shall not meet again, but I take my leave of you with gratitude and with my blessing."

Selina was minded then that she still had the two bells that summoned the stag and the unicorn in the pockets of her tabard, and she gave them back, though with some reluctance for she was sorry to part with them. Had she not, for Lucius did not demand them, she wondered, if like the other conjured things, they would just disappear. But Lucius took them with no more than a nod of acknowledgement, so she would never know for sure if that was the case.

Then he sent them on their way with, "Go forth now through the portal 'ere I seal it for good and aye."

And this they did, and 'twas as easy as going through any doorway. Then, most suddenly, all three found themselves in Selina's chamber.

CHAPTER TWENTY

Despite the apparent ease of passage departing the Tapestry, the transition left them more than a little unsteady and disoriented. They were returned at last safe and sound to their own world, but felt as if they had yet to attain their land legs after a lengthy voyage. All three found the covering on the chamber floor no more flat and stable than a flying carpet. But on consideration, Selina accepted that after all that they had so recently endured, 'twould be entirely unreasonable to expect things to be otherwise.

And it was surely also the case that the complete and final withdrawal of animation from the web as they were catapulted from it created a kind of vacuum. The pulling sensation that always accompanied the rending of the membrane dividing the two worlds was climacteric. It caused powerful suction waves to follow after them in their departure, making them feel distorted and stretched in body and mind. As the wall hanging covered the height and breadth of the whole end wall of the chamber, 'twas a considerable reverberation.

But at last, losing the sense that she was like unto a tumbler or a tightrope walker, she regained equilibrium and knew that the first thing she must do before anything else was to return Allan's periapt to him. And when he had it, he wasted not a moment in restoring it to its rightful place at his neck. Gifted to him at birth, 'twas as if it were so much an essential part of him that, like the clock that runs down without its winding key, he cannot properly function without it. Then she unbuckled the tight strap from the mandore, that she may give the instrument back to Tristram that he too be fully himself.

She could see then that the Tapestry that closed itself off so decisively when they were flung from it already had a different look, just as Lucius had foretold. Because it dominated the chamber by dint of size alone, any change was immediately apparent, and what could be now seen was that the vibrancy that was its hallmark was gone, and 'twas presently no more than a sublime piece of craftsmanship. She particularly remarked that in the foreground there was no sign at all of the errant figure that appeared so out of place in paradise. For, of course, he be unwoven from the tableau, no longer lost and forlorn but found and liberated, and here in the chamber.

But even as she contemplated the reductive metamorphosis that had taken place, the first sunbeam heralding the dawn of a new day came in at the window to shine full and precise upon the exact centre of the Tapestry. And in that very moment each caught their breath, for 'twas then that they became aware that this penetrating ray of light marked not just the temporary cessation of animation that every morning brought, but the permanent closing of the portal. None might enter forthwith; no chatelaine with a key at her belt might gain access, for there was now neither lock nor door to open. The way was sealed fast for all time. There was no going back.

She looked to Allan then, and he returned her look, knowing what must come next, that which consumed his mind and was his paramount intent – the reunion with Isabella.

Though he was not without awareness that for him this was a different thing than 'twould be for her, for his long withdrawal into bewitched slumber seemed to him no more than the passing of a single night, and his separation from his new wife but a most recent event. Therefore, he was most eager and impatient to go to her, having no uncertainties to contend with. She, on the other hand, had lived near half a century in isolation and despair, and though she had not changed physically, of a certainty such travail must have wrought great difference in her in all other ways. His look to Selina then was for guidance as to how best it should be done that he cause Isabella no distress. She counselled that 'twould be best that she go first to Madame and acquaint her with all that had come to pass, then allow her as much time as she needed to compose herself before he joined her. Asking both then that they wait on her while she prepared the way ahead, Selina stepped into the passage to make the short journey to Madame's chamber.

But she was not within, and must therefore be yet in the chapel with the priest. For, Selina reminded herself, 'twas but break of day, and no doubt both still remained at prayer in observance of their all-night vigil.

Indeed, she found 'twas so. The priest was on his knees before the altar. Isabella was on her knees in the first pew. Both started at the sound of the lifting of the chapel door's latch, and in a trice Isabella sprang to her feet and turned to face her. The priest, stiff from so long on creaking joints, took longer to stand upright, but both looked at her with the same expression. Their faces were full of wonder and disbelief; they could not trust their eyes nor accept the evidence they saw before them. For her coming represented the fact of Divine intervention, and was nothing less than a miracle in answer to the fervent entreaties that they dared not hope be granted.

'Twas the priest who spoke first.

"Praise God! You are returned to us and you look whole and sound."

Then Isabella too found her voice, though its sibilant quaver was nothing like her usual tone, and as she asked only, "Pray tell me, did you find Allan?"

Selina, wasting no time in preamble, went directly to the point.

"Madame, I did, and the lost troubadour too. Both are full well and presently in my bedchamber. I counselled Allan that I come before him that you be given time to grasp the situation, lest it be too great a shock if 'twere done otherwise."

As Selina had fallen to her knees when the witch was slain, so now did Isabella resume again the posture she had just quit. And more than that, she fell to noisy and unrestrained weeping, as the mighty dam of self-control and stoicism that grow stouter over the years at last gave way and burst asunder.

Selina, likewise in an unrestrained response that paid no respect to station, at once attended her, and, wrapping arms tight about her, stilled the shuddering shoulders as she reassured her.

"My Lady, the sorceress is slain and all her spellbinding undone. Allan was bewitched these many years into perpetual slumber, but he has awakened as if he had but passed a normal night's repose, so for him 'tis as if he was with you only yesterday. He is in great urgency to come to you."

Before Isabella had time to answer, the chapel door sighed open again. This time it gave way to Abigail, who, having heard the racking sobs of her beloved mistress, came in torment, expecting to learn quite other news.

Raising herself back again to her feet, Isabella called the chatelaine to her and in tight embrace reassured her that they were but tears of joy. For unbelievably that for which they have long prayed had come to pass. The witch be dead and gone, the past undone, and Allan, her husband, even now awaited her in Selina's chamber.

Abigail groped her way from Isabella's enfolding to sit down heavily on the nearest pew. If Madame felt overwhelmed the chatelaine was no less so, for 'twas clear that she too had not dared hope for such outcome and was at a loss for words. But when she also had her voice returned to her, she surprised Selina, for it is to her that she turned first.

"Child, you have done a wondrous thing, and though 'twas preordained, the outcome was never certain. What we demanded of you afforded you no personal gain, yet you did not turn from a task that mayhap cost you your life.

We asked everything of you, and you gave it. Our motives were fuelled by our own great need which left no space to consider what the cost was for you, who personally profited not at all from the result.

"While I waited out this last long night in my chamber, I realised that we lost sight of such facts. But nevertheless 'twas indeed only you who could accomplish what none other could. In all these long and miserable years, we languished without hope till you came to us, and I trust you find some recompense in the great good you do and the joy you bring, for we cannot repay such considerable debt in any other way."

With that said, she struggled to her feet and astonished Selina by dropping her as deep a curtsey as age would allow.

Selina, much moved, assisted her back to the pew, and, taking position alongside her, she then invited Isabella and the priest to also be seated whilst she regaled them with a full account of all that had come to pass since she was last in their company. None had commented on her strange apparel, but she explained its purpose now. And she told all else that had befallen in the span of a single night, leaving nothing unremarked.

When her task was done, she waited then on them to profess further need of detail than she gave in a first telling, but none spoke for a space while they pondered on all they had learnt. Then Isabella stood slowly but deliberately.

"I have heard all I have need of with regard to what befell Allan, and that he misconstrued our separation such that it seems to him we have been parted for but the space of one night. And such apprehension makes all simple, for with his sense of only briefly interrupted continuance, there can be no strangeness between us as would result from his knowledge and experience of the true length of the span. 'Tis clear then that he has not changed at all, and why would I linger another second thinking on what was the best way to conduct myself when I have had so many years praying for and anticipating this moment. I have rehearsed it a thousand, thousand times in my mind and have no need for further preparation."

Selina stayed her for a moment.

"Let me first fetch Tristram, the troubadour, away that you have naught but your own two selves in attendance."

And this she did, for the reuniting of Isabella and Allan was a most private and exclusive happening. It could be imagined full well, but it could not be witnessed.

Then she, Tristram, Abigail and the priest repaired to the hall, heartened to find the breakfast fare was already laid out. 'Twas well that as ever there was generous amounts of everything on offer, for they were of good appetite. Selina had not partaken of aught since the midday meal the day before, the priest of similar duration as he fasted to add credence to his prayers, and Tristram had not eaten for a two-year span and suddenly was ravenous. Abigail was the only one at table that, as ever, had little interest in the victuals.

As she tore again the warm bread in her hands, Selina had sudden awareness that the company she had yearned for when she be at meat, was here about her now and all with much to contribute to avid discourse.

The priest must hear again each and every detail of the part the cross he consecrated for her played in reflecting back to the witch her own evil intent. The relating of such divine retribution was most pleasing to his ears.

Abigail likewise insisted on the retelling of the finding of Allan, that after so long he nevertheless woke on the instant to Selina's touch, with nary a sign of any harm done. That she attributed to the blessedness of the Tapestry itself, and the purity and incorruptibility with which the weaver had imbued it. For it was assuredly a fact that because of it, despite Sibylla's witchery, Allan was preserved in all aspects exactly as ever he was.

Tristram also rejoiced to at last be free when he had fear of permanent confinement in an Eden that for him was no paradise. But Selina was also aware that, like Allan and Isabella, he had a great necessity to speak with her with none other present, for what needed to be said pertained to themselves alone.

When hunger was satisfied and enquiry likewise, Abigail said she must retire to her bed for a spell, for she was full weary after a sleepless night. She must also be in a fit state to encounter Madame's husband when he presented himself.

The priest too said he was obliged to leave them, and would not wait on Allan's coming, for the duties of his parish called him and they could not be denied.

Thus, at last, Selina and Tristram were alone at table, and he wasted no time in holding forth, for 'twas plain he had much he needed speak of.

"I have had no opportunity to give thanks to you for all you did. For not only have you freed me from an entrapment that I feared most profoundly was everlasting, but you also plucked me from the witch's clutches. Thus, you have twice saved me, but then again, as much and more than such preserving of my life, 'tis your very self that demands my greatest gratitude."

When Selina held up her hand to stay what she clearly regarded as an extravagant and overzealous thanksgiving, he in turn shushed her, for he was determined to have his say and 'twas certainly not done yet.

"No, hear me, pray, while we have the chance, for there is much I must lay before you. And in the start of the telling I need to go back to the time before this misadventure befall and 'ere I was lost in the Tapestry, for in that time my life was a different thing entirely and so was I.

"Ever then was I travelling, going from one place to another but staying nowhere longer than the length of time it took to relay the news, narrate my stories and perform my repertoire. Then, when the show was done, but before the adulation was likewise spent, I was on the road again, making sure regret at my departure followed on my heels. Thus, my return was eagerly anticipated and the attendant hospitality reliably lavish to ever tempt me back and encourage me to stay. My journeying from manor to stately home became like unto a royal progress. 'Twas a charmed life, and the result of such pampering was inevitable – I became spoiled, vainglorious and heedless. And there being no reason that I could see to be other, I would have continued thus. The imprisonment in the Tapestry stopped me in my tracks and brought a decisive end to thoughtless self-indulgence. I baulk at calling it a blessing in disguise, but 'twas true that only something beyond my control, and as extreme in consequence as this proved to be, could make me think twice, and then think yet again on the values by which I lived my life. Two years afford the space for much reflection, a time when I could neither escape the situation nor my own mind's unravelling.

"'Twas irony too that the sweet souls who dwelt in the Tapestry were almost reflections of myself – they were most pretty to look upon and exceedingly charming to encounter, and they ever presented an unfailing good humour and willingness to disport themselves. But hey, ho! None will remember you on the morrow nor have any desire to know your name or aught about you. They entreat you to join them but if you do not they mind not at all, for then they just turn to another in your stead and there be plenty round and about to engage with. The one difference between us in how we conduct ourselves be that they do all in innocence, knowing nothing of guile, whereas that was my essential ingredient. And if Lucius's creations lack soul, and I in contrast do have my God-given soul, I either forget or ignore that I have it.

"I had two conceits, first my virtuosity on the mandore with the ballads I compose and sing, but second, and of equal value to me, was the power and appeal of my own person, which was a currency that enriched and inflated my vanity. In the Tapestry neither of these things held sway. For 'twas clear they found my melancholic madrigals of little use for dancing, and I was no more attractive to look upon than any other, so merited no special regard. Thus, while I had no choice but to remain, the very things that defined me in my own estimation were stripped away. I depended on the adulation of others, for how they see me was how I then saw myself.

"Thus, I lost my freedom and I lost my identity, never then was anyone more thoroughly lost than I. But by and by, what I found in their stead be other parts of myself that had also been lost, but which could now evidence themselves without hindrance. And 'twas like discovering a new land that was there all the time, unseen, unexpected and unexplored. But being a habitual traveler, I did explore it and found it to be my own true home, so that like Allan and his kin, I would gladly leave all that went before without regret, and settle in a new place that my heart recognised.

"Yet though I had changed, the situation had not, and such transformation was given no opportunity to be put to the test and must therefore languish untried. It seemed most capricious of destiny to contrive such a powerful reformation only to have it go to waste. So, I revived then my neglected faith, and prayed with all the intensity of devotion that I could muster, that deliverance would come and give me the chance to demonstrate my reborn will to do good. I would be the Samaritan and not he who passeth by on the other side, as was previously my wont.

"And 'twas then that you appeared most assuredly as answer to my prayers, for you came like a shining angel and with the strength and knowledge to defeat the witch. And by your hand was her undoing, and Allan and I both were set free.

"Though I was in awe of you, I discovered you were also most fully human, and as much the victim of fate and circumstance as was I. Your joy in the company the Tapestry afforded was a delight to behold, for 'twas clear you were parched of companions far too long. I bore witness then to the fact that, though you be angelic of a certainty, 'twas with human frailties, and such vulnerability meant you were assessable. I need not put you on a pedestal above mere mortals where you were unattainable, for though you brought about my salvation, I in my turn can offer you much that also was like unto a saving grace.

"If I am free to go now, to strap on my mandore, take my leave and wend my merry way, so too are you. None here would think to try and detain you when you have done all that was asked of you and more. Those who tasked you with the finding and liberating of Allan have no need of you now. But I have great need and I cannot depart without you, for, as I have told, I am not he whom before I was. Where he was self-sufficient and self-serving, I find you are most necessary to me, and, rather than being entire unto myself, I am no one at all if I have not you beside me. So, I ask of you, come away with me. And wherever we might choose to go hereafter, surely we shall start our travels by first journeying back to your hometown to have encounter with your brothers.

"I am emboldened to speak my mind in no uncertain terms. For it is apparent, is it not, that I speak not just for myself but for us both."

Selina, too overcome by much feeling, could but stretch forth her hand to cover his own and nod her head in dumb agreement. The very thought of making the journey to be again with her brothers and with Tristram alongside, not just for that occasion but for all future travel, or for none should they chose to stay, was truly a most gladdening thing.

She took him then to sit with her in the garden, first gathering crumbs from the table into the lap of the tabard she was still wearing. And the birds as ever came to her willingly and she saw their bath was filled with fresh water, and whoever tended it all had hung a net of lamb's wool and feathers that they had material to build their nests. She gave thanks then for whoever it was that minded the garden and made it the sanctuary that it was, nor neglected the needs of the birds. And she gave thanks too for the little garden she had left behind when she had departed following her grandmother's death, for it also was a blessed thing, and she had sincere hope that the new incumbents would find it so. She could not stop there, but must extend her thanksgiving for all the good that had come about – that Tristram and Allan were saved and Isabella's anguish be at an end.

And, in a while, they would behold Isabella and Allan come into the hall, and that indeed would be a moment to be marked, but 'twould be no more or less than the moment she had just shared with Tristram.

CHAPTER TWENTY-ONE

Come the evening, nothing was as before. Abigail certainly was not herself, and insisted on going forth in ungoverned delirium like a trumpeting herald. She loudly informed all that Madame's husband as was lost be found and come home, and thus, praise God, Lady Isabella now also was released from her long period of confinement and restored to them. She further instructed them that as there was no more call for her isolation with the attendant locking of doors, from henceforth they would all be left unfastened and free access and warm welcome accorded to every dweller in the settlement. In confirmation of such statement of open house, she unclasped her heavy key-hung belt and set it down with finality upon the chest in the Great Hall.

She had also given the kitchen notice that a late family repast be prepared to honour Lord Allan's homecoming, and that 'twould be a marvellous thing on such occasion to witness him filling his long-empty chair at table. The very evident flesh and blood of him seated therein, at last dispatching all the scurrilous rumours as had been bandied about since his disappearance.

And as proof of who he truly was, on the morrow he would present himself to all, alongside Lady Isabella. And as it would also be the first time she had set foot outside the manor since the days when her father was Lord, there would be few who had any more remembrance of her than of him.

Thus, these two would meet and greet everyone in their employ as if it was the first time of encounter, and indeed for most it was exactly so. But if they came before them unchanged in appearance from that which they were half a century ago, it must cause confusion and disbelief, and if the reason was not confessed mayhap they would even be deemed impostors. Against such false conception, the tale would be told in full account, for already it was planned to make tomorrow a holiday, with everyone invited to a festival and feasting in the Great Hall. 'Twould be but the beginning of many such celebrations, with invitations sent forth to neighbours both old and new, as the previous state of affairs was reestablished. Certainly no time was wasted in dispatching a messenger on the swiftest mount to Allan's kinfolk, alerting them and calling them thither.

Allocated a new chamber, Selina at last shed her jester's costume, and, as she lay it aside, a gentle knock at the door revealed Flora with the handle of a basket over her arm. It exuded the heady aroma of exotic perfumes and unctions, and alongside there was an array of jewelled ornaments for garments and hair. Her limb was also burdened with a selection of fine dresses.

Of a certain Abigail was intent to prove that whatever the impairments of age they could not diminish her determination to honour this great event. And, with no detail lacking her attention, Selina was most particularly favoured.

Inviting Flora within, she bade her be seated on the bed, and, sitting close by, sought to draw forth knowledge of what was known in the household regarding recent happenings. Flora confessed that all within and without the manor were consumed with amazement and excitement. But such brief news as Abigail had related left so much unsaid and with so many questions unanswered that none could make good sense of it.

Selina reassured her that 'twas true that Allan was found and rescued and that Lady Isabella was also liberated from her incarceration. Tonight, they would take their place at table and may thus be seen by all who attended them. And on the morrow, they would preside over such a public rejoicing as had not taken place in the settlement since their wedding. And that surely would be the occasion when Lady Isabella would speak of all that had come to pass since that day. When the joy that they foresee, turn about by dint of Sibylla's curse, to become instead the very opposite.

But halting further discourse, she said 'twas time now for her to prepare herself that she look fitting for the occasion 'ere she join them. And 'twould not only be in honour of Allan and Isabella, but for Tristram too, for she was wont to have his good regard. Of all the fine new apparel presented, she chose to wear the simple red dress that had previously pleased her so well, and when she had it on, Flora spilt the contents of her basket onto the chest beneath the window and laid all out that she may make use of, whatever attracted her.

'Twas clear Flora was much caught up in the preparations and requested shyly that she be permitted to dress her hair. Selina handed her the brush and comb willingly, saying it be in a fine tousle after long confinement in the jester's cap. When Flora had brushed it into good order, she suggested that she left it unbraided, for it looked very well as it was, and rather than constraining it with plaiting, to permit it to be but loosely restrained with jewelled hairpins. Selina readily agreed, and of the many fine offerings laid out for her pleasure and adornment, selected naught but the hairpins that she felt more her own true self.

Though she no longer had certainty who that self truly be, for since Jacob fetched her here so much had befallen that in no wise could she not be much changed. Smoothing down the skirt of the dress before she went forth from the chamber, she realised that a part of that change was that now she felt at ease in such apparel. Previously she saw herself as an upstart pretender tricked out in finery to which she lacked any entitlement. Now such awkwardness was no longer the case, for with the proving of her worth came the confidence that she was the equal of any man or woman so attired. She may then enjoy these rewards for truly they were full-well earned, if not by birth then assuredly by deed.

Tristram had also been given a chamber and fresh linen and hose from Allan's store, for he had enough to spare. All his apparel and other personal items, having been sent to the manor ahead of him on the occasion of his marriage to Isabella, were even yet preserved in chests and closets. And, upon her instruction, they have been scrupulously maintained against his return.

They would both of a certainty stay for this night and the festivities on the morrow, but afterward they would be compelled to take their leave and travel to her homestead for her own reunions and celebrations. The overwhelming euphoria that accompanied the anticipation of such meeting with her brothers, and all those whom memory ever held dear, created a thrilling that coursed through her and ignited an avid impatience that could not countenance long delay.

And what thereafter?

Tristram's life hitherto had been as a travelling minstrel. By its nature it was a solitary and rootless existence. What part could she play in such a way of being? For either she went with him and found a purpose, or alternatively Tristram could stay put in her hometown and find some employ that suited him there. She admitted that neither option sounded convincing nor ideal; notions having no more value than makeshift compromise. But such considerations were for the morrow. This time was to rejoice with Isabella and Allan, and with that intent she departed her chamber and made her way down the winding stairway to the hall.

Here 'twas the very opposite of how things had erstwhile been, for rather than echoing emptiness, there was bustling activity as many went back and forth from the kitchen, carrying loaded platters through wide open doors. Before the fireplace that still had a log or two ablaze against the chill of evening, Isabella, Allan and Tristram were gathered along with the priest. Abigail, who though she looked well content also seemed ever more frail, was accordingly seated in a cushioned chair alongside.

Isabella, free from confinement and free from the veil, looked inebriated but not with wine. She was intoxicated with a delight that she clearly found hard to contain, as it must ever try to pour forth in what might be construed as an unseemly manner. She resembled a child who had been given too many sweetmeats, but Selina, who had herself just been subject to like emotion, understood her full well.

Isabella beheld her as she came into the hall from the stairs, and, stepping forward, held out her two hands, bidding her come swiftly to them. She was dressed in a most sumptuous gown of gold silk, the bodice richly embroidered with seed pearls and crystal beads. The hem extended to a short train and was likewise embroidered and trimmed with miniver, as was the padded band that encircled her head. Allan was no less arresting in a dark blue velvet tunic and fine suede leggings dyed to match. The depth of colour emphasised the fairness of his hair and reflected the blueness of his eyes. His gemstone was hung on a heavy gold chain about his neck, its entwining as complex and intricate as was all the art from his native land. 'Twas clear these garments were fashioned for their wedding trousseau long since, but had only now been brought forth to fulfil their purpose.

Though much time had passed for all others since that day, for Isabella and Allan it had stood still. For here they were, neither aged nor in any way changed from that which they were before Sibylla cursed them. Though all about them had been much altered as Father Time imposed his will, till this day they were beyond his reach. Not so now, for with the Tapestry sealed and its magic properties withdrawn, they too would become subject to natural law.

As Selina reached them, Isabella addressed her in a voice charged with much emotion.

"Selina, there be naught I can say or do that will ever be enough to honour our debt to you. 'Tis even now, whilst I am in the midst of it, hard to believe that all is made well and good by your doing, and 'tis not one of the dreams I was wont to have – fantasies that cause me great anguish on waking. But with the realisation that it is nothing less than the absolute truth, and not a false construct that my mind conjure, it releases in me a rapture of such magnitude that I am hard-pressed to restrain it. And, overwhelmed by the joy it evokes in me, how can I stop it bursting forth?

"I told you in the beginning that I have considerable means and it is my pleasure to reward those who serve me well, and assuredly none have served me better than you. So, name whatever you want or wish for, and if it be in my power to grant it you shall have it. For what price can be put on the salvation of souls in torment? I would have given all that I had in barter for my father's life. I certainly owe you no less."

All gathered looked to her then in waiting to hear what she would demand in payment, for she was free to ask much, and they knew that, coming to this place as a hapless orphan, presently she had nothing at all.

Selina, before she gave answer, moved to stand alongside Tristram as a statement that all she asked concerned him too. And they should bear in mind that he also was owed for the two years that he was lost in the Tapestry by their ploy.

"Madame, 'twas destiny propelled me to come here and engage in what needs must be done. I was given no choice in the matter, but the outcome of itself be reward enough and I could ask for nothing more than that. But in truth, henceforth there be such things as I will necessarily have need of, and these I would request that I be enabled to begin afresh in a life that currently is bereft of all resource.

"Tristram and I will travel the day after tomorrow to find my brothers, who I have sorely missed these last years, and who I yearn to see and be with again. They, being all the family I have left, are most precious to me. Therefore, if you gift us two horses for the journey, and, should it be needed, a sum that will buy us lodging on our way, that will be sufficient for the moment. But thereafter, when I am come again to my own domain, there will be further needs that are apparent. Having lost my parents to the Pestilence, I have no home to return to, and my brothers are settled now in their own abodes. 'Twould fulfil my dearest wish were I to have a little dwelling of my own there in that place, for 'twas where I was born and raised and where heart and soul shall ever belong.

"And, other than my own needs, I would also ask a boon for Jacob, for he afforded me great comfort on my coming and afterward. Please see that he is ever secure within the settlement, and that his daughter who has employ in the bakehouse shall be given such tasks as she enjoys best and a goodly wage for her labours. And that his granddaughter Flora be granted special favour, for she strives very hard for one so young."

Isabella reached out and gasped both her hands.

"All you request you have for the asking. When you are come again to your own hometown, seek out a dwelling that pleases you, but let it not be of humble proportions.

Rather choose a sturdy and spacious house as will serve you well for a lifetime. Let it be of elegant design, pleasing to the eye and providing room to accommodate all the needs of a full life, and if there is not such a place then we shall employ architects and builders that they fashion it according to your instruction. And you shall never be in want, for should you be, just let it be known and all you lack shall be given you."

Then, as she released Selina's hands, Allan stepped forward, and, taking her right hand, he bent over it and touched his lips to the back. Then, raising his eyes to her face, he added his own tribute.

"But let us not be deprived of your company. For both you and Tristram are my comrades-at-arms and such a bond ties us together for our lives' length. Pledge then that you will return most regularly to renew our fellowship, and mayhap, if he choose to indulge us, to have Tristram enchant us with his mandore, for I believe he has an uncommon gift."

Tristram promised then to entertain them and all their guests on the morrow at the great gathering that was planned. And upon such oath, they all took their places at table. Isabella and Allan being seated at last side by side in the grand and stately chairs that for so long had served no purpose other than to gather dust. With Tristram and Selina settled on one side, and the priest and Abigail on the other, the servers came eagerly to offer a variety of elaborate dishes. Their flushed faces evidence not just of the heat of the kitchen, but the exhilaration of the occasion. None had seen, nor thought to see, such activity return to the manor.

Nor could they take their eyes from Madame in her beauty. The tales of her disfigurement proved naught but foolish imaginings spawned by idle gossip. Likewise, Lord Allan, previously condemned as a scoundrel and a coward, clearly was nothing of the sort, for with his fine stature and golden hair, he was both noble and unusually handsome.

Selina and Tristram too were eyed with curiosity and wonder. Even though they had heard but scant detail so far as to how they were instrumental in bringing about this amazing change of fortune, they knew it could not have happened save by their action. For of a certainty, Selina was brought hither to undo the casting of a witch that had the lord and lady bedevilled by her sorcery for more than half a lifetime. It signified then that she too must be an enchantress. Such a conclusion earned their respect, and with it more than a little care in attending her, that she was not provoked into demonstrating her art should they be found wanting.

Though the fare was exceptional, most especially bearing in mind the abruptness with which it was summoned, those at meat were too consumed with other more absorbing distractions to give it its proper due.

Allan enquired of Tristram if he intended to pick up his life as it was hitherto. For though he was lost from such pursuits for a span of two years, that would not be long enough for him to be forgotten by those he was wont to entertain, but 'twas time enough that they might pine for his coming and look to find out where he was.

Tristram, however, admitted that in that two-year span so much had changed that 'twould not be possible to just blithely continue as before.

Surely, for all as were gathered together at table, their lives and themselves were so much altered by what they experienced that it must be that only a new beginning could take such change into account. The old ways no longer sat easy. For, reconfigured in mind and spirit, the pursuits of who and what they had been before no longer fulfilled or satisfied who they had become.

Yes, his music defined him and ever would, but how he presented it and conducted himself in so doing was open to a wide variety of options. Footloose and with the freedom of the road, the life of the troubadour was like unto that of the vagabond, and mayhap after a span its essential singularity began to lose its thrall.

And then Tristram more particularly addressed the priest.

"One can also grow weary of a fawning deference that is appropriate with regard to a saint in church, but excessive when applied to a strolling player."

When he made this observation, Selina's grandmother's itinerant mummer came to mind, and she was therefore much inclined to support his point of view.

The priest, who was as pink-cheeked as the servers, though mayhap more because of the fine wines and mead than because of other causes, nodded sagely in agreement.

Tristram concluded with a spreading of his hands and a smile, and he owned, like Selina, that these concerns were for a later date, whilst this time now was solely for celebration, so let no weighty matters obstruct the revelry.

Nor thereafter did they, and with Isabella's exuberance finally given leave to express itself, 'twas then a merry time was had by those at table, and servers alike, for good cheer of its nature was inclusive, not selective nor partial. And Abigail and the priest, relaxing their normal sobriety, also entered into the spirit of the occasion. But all present being lightheaded from dearth of sleep as much as from rejoicing 'twas not so very difficult.

Nevertheless, weariness could not ever be held at bay, and thus before the church bell sounded the twelfth stroke that marked day's end, Isabella and Allan rose from table and went forth hand in hand, followed by Abigail and the priest, for the full day planned for the morrow dictated an early start for all. The priest would lodge in a chamber alongside the chapel that he may conduct a thanksgiving mass at daybreak, and Abigail, who looked exhausted, was clearly far too long from her bed.

Selina and Tristram stood as the others took their leave, but, being of like mind, did not at once follow after them in departure. Despite the demands all they had endured had made upon them, they lacked the fatigue that drained away their reserves of vitality, and, rather than retiring, they were compelled to remain a while longer where they were. Then, they moved back to stand once more before the fireplace, that the servers were free to clear the table, and because here they were also beyond the hearing of those so engaged.

Tristram confessed then that in all rightness he should be keeping company solely with his mandore, for tomorrow's eve being such a great event it was necessary that he compose a special work to mark the occasion. And even though he had not lost his skill in any part due to the Tapestry's endowment, 'twould still be a task as must take a considerable length of time.

But he also confessed he had as much pressing want to spend his time with her, which made it most hard to call forth the professional discipline that was required. For there was a multitude of things he could not wait to hear tell of, and that he in turn must acquaint her with. No detail of her life could be insignificant, for he wanted nothing left unknown, and had pressing need to reveal all he was, had been, and wanted in the future to be. It required an essential baring of the soul, a stripping away of everything that was not true nor honest. A time for pledging and for confessing. For owning your failings that you may then choose to disown them, and embrace in their stead rarer and finer attributes.

Selina reassured him that they had a lifetime to acquaint themselves each with the other, so let them retire to their chambers now that he had the time he needed to honour this most special occasion. For in this he had not the luxury of years, but of only a very finite amount of time in which to achieve his best endeavour, and it demanded no less.

And so reluctantly they withdrew each to their own chambers, and, though it was at Selina's insistence, in truth she found it no easier than Tristram.

All that had come to her since her grandmother's death was more than she could have ever believed possible, even in her most extravagant supposing. So, she was like unto Isabella, and the outpouring of hitherto suppressed hope and longing which now was released by their fulfilment overwhelmed her. She was given so much and all at once; it afforded no time for gradual readjustment. One day she was this, the next day she was that. 'Twas as dizzying as when they were flung from the Tapestry.

But hapless orphans are wont to doubt their entitlement to good fortune and, like Jeremiah, apt to fear it was a mistake, or a deliberately cruel jest of fate that will snatch away the gift 'ere you have a chance to grasp it. And was not the Pestilence the prime example of the destroyer of wishful thinking?

She upbraided herself then that she be so miserly in her joy, and she threw off dull care with a spinning around that spread out her red skirt in the manner as delighted her when first she put it on. And it mimicked too the way she span in her jester's costume to consternate the witch, which raised in her both justified pride and mirth. Then she was restored to good humour and thanksgiving and shamed to doubt her blessings. As she climbed into bed and prepared to blow out the candle on the stand alongside, she looked to the end wall where the Tapestry would be were she in the old chamber, and she sighed in regret that all that it was in its beauty and perfection now was no more. But those that dwelt within were not lost, but instead gifted with real life somewhere and that was a marvel. She thought on the stag and the unicorn with their strength and beauty and wondered in what guise they might be born, and if they would have existence in a world that resembled the Tapestry or some other domain entirely. And in remembrance of them, she blessed them, and then, surrendering to her own body's needs, fell into fast and dreamless sleep.

Chapter Twenty-Two

Waking and rising at first light, Selina began at once to make preparations for the day ahead – a day which promised to be like none other for any as attended it. Choosing a gown of fine, pale blue silk, embroidered all over with birds and flowers of diverse kinds, she fixed her hair on the top of her head in a twist which she then embellished with a garland of hand-wrought blossom from the basket. It seemed the perfect apparel to honour both the spring day and the great occasion.

But when she descended into the Great Hall, she found only the priest at table, the others still abed or elsewhere. He clearly was in exalted mood, preparing for the mass he would soon conduct in the settlement's chapel. A service open to everyone as dwelt there. And no doubt with the day being declared a holiday and all free to attend, many would come. Selina had suspicion that 'twas likely they were there as much in hope of learning more of the truth of the extraordinary happenings from the priest, as to make their devotions. For though 'twas said that Lady Isabella would give a full account at the great gathering in the hall later in the day, that was too long to wait if there was the hope of earlier enlightenment.

When he departed to fulfil his duties, well aware and not averse to the fact that he was more eagerly anticipated than would normally be the case, Selina declined to go with him. She must wait on Tristram.

That there was as yet no sign of him did not surprise her. For he retired to his chamber not to get his rest, but to prepare his tribute to Isabella and Allan.

She was uncertain as to what she could do till he came. For though she was now free to go where she would, she feared that, should she decide to explore the settlement beyond the manor walls dressed as she was in her fine clothes, she would draw attention to herself. And mayhap, unprotected by an escort, she might be surrounded by curious inhabitants who would insist upon pressing her for answers to the many questions that all were asking.

'Twas a wry thing, was it not, that those she had desperately sought to have contact with, she was now reticent to approach for fear she would be overwhelmed?

Abigail, if she was up and about, which surely would be the case on such a day, must already be in the kitchen, involved in the preparations for the planned feasting.

Isabella and Allan were most likely taking breakfast in their own chamber and thus, strangely, with so much activity going on all around her, she was presently once more on her own. But if she was leaving on the morrow, 'twas an opportunity to sit once more in her garden before she went. For, as with her own little garden at her grandmother's dwelling, she would leave it behind, and so she needed to have the pleasure of it and the birds one last time, to express gratitude for its tranquillity and beauty, and to say goodbye to it.

And it was there, some hour later, that Tristram discovered her, with blackbirds, robins, titmice and all manner of other birds who had found food and sanctuary there gathered on their table and round about her feet.

He did not appear as if he suffered from lack of sleep, in fact he admitted that it was indeed peculiar to take repose once more in a bed, but he had completed the tribute that he would present at the gathering that eve.

'Twas like unto her own empowerment, he said, for, when she confronted the witch, what she needed came to her, born directly from pure inspiration, and so 'twas with him. The tribute presented itself almost already fully formed and with but little effort, from some creative part of his own being, or possibly from some other source without that he was able to access.

He further enlightened her that in the receiving of that inspired knowing, he also was given an additional gift.

"As troubadour, I am required to relate the news of what has taken place in one domain to another. This night, after Lady Isabella has relayed to those assembled the story of all that has befallen twixt herself, Allan, the witch Sibylla, Lucius and the Tapestry in the long span of years since their wedding, I shall then present that tale translated into song and rhyme.

"But here be the novel thing. Alongside my telling in music and verse, you shall act it out in mime. You have the jester's costume, and who knows the movements and gestures better than you? For you will not be play-acting, but reenacting the actual way it was."

Selina, about to protest that she knew nothing of theatricals, stayed herself in recognition of the fact, that as Tristram reminded her, she had given a performance that consternated a sorceress. And what she did then she could do again, though for a different purpose. She required no schooling in the art, just remembrance of the situation. When she thought on it, she found her body responding, ready to conjure again the mischievous prancing of the fool.

And had she not perhaps inherited her grandfather's gift, passed down to her in their shared kinship? If that was the case then he bequeathed her his art as well as his resourceful spirit. Just as her grandmother had supplied the remnants without knowledge of the boon they would be, so the mummer had also enriched her without intention, for he never knew of her existence.

Maybe all that had played out in her grandmother's life, her mother's life and her own thus far, had in it a pattern and an unfolding that you could only understand and appreciate when you looked back, for while in the midst of it there seemed little to recommend it.

But if one thing begat another in an impulsion of inherent possibilities, where might this momentum be leading? The jester's costume seemed an obvious and rational choice with regard to what to make of so many diverse bits and pieces of material. 'Twas only later that the true reason was apparent, when it confused the witch. But that was not the end of it, for now she saw that it had a further role in what came afterward.

Had she not considered that she had no part to play in a travelling minstrel's life, and the minstrel had no place in a life that restricted such travel, but if she had her own unique part to enact, presenting in mime the depiction of the stories he sang and told, then that was where this had finally brought them. 'Twas spelled out plain; this was what they should do next. If all went well this eve and their dual performance was applauded, then that would be the seal of approval that prove the point.

Exhilarated, she insisted that at once Tristram fetch his mandore, whilst she returned to her chamber and donned again her jester's costume. Then they would use the quietness of the garden, where undisturbed they could rehearse their presentation.

And she was amazed at how easily and naturally it all came to her. Tristram's telling of the tragic tale with voice and instrument stirred her to extreme response, and with but little need of experiment nor tentative movement, she allowed the story to dictate to her body.

Just as she found an inner knowing already present and waiting when she encountered Sibylla, she found interpretation of tale and music, likewise stored within her and primed for expression. She acted out in perfect display every twist and turn of the saga, and in the doing knew she had found her life's work and her purpose. 'Twould appear she was born for this.

*

And that eve at the great gathering in the hall, it seemed all there assembled, and they were very many, must agree.

When the feasting was nearly done, Lady Isabella rose to her feet and gave a full account of why she was so long confined and could not be seen. And she told of the bewitching which had ensnared her husband, Lord Allan, likewise, causing his absence from them these many miserable years. She acquainted them with Sibylla's evil sorcery, with Lucius's magic Tapestry, and with Selina's immense courage and ability in overcoming evil in direct confrontation with the witch. And last, she informed them of how the spellbinder, who tortured and ensnared them with her cruel contempt for their blamelessness, was finally slain, and how it was most assuredly divine justice that she had inadvertently turned her loathsome magic against herself and died by her own hand.

At the completion of the telling, with all in amazement at what they had heard and full of rejoicing at the outcome, 'twas then that Tristram bade them stay yet attentive, and hearken to the tribute that had been specially composed to mark and honour this glad occasion.

And when all were hushed and intrigued by the colourful jester that had appeared from a side chamber, only at that moment did Tristram assume his stance. Then such notes that he at once brought forth from his instrument in melodious cascade vividly evoked the pain, sorrow, grief and despair that these tormented souls must suffer. But thereafter, with change of pace and tone, the plucked strings evoked in their place the rise of hope that came in their stead, giving birth to brave defiance as they dared challenge the witch and her curse. All those assembled were themselves bewitched by the exquisite melodies which described so perfectly all that Tristram informed them of in his verse.

But alongside, Selina demonstrated in dance and mime all that the troubadour related in song. She had made a mask on a stick that depicted the sorceress's face, and had another for the tiger, and these she employed to embolden the drama so none could be in any doubt what fearsome encounters they must have endured.

And indeed, it was a most illustrious performance that presented in its art the truth of that which Lady Isabella had confessed, and there was nary a one that remained unstirred by what they witnessed. Many came to them thereafter and spoke with them, and those of noble birth were compelled to beg them to come to their manor or stately home and repeat that which they had rendered that eve.

And why would they not? For their acting out of that which they had experienced together was a moment of recognition for them both. The vanquishing of the witch had sealed their commitment, each to the other, but not as Allan had said, as comrades-at-arms, for them 'twas a different thing entirely. Then the discovery that what they established in that endeavour extended to embrace a perfect partnership also in their performing art.

Who could doubt that in the whole of Christendom there was no more perfect match? Of a certainty, they were blessed.

*

On the morrow, when the time had come for them to depart, Isabella and Allan attended them, making sure they had all they needed for the journey.

Their horses, freshly groomed and bridled, were selected by Jacob, not only for their good temperament but their good presentation. Selina, who had never ridden other than on the back of a pack horse, was awed to own such a handsome steed.

And Jacob himself would accompany them with a small covered wagon which Isabella insisted they had need of. 'Twould purvey the fine clothes that had been fashioned for Selina, and the many other gifts as had been pressed upon them. And not just for themselves but for her brothers, for she could not go to them empty handed.

Selina was delighted to see 'twas the same old but willing nag as would pull the cart, for Jacob informed them that the distance to her own domain was but half that of the journey they made from her grandmother's dwelling. The wagon was also a far lighter vehicle than the carriage. But the truth also was that the nag enjoyed being in employ between the shafts. Being an honest creature, he was glad to earn his keep, but also sometimes to travel further afield than his normal allotted span, as long as it was Jacob in the driving seat. For the daily round at home, venturing no further than field and back, lacked variation and he still was curious and glad to encounter new experiences if they were not overtaxing.

It seemed also somehow fitting that she went as she came, with Jacob and the nag. Though she had more to convey in her leaving than her coming, when she brought only her grandmother's chest and workbox.

At first light this morn, upon her rising she had taken particular care, before all was packed away, to select habit as was best suited both for the journey and for the meeting with her brothers. For it being four years gone since they last laid eyes on her, and she being much changed and grown, 'twas necessary to her that she made a good impression when they beheld her afresh. But she chose modest attire that she looked, like her mount, well presented rather than over-dressed, less they think in her changing she had become vain.

Whilst she prepared herself, Flora came to the chamber, not to attend her but rather in a great excitement. She had come direct from a meeting with the chatelaine, for it seemed Selina's instruction with regard to herself had been put into immediate action.

Abigail was to retire forthwith, for 'twas plain she was no longer able to serve Lady Isabella in the way it must now be done. There was no longer need for keeping the keys, but Madame would have particular want from henceforth for a lady's maid as she came back into the way of life that made all the claims upon her as such station demanded. Abigail would train her in every aspect of such employ till she was fully informed and had no further need. She would be fitted for new garments, and given a chamber within the manor house that she was in close attendance when required. But her hours would not be so over-burdening that she had neither the time nor freedom to visit home and friends. Flora thought she had gone to sleep last night and woken not from a dream, but to find herself inhabiting one.

She took from her apron pocket something wrapped in a muslin cloth and thrust it into Selina's hands.

"I like to embroider and I have fashioned this for you to take in remembrance, though 'tis naught beside what you give to me."

Then, with an avowal that she would be there at her departure, Flora made a hasty retreat, for despite the need to demonstrate her gratitude, she was made awkward by shyness.

Selina had no doubt that with her new role, she would soon grow out of all such reticence. Then she carefully unwrapped the gift to find a pin cushion fashioned in the shape of a blackbird, with beak and eye rim picked out in gold thread, and where the wing coverlet would be 'twas embroidered in fine detail a little crock filled with primroses and violets. She was well pleased with her present, and all it represented, and it would find its place perfectly in her grandmother's workbox.

Then, after all had been attended to and they were gathered at the entrance to the manor, with Jacob having stowed everything they were taking with them, he climbed up onto the driving seat to wait upon their signal.

Flora was there as she had promised, with Abigail close by her. She came forward a little unsteadily, but nevertheless determined to take hold of Selina's hand and grasp it firmly.

"Do not keep yourself from us too long, for you are like the Tapestry, woven into this place and into the hearts and minds of we who dwell here."

Then Isabella embraced her and Allan bowed over her hand, before he gripped Tristram's and put an arm about his shoulders.

Parting is painful, that is sure, and they had some difficulty in turning about to mount their horses who were waiting patiently. Not so the nag who had stood still for long enough, and let his impatience be known with a series of snorts that informed those assembled that as far as he be concerned 'twas time to be on the road. His prompting was the spur they needed, and as they mounted and wheeled their horses to face the road, Jacob clicked his tongue to the nag and they were under way.

Many came from the settlement, forsaking whatever employed them in order to cheer them off, and, it being declared a holiday, they were a goodly number. And Selina was aware of how different 'twas when she departed her grandmother's domain, where none at all attended her leaving, nor even took note she was going.

Now here she was, in fine attire on a fine horse and with Tristram beside her, very much her fine fellow. Like Flora, it seemed such things as befell her were beyond all credibility.

Jacob told them that with an early start and good going underfoot, they would reach her hometown by midday. And 'twas good for him too, as after a rest and sustenance there was plenty of time for an easy journey home for himself and the horse.

As he took up position in front that he led the way, Selina and Tristram fell in behind at an easy pace. She had a constant thrilling that vibrated her whole being when she embraced the knowledge that they were travelling to her own beloved hometown and to Edward and Daniel. And that these, her brothers, would be instrumental in helping her find her own dwelling place there.

But if she had employ now as a mummer to perform alongside Tristram, then travel was essential to such a way of life, and meant they would take lodging wherever they found themselves, but certainly would have no fixed abode as they plied their trade. After her years of cramped confinement, such freedom was in no wise unwelcome. And alongside such lack of restraint, there was the knowledge that when they needed respite from the road and the performing, then she would have her own home to go back to. A place where they may remain for as long as they wished, or till the call of what they did compelled them back to their travels. For there was no doubt, having acted out her part but once, the thrall to continue was so compelling it defied denial.

So, if she had the best of both worlds – the steadiness of home and family as safe anchor, and the excitement of venturing abroad, choosing to perform at such places as were most pleasing or interesting – it would seem she had been gifted a charmed life.

Yet because she had come to see that life was not entirely chance, nor was it composed of random happenings, but rather things unfolding in a pattern that appeared to be behind all that came about, she resolved to adopt no hard and fast stance. Rather 'twould be more to wait and see what came next of its own accord, rather than to plan ahead.

Because the Pestilence had struck down her parents, she must take up residence with her grandmother, and had she not been there, Isabella's priest would not have discerned that she was the one to vanquish the witch. And in the doing of that, she found Tristram and thereafter her gift of interpretation through mime. Out of disaster came profound blessing, but most assuredly at the beginning she saw nothing ahead of her but subjection and isolation.

She departed with many gifts, fine attire and ornaments, and flagons of the best mead and wine for her brothers and the feasting that would attend her own homecoming, but she took with her also two other gifts that could not be conveyed in Jacob's wagon. The ability to vanquish Sibylla and the knowledge of dance and mime. Though she be untutored in both, they came to her in complete and perfect presentation.

The art of mime she would demonstrate each time she performed with Tristram, but what of the other? Would it ever be called back into usage? No doubt there were other witches and wizards wreaking havoc where they would. And if there were and she heard tell of them, would her gift be obliged once more to engage? Or was it only Sibylla she was destined to confront?

If all things unfold in their due season, she had no need to ponder on such possibility, 'twould come about of its own volition. She left it then in God's lap and gave her full attention to that which was presently here and now. For indeed, it was more than sufficient.